Melanie couldn't understand…how did she get here, and why?

There was something here that didn't make sense. Not long ago, she'd been in her apartment, getting ready to go to work. But when she'd opened her eyes, she saw Trinity Church in front of her, from a freezing cold bench in Copley Square with a crowd of people gathered around her, dressed oddly and gawking at her. She knew that this man had stepped forward, a doctor who looked so much like Justin, and taken charge to get her to the hospital. But why? How had she gotten to Boston? And then, as if a flash of cognition had struck her like a bolt of lightning, she had a thought that was more frightening than enlightening. Could it possibly be? She had to ask.

"Dr. Thornwell?"

"Yes?"

"What is the date?"

"Oh my, you really have had a head injury, haven't you? It's February tenth."

"What year?" Melanie was shivering again, but not from the cold.

Thomas leaned down close, and Melanie saw that his eyes were an interesting green, with brown and gold flecks, and his hair dark brown, almost black. She was mesmerized by his eyes, but she also noticed that the doctor had a look of surprise on his face, his eyebrows arched, his mouth slightly open in an oval, the tip of his tongue placed over his bottom lip. That look worried Melanie a bit, but she just wanted an answer.

"You don't know what year it is?" It was hard to tell whether his tone was exasperated or sympathetic.

"No."

"You must have hit your head hard. It's February 10, 1886."

Rushing to work in New York in the winter of 2016, Melanie Swift is hit by a truck on the icy city street. Drifting in and out of consciousness, she "wakes up" on a freezing bench in Boston, shocked to find that, not only is she in a different city, but that it's the year 1886. There, she meets a young doctor who falls in love with her and takes her to live in his home with him and his sisters. Confused and homesick, Melanie tries to adjust, but she can't give up hope that she'll somehow be reunited with the man she loves in her own time. But what if she's forced to live out her life in the past? Should she give in and learn to love the man who so clearly loves her, or continue to pine for a man who won't even be born for another hundred years? And, most importantly, how can she be sure that her actions in the past won't change the future in some terrible way?

In *Time Out* by Rebecca Marks, Melanie Swift gets hit by a truck on the icy streets of New York on the way to work in 2016 and wakes up on a park bench in Boston in 1886. The first person she meets happens to be a doctor, Thomas Thornwell, who discovered her on the bench in the freezing weather dressed in only the hospital gown they put on her in 2016. Luckily Thomas acts quickly and has her transported to the local hospital before she freezes to death. But Melanie knows right away that something is wrong. Instead of a warm gasoline-powered ambulance, Melanie is taken to the hospital in a horse-drawn ambulance. Then there is the way everyone is dressed. But she is shocked, nonetheless, when she asks Thomas what year it is and he tells her it is 1886. Not only doesn't she know how she got there, she doesn't know how to get back to her own time and the man she left behind—the man whose memory won't let her love Thomas as he loves her. Though quite a change from Marks's other series, the *Dana Cohen Mysteries, Time Out* is cute, clever, and highly entertaining. A real treat. ~ *Taylor Jones, The Review Team of Taylor Jones & Regan Murphy*

Time Out by Rebecca Marks is the story of a young woman who goes back in time from 2016 to 1886. Our heroine, Melanie Swift, rushes off to work in New York in the winter of 2016, where she falls in the icy street while hurrying to the bus stop and gets hit by a truck. She drifts in and out of consciousness while being transported to the hospital and then slips into a comma. When she wakes up, she is freezing and immediately knows something isn't right. Instead of being in a warm hospital bed, she is on a cold park bench, in Boston of all places. She has no idea how she got there but is grateful for the doctor who happens to pass by on his way to work. He finds her on the park bench and summons the ambulance, which turns out to be a horse-drawn carriage. When she starts asking questions, clearly confused as to how she got to Boston from New York and from 2016 to 1886, they think she hit her head too hard. The young doctor who found her falls head over heels for her and takes her into his home once she leaves the hospital. But Melanie wants to go home to her own time and the man she loves there. She doesn't want to stay in the past, but she doesn't know why she is there, how she got there, or how to get back. *Time Out* is a light-hearted, fast-paced, and intriguing story, filled with charming characters and some wonderful scenes—a delightful and entertaining read. ~ *Regan Murphy, The Review Team of Taylor Jones & Regan Murphy*

ACKNOWLEDGMENTS

Thank you to my faithful pre-readers—Matthew Schneiderman, Sue Machler, and Elaine Lansky—who have learned that I really *do* want the constructive criticism! It makes my books much better. Also to the pals in my writing group—we're all in this game together. And as always to Jimin Han and Pat Dunn from the Sarah Lawrence College Writing Institute—mentors extraordinaire. Also to Jim Gallagher for another wonderful cover, and to Faith, the amazing editor at Black Opal Books, who commiserates with me on the treacheries of the English language.

Time

Out

Rebecca Marks

A Black Opal Books Publication

GENRE: PARANORMAL ROMANCE/TIME TRAVEL

This is a work of fiction. Names, places, characters and incidents are either the product of the author's imagination or are used fictitiously, and any resemblance to any actual persons, living or dead, businesses, organizations, events or locales is entirely coincidental. All trademarks, service marks, registered trademarks, and registered service marks are the property of their respective owners and are used herein for identification purposes only. The publisher does not have any control over or assume any responsibility for author or third-party websites or their contents.

DEDICATION

With great love and affection, I dedicate this book to the city of Boston, where I lived for many years. That such a small city can be so rich in culture, literature, and educational opportunity is a wonder in itself. That this book enabled me to delve into the life of Boston in 1886 was another wonder. In spirit, I will always be inextricably and happily connected to Puritan John Winthrop's "city upon a hill."

Chapter 1

Today Melanie Swift was giving a big presentation for the CEO and a bunch of other upper level managers. This didn't happen often, so she was freaking out big-time as she gathered all the materials she'd worked on most of the night. She caught sight of herself in a mirror as she flitted around the house, knocking down glasses she'd left on tray tables, tripping over the slippers she'd abandoned in the middle of the living room. She noticed that her blue eyes had deep circles underneath, and they were sunken into her head. She hadn't slept much the past couple of days.

"Crap," she said, as she ran into the bathroom, almost tripping on the area rug that she'd put down in the hallway. She started applying concealer under her eyes, but some of the white crème slid onto the bridge of her nose. "Shit, it's impossible." She wiped her face with her hand, and then ran her forearm under the running water, which had gotten too hot. "Ow!"

The skin on her arm above the wrist turned bright red. Her small bedroom looked as if it had survived a tornado—clothing, makeup, and shoes strewn around. It had come down to three suits: a black one, a red one, and the one she had ended up with, a robin's egg blue one that offset her newly coiffed, newly streaked blonde hair, and a soft white silk blouse that clung to her curves. Back at the mirror she pulled the skirt down a little. She was tall, and it wouldn't be appropriate to show too much leg, although…they were all middle-aged men.

On Saturday, she'd used a Groupon to go to a trendy salon on Madison Avenue and get the full treatment—haircut, foils, a facial, mani and pedi—and the stylist, Chloe, according to her nametag, had surveyed her handiwork afterward and pronounced Melanie a dead ringer for Charlize Theron. Charlize Theron! *Good way to get a customer to come back*, Melanie thought. But maybe she *did* look like Charlize Theron. Anyway, if today worked out the way she hoped it would, she wouldn't ever need a Groupon to go back to that place again. Not bad for an art history major.

Jesus, I have to get a grip. Not like I'm the first person ever to go through this. Besides, I'm prepared, really. She glanced at the kitchen clock. Quarter after six. She was glad the bus her company provided left early, so she could get to work and rehearse her presentation before the meeting. She knew she should probably eat something, but the thought of putting anything in her mouth made her stomach churn.

Okay, okay, breathe. Calm down. She wished she could do one of those hot yoga classes now, just to sweat out some of this stress; but of course that was not possible. She pulled her rain coat out of the closet. It had been sleeting, and the streets were slushy and treacherous. She couldn't find her waterproof boots, so she slipped her heels on. She'd just have to watch out for deep puddles. She grabbed her bag and a banana, and wriggled into her coat as she headed for the elevator. The doorman smiled and tipped his hat as she flew out the front door, not waiting for him to open it.

"What time is it, Joe?"

"It's six-twenty-eight, Miss Swift."

"Oh, God, I'm late."

"Did you want me to grab you a taxi?"

"No thanks, I think I can make it. Bye!"

Breathing hard, she never turned to face him. She didn't even wait for him to wish her a good day the way he always did. She hoped he wasn't offended. It was only because she'd been able to get an entry-level job at this hedge fund that she could even afford to live in this neighborhood. The good friends she'd made at college would be judging her harshly now. They'd all majored in liberal arts and held themselves above the vagaries of a materialistic world. But she had to admit, she loved doing the things she'd never be able to do if she had gotten an unpaid internship at a museum or a ten-dollar-an-hour job in a gallery. Let them ridicule her sellout from their tiny walk-ups way uptown or in Queens.

It was freezing outside, and no one had been out there yet to salt and chip away at the frigid mess. Melanie's scarf was too thin. She shivered and pulled her hood closer around her head as she watched her breath crystalizing. Juggling her laptop and the heavy bag full of papers, she made her way over the slick, icy sidewalks, pushing on toward the bus stop.

She couldn't wait to see Justin today. He'd help calm her down. He was a good friend, and she'd confided in him how nervous she was about this presentation. He'd been at the company for a couple of years already, assigned to her as a "mentor," but there was an undeniable attraction between them, even though she tried to fight it, to be more in line with company protocol. She giggled when she thought of all the times she'd doodled in her notebook during boring business meetings, "Mrs. Justin Hilliard," like some middle-schooler. Anyway, he'd promised to sit with her on the bus today, to help her with nerves.

To take her mind off her presentation, she allowed herself to think about Justin, just a little. She was starting to have feelings for him that superseded a crush. He'd given her some clues that he might be feeling the same way, but he hadn't asked her out. If she succeeded today, she decided—if everything went well—she'd invite him out to celebrate. It was a good excuse. She'd tell him it was to thank him for the support and advice he'd given her.

Walking fast, trying to run where the sidewalk was fairly well cleaned off, hanging on to her bag, praying not to slip—she had the bus stop in her sights. As she hurried to get there, the stinging, biting ice pellets slammed into her face, making harsh, stabbing attacks, edging under the fur lining of the rain coat hood, which she had tied under her chin. As Melanie began to cross the street, a pick-up truck came around the corner too fast. She hardly noticed it and didn't feel herself losing traction until she was almost at the edge of the curb and stepped into a pile of freezing slush. She stomped down to get her balance, but the high heel on one shoe cracked and broke off, making a splat sound, and she crashed down hard, bags, computer, papers flying in all directions. *Oh my god, I can't control where my body is going*, she realized, horrified.

She felt herself slipping into the street, head first, as the truck approached. She heard the brakes screech and screamed for it to stop, but it skidded into her, smashing her head and her body with a force she could never have imagined. Then everything went black, and she couldn't move, couldn't talk—but she could hear everything.

"Melanie? Are you all right?"

It was a ghostly voice, coming from behind her, but the heavy, quilted hood muffled it, and she couldn't respond, anyway. She tried to turn her head toward the voice, wondering whether it was Justin's. Maybe she could still get to work on time. She didn't feel any pain.

"Melanie! Oh my God! Someone call nine-one-one, please!"

Maybe this was what it felt like to be paralyzed. She thought she felt slush seeping into her mouth and nose. It tasted like dirt, but she couldn't make her mouth move to spit it out. She heard others screaming, asking if she was okay, but she couldn't respond. Her conscious self seemed leave her body, and it was as if she was somewhere else.

She knew she was lying there in the street, but she couldn't see anything.

The truck stopped. The distraught driver emerged gasping, holding his hand up to his mouth, the driver's door still open, and the alarm bell dinging to remind him to close it. Melanie couldn't see him, didn't even know he was standing over her, pacing from side to side, his eyes wild with fear, talking fast on his cell phone in a language she didn't recognize. Now a small crowd had formed, despite the early hour and the terrible weather. Melanie heard a buzz of voices, but she couldn't make out any words.

She heard Justin's voice again, yelling at the nine-one-one operator to send an ambulance, "Hurry, please!" he was yelling, or maybe she was dreaming, "She's badly injured. She's not moving."

She had no idea how much time passed, her heart beating loud and fast in her head. She gagged on the icy water. She had been cold at first, but now her body was numb, so the cold didn't bother her anymore. Was she delirious, wondering whether her pounding heart counted as aerobic exercise? She wouldn't have to go to the gym today. That made her happy for a moment, until she tried to move again but couldn't.

"I'm a nurse," she thought she heard someone say, and that was comforting. "Don't try to move her. She could have some very serious injuries. You don't want to make them worse."

And then Justin's voice, definitely Justin's voice. "But what if she drowns with her face in the water like that?" And louder, "Melanie, honey, can you hear me? Please nod your head or something."

Justin sounded hysterical. She wanted to comfort him. He'd called her *honey*. She would definitely ask him out.

Melanie tried to move her head, but after having edged her nose out of the frigid water so she could keep breathing, she was still immobilized, and she was getting scared. She had a fleeting thought that it would be nice to go to sleep, but she kept hearing Justin say, "Stay with us, Mel, the ambulance is on the way. Please stay with us."

He sounded so desperate that she decided to do what he asked. She wasn't sure why, but it seemed like a reasonable request. She would sleep later.

The siren shocked her out of her stupor, but when hands started to move her gently onto a hard board, she whimpered. It wasn't exactly pain that she felt, but she didn't want people touching her.

"Sorry, miss," someone said in a foreign accent, but she couldn't tell where it was from. "We don't want to hurt you any more. Just try to relax. You'll be at the hospital soon." Someone was wiping off her face off with a cloth. "Can you tell us your name? Where you live?"

"Her name is Melanie Swift," she heard Justin say. "She lives right up the street. Is she going to be all right?"

Relax? Hospital? There was no time to go to a hospital. She had to get to work. She tried to answer, but the only thing she could manage was a groan.

"We know you're uncomfortable. You'll be warm and dry soon. We're getting you to the ER as quickly as we can. They'll take care of you there. It's going to be fine." As he talked, he continued to nudge her body out of the street. Warm and dry sounded good. She felt herself being hoisted up on the board, a rigid brace secured around her neck and a mask attached to her face, blowing something cold into her nose. She tried to wriggle out of the brace and the mask, but she couldn't move. A bump made her try to grip the board, but her arms were immobilized.

"Be careful!" she heard Justin yell.

Thanks, Justin. Be careful.

"It's slippery," someone else said. "Don't drop her."

Finally, she felt herself being laid down on a gurney, and then wheeled away across a bumpy road. Her eyes were closed, but she could tell there were bright lights flashing all around her. It was a little warmer, but she was still shivering. The mask on her face made it easier to breathe now, so she stopped fighting it. She tried to take deep breaths, but it hurt her ribs. Then she was lifted into the back of a vehicle—the bus? She felt optimistic. She hoped her suit hadn't gotten dirty.

"I want to go with her," she heard Justin say.

Of course, he'd go with her. They both had to get to work. It must be getting late.

"Are you family?"

"No, I work with her. I'm a good friend. Please let me go with her. I'm sure she's scared."

"She's unconscious and in shock, sir, so she isn't scared right now."

Melanie *was* scared, so she was relieved when they finally said yes.

It helped to have Justin with her. She tried to open her eyes to smile at him, let him know she was relieved to have him here, but her eyes were shut tight, and she couldn't get the lids to move.

"Sir, are you going to be okay? Is this your girlfriend?" The accent was talking to Justin now.

"Yeah, sure—I'm just really worried about her," he said, his voice breaking with emotion, "This fucking accident never should have happened."

She could imagine him staring down at her, a look of terror on his face, his eyes drawn into a narrow squint, his lips almost invisible, and his skin pale and gray. She was frustrated that he was so concerned about her but she couldn't seem to get the words out to reassure him, tell him she liked him a lot, maybe loved him. She tried to raise her eyebrows, to signal something to him, to calm him. But it was impossible.

"Hang in there, honey," he said. She could hear him, even over the din of the sirens and the clacking of the tire chains along the icy road. "We're almost there. They're going to help you. I need you to be all right."

Where was she going? Was this vehicle taking them to work? Anyway, she trusted Justin to keep her safe. There were two other people—by their voices, one man and one woman—the man with the accent leaning over her, poking her, checking the mask on her face, which she tried again to shake off but couldn't. Both of the people seemed professional, friendly, and reassuring. As they leaned down and she studied their voices, she thought they sounded confident. They had stuck something in her arm, and it felt cold. She wondered why it didn't really hurt.

"Is she in pain?" Justin asked one of the people.

"She's in shock," he replied. "So no pain. She's still unconscious. Her blood pressure is very low. It's a serious head injury."

Melanie wondered if they were talking about her. She tried to sleep, but all the noise and the constricting medical equipment kept her awake.

"Does she have family we can contact?"

Justin said something, but she wasn't sure what. She wanted to tell them that her family didn't live around here. She was from New Jersey. Her parents had been divorced, and her father had moved to LA years and years ago. He hadn't been in touch with them since she was a small child. Then he had died, but right now she couldn't remember what from. Her mother lived in Princeton now. She would give them her mother's telephone number, except, for some reason, she couldn't remember it, which was kind of funny, since she called her mother all the time.

"Her mom lives in New Jersey," Justin said. "I'll find out how you can reach her."

Melanie tried to open her mouth to say something, but her lips were stuck shut and nothing came out. Except for the other-worldly sound of the siren, it was quiet now, but moments later the activity level around her increased again. She felt the gurney moving, felt the wheels bumping as they caught slightly in the grout lines of the sidewalk. Then she heard the words for the first time. "...unconscious, possible brain injury, broken ribs."

She could hear them when they were close-by, but the

voices drifted off as people held their hands over their mouths or turned their backs to her. She knew she was going somewhere fast. Felt the whoosh of a door opening, and then the harsh outside air changing to warmer inside air.

"CT scan."

That was the next thing she heard. Okay, they were taking her to get a CT scan. She knew what that was. Her uncle had had one when he had a stroke. Her uncle got better. He'd said the CT scan didn't hurt. Okay, a CT scan. They would figure out she was all right and let her go. She suddenly realized she wouldn't be at work in time for the meeting. She tried to grab the gurney again, but none of her muscles worked at all. She tried to cry. It didn't happen.

Next, there were people all over her, removing her clothes. She heard cloth ripping with a terrible sound. She felt frustrated that her expensive suit was being ruined. She tried to protest but couldn't. The worst part was not being able to communicate.

She still felt no pain, but she couldn't move, and finally she just stopped trying. She couldn't tell how much time had passed, but she wasn't bored, which was surprising. Boredom was something she hated, and she was easily bored. She had to be doing something, had to be moving, had to be rushing, energized.

She tried to count the seconds—one-one thousand, two-one thousand—but she kept losing count at about three. After a while the CT machine moved again, and then it went down, just as it had gone up in the beginning. She worried she'd feel the way she did on a roller coaster, as if her stomach didn't move quite as quickly as the rest of her body. But this was a slow movement, and it didn't take long. Finally they moved her out of that room and back to a bed. She hoped Justin was still there and was happy when he spoke to her.

"You're going to be okay, honey. I won't leave you," he said.

"We suspect some brain swelling." That was the next thing Melanie heard, but she didn't know who was talking. "CT results will give us the whole picture."

"What does that mean?" Justin's voice.

"We have to watch her very carefully."

"All right. I'm going to stay here until her mother arrives. Is that okay?"

Melanie wished she could hug him, tell him how she felt.

"Yes, that's fine. Her mother's on the way."

"Okay, good." Justin's voice was still a little choked.

Her mother was coming? Why had they called her mother? Her mother had a job and an apartment to take care of, and she would have had to come all the way from Princeton.

"What are you going to do for her? What is the prognosis?"

Justin's voice got closer. She heard someone say they couldn't give him any information, he was not a family member, there was HIPAA to be concerned about. But she wanted to know the answers too.

"Oh, Jesus, there are tears coming out of her eyes. Please help her. Melanie, honey—can an unconscious person be terrified?"

After that, voices floated in and out. Justin's voice, other male and female voices, sometimes bending down close, sometimes farther away.

"Here, honey, I'm slipping this in the pocket of your hospital gown," she heard Justin whisper close to her ear, as an object was inserted into her pocket. "Then when you wake up, you can call me."

She felt herself being moved around, needles being stuck into her. She tried to sleep. She thought she heard Justin say goodbye, but she didn't know if that was a dream. Soon after, she heard her mother.

"Oh God, what happened to her? She looks terrible. Can I touch her?"

"We're sorry, Mrs. Swift, but she's critical. We're not sure whether she'll need surgery, but we're hoping she won't. Will you sign the release just in case? Is she allergic to any medications?"

Now Melanie heard her mother crying, which was odd, because she couldn't remember ever hearing her mother cry before.

"Can she hear us?"

"She never regained consciousness, Mrs. Swift. It's hard to say whether she can hear."

"Would you please just wipe the tears away from her face? Her face looks so terrible, as if she was beaten up. She's so pretty—will her face be scarred? Why is her skin black and blue? Did she get hit in the face? Can you just tell me what you're going to do for her?"

"The CT scan results look promising. Likely, we will lower her body temperature and keep her in a medically induced coma," the male voice said.

"What does that do, Doctor?"

"With traumatic brain injury," he said, "the brain often swells from the trauma, but unlike a swollen arm or face or leg, there's no place for it to go. The skull is too hard a capsule. You don't want the brain to swell downward and endanger the brain stem, right?"

"I suppose that makes sense," Melanie's mother said.

"Also, inflammation can cause the brain to press into the skull, which then can increase the pressure even more. This could cause the blood supply to be cut off. All the outcomes can be critical or even fatal."

"Oh no…" her mother's voice trailed off.

"So when we put a patient into a medically induced coma and lower her body temperature, it gives the brain some time to rest and heal, for the swelling to reverse itself. Our goal is to save as many brain cells as possible so that when she comes out of this, she will be back as close to normal as possible."

"How low will her temperature be?" her mother asked, her voice sad and resigned."

"Only the low-to-mid-nineties. Not lower."

"Won't that make her terribly uncomfortable?"

"She won't feel anything, Mrs. Swift. You don't have to worry. She won't have any pain or discomfort."

"You know this for a fact?"

"She will be anesthetized."

"As long as she is not in pain. I couldn't stand thinking that she went through this and she's in pain too."

"Believe me, it would be much worse for her if we didn't do this."

"I guess we don't have time for a second opinion." Then her mother gave a short, embarrassed laugh. "No, I know we don't. I trust you. I'll sign the release."

"Thank you, it's the right thing to do. But I'm afraid I must ask you to leave now. There's a family waiting room right down the hall. We'll be sure to keep you informed of everything that's going on."

Melanie heard footsteps and the soft closing of a door, and her mother's voice became fainter. Then she felt something brush across her skin, but she didn't know what. Perhaps they were drying her tears, as her mother had requested, although she hadn't realized she'd been crying. She strained to hear the voices but couldn't.

Next there was a flurry of activity, a door opening and banging, shoes squeaking, and she felt herself rolling along the floor, fast. She prayed she wouldn't fall. She heard a beep, and a heavy door made a rumbling sound as if it was opening. Then she was rolled somewhere again. She felt as if she was dropping downward, which scared her even more. The door opened again with its loud rumble, and she was being rolled on a flat floor into a room. She sensed a very strong light in there, but she couldn't open her eyes to look. Then there were voices, some hushed and some loud, and activity she could feel around her head. Someone put something over her face, and she wanted to brush it off, but she couldn't. Then there was blackness and she was no longer aware of anything.

Chapter 2

Melanie was shivering, could feel her entire body shaking. She huddled, clasping her arms around her, to try to trap some warmth, but it wasn't working. She was so cold that she started to moan, but the moan sounded to her as if it was coming from outside her body. She had no idea there was a small crowd gathering around her, but their voices became louder, and after a few moments she struggled to open her eyes and look up. The group created a kind of dark, human fence around her. The men were strangely dressed, some with top hats, shiny canes, and long black coats. They looked like confused statues or actors in a movie. The women had on long, dark dresses that almost touched the ground but allowed their black, pointy-toed, button boots to stick out when they moved. They wore heavy looking, gray and black wool coats that were buttoned all the way up to high ruffled necks at the top and reached down below their calves.

"Look here, she's opened her eyes!" one of the men said, his tone of excitement cutting through the frigid air.

Melanie watched as their breath became clouds of steam. Her teeth were chattering, and she couldn't control it. She almost didn't notice when another man, dressed in white and younger than the others pushed through the crowd.

The handsome young man bent over her, looking into her eyes. "Are you all right, miss?"

"What?" Melanie asked. She did a double take. "Are you…" He looked so much like Justin, but there was no way. Justin never dressed like that. She didn't finish the sentence. Her voice was a hoarse whisper.

"Oh, she speaks English!" a woman in the crowd commented, her tone loud and excited.

The young man turned around and raised his arms to quiet them all down. The crowd hushed for a moment. "I'm a physician, miss," the man said, turning around to face her again. "I was on my way to the hospital. I'd like to help you."

"You're not Justin, are you?" Melanie asked, sighing.

"Where did you come from?" he said, ignoring her question.

"New York," Melanie said." She wasn't ready for the titters that rose from the crowd, which was now increasing in number. She tried to shield her face with her arm but quickly restored it to its place around her shivering body.

"Strange outfit for New York," one of the men with a cane said. "I thought they were fashionable there." More laughter from the crowd.

"Hush!" The young doctor put a finger to his lips. "I'm trying get some information from her."

Melanie stole a look at her surroundings. The snow was packed densely on the ground, and she was sitting on a cast iron bench that felt even colder than the air. She tried not to touch it with her hand, worried that her hand might stick to it. She looked above the heads of the crowd and out toward the horizon.

"Is that—" Melanie hesitated. "Is that Trinity Church over there?"

"Well, yes, of course. Why do you ask?" The doctor was wearing a long overcoat. He removed his wide wool scarf and arranged it over the front of her body, placing the ends around her shoulders.

"Where am I?"

"You're in Copley Square. Where did you think you were?"

"I'm in Boston?"

Now the crowd was chattering and laughing more than ever as they leaned in to hear her, despite the doctor's vain efforts to quiet them down.

"Yes, of course, Boston."

Melanie took a deep breath to try to regain her composure, but that hurt her ribs so badly she thought she might pass out. "Oh, God," she said.

"Maybe we should get the asylum men," said the man who had commented on Melanie's clothing, "I think the girl's delirious."

The doctor raised his hand again. "This poor young woman is freezing to death. That could wreak havoc with anyone's mental faculties. Does anyone have a muff she can use? Her hands are like two blocks of ice." The crowd grumbled in unison, but someone did part with a muff, which the doctor helped Melanie put on her hands. It was still warm inside, and she was grateful.

For an instant, Melanie thought she might be hallucinating, but it was hard to deny Trinity Church. She'd studied it in her art history classes at Harvard. The church, with its rough-hewn stone exterior and red clay roof was the archetypal example of the Richardsonian Romanesque style. Those wonderful lectures coursed through Melanie's head, momentarily making her forget about her physical condition. She felt woozy, the way you did when you first woke up from an afternoon nap. She had no recollection of traveling to Boston. How could she be here without knowing how she had gotten here? She was afraid to cry, because the tears might freeze on her cheeks. Plus, when she breathed, her chest hurt.

"We have to get her to the hospital. She's freezing and confused."

Some of the people in the crowd, which had now expanded to about fifteen men and women, nodded their heads.

"Can you tell us your name, miss? Can you walk? My name is Dr. Thornwell, and I want to help you, but you need to help also, if you can."

Melanie tried hard to move, but either the cold or the stiffness in her muscles and the pain in her ribs and head prevented her from manipulating her body, which ended up collapsing across Thornwell's torso. He pushed her up gently.

"My name is Melanie."

"Melanie what?"

"Melanie Swift. I can't move," she said, her voice weak from the cold. "Please don't let me die." She gasped. "I don't know how I got here. It hurts when I breathe."

"Will one of you please help?" Dr. Thornwell scolded the crowd, their feet welded to the ground as if immobilized by inertia. "We need to summon the ambulance, and soon. She could get frostbite."

Those last words seemed to mobilize the crowd. "I'll go to the fire station on Boylston Street and have them telegraph the hospital to send it," one of the younger men said. "It won't take but a few minutes for me to reach there if I run."

"Thank you," said the doctor, as the man sprinted away. "Please, can someone lend a coat that I can drape around her? You will have it back as soon as the ambulance gets here."

One of the men offered his coat, which Thornwell used to cover Melanie from her chin down to her ankles. After being swaddled in all the clothing, Melanie felt a little warmer, but her head still throbbed and she wanted to go to sleep. The doctor continued to talk to her. "Don't sleep, Miss Swift, all right? You need to stay awake or I'm afraid we won't be able to wake you. Keep your eyes open. The ambulance will be here soon, I promise."

Melanie tried hard not to close her eyes, although she couldn't open them too wide, because the light hurt them.

Her head was pounding, as if it had been caught in a tight vise and squeezed until her skull might break. It hurt everywhere, on the top, in back. She wanted to put her hands around her head to try to make the pain stop, but she couldn't move her hands, ensconced as they were in the woman's muff. She didn't know if she could trust these strange people—from the little she'd been able to see, they were dressed oddly, their accents weren't familiar, and some of the expressions they used sounded a little old fashioned to her. Nevertheless, she didn't have a choice. She had no idea what was going on, and she knew she needed help. At least this doctor who looked like Justin was willing to help her. She hoped she wouldn't freeze to death before they were able to get her to the hospital.

"Ah, I hear the horse," said one of the outliers in the crowd, who had appointed himself temporary sentry.

"Please step aside so they can get to her."

Thornwell used his arms again to part the crowd, and the people dispersed, some of them walking off down the snowy street, not sticking around for the end of the show, others just moving over a few paces. Soon the sound of clopping hooves was unmistakable. Melanie wondered what a horse was doing outside on such a cold day. She wondered where the ambulance was.

A high whinny accompanied a man's voice. "Whoa, Bella! Whoa." Two fast hoofbeats on what sounded like cobblestone ended the horse's complaint. Then Melanie heard the sound of people running, and the increasing volume of the footsteps told her they were running toward her. She tried to shrink into a ball, afraid of what was going to happen next.

"What's the story here?" A man's voice, and he was very close.

"My name is Dr. Thomas Thornwell. I was on my way to work, and, thank God, I found her. I'm not sure, but she was here on the bench. She has hardly any clothing on, she's shivering, and she couldn't walk. Something happened to her, but I don't know what. She isn't even wearing shoes, only those cloth slippers that look very flimsy. She needs to get to the hospital quickly or she'll die of exposure. I tried to keep her from going to sleep, but I'm glad you got here, because I don't think she could have held out much longer."

"Okay, Doctor. Is it all right if we take her to Boston General?"

"Yes, I work at Boston General. I'll ride with her in the ambulance."

"Do you know her name and where she came from?"

"Her name is Melanie Swift, but the only thing she said is that she's from New York and doesn't know how she got here."

Melanie was relieved that he was going to ride with her in the ambulance. But what happened next was completely unexpected. Two men in uniforms she couldn't identify approached the bench where she was huddled and, within seconds, had lifted her gently onto some kind of platform on wheels. She had a flashback to a time she couldn't place, where people were lifting her and moving her. Her body went rigid. She had no idea why, but she knew this had happened to her recently.

"Miss Swift, it's all right," said one of the men. "We won't hurt you."

In fact, they were being so gentle, Melanie almost couldn't feel the bumps as the squeaky wheels brought her toward the horse, who was snorting softly. She could see that the animal was a dark reddish roan color, with a flowing black mane that trailed down either side of its head in graceful waves. The horse's breath froze in the air as he snorted. She hoped that mane kept him warm. As they pushed the platform where she was resting onto the wagon, she realized her head was still throbbing and her entire midsection was sore—her back, her thighs, her ribs, and her neck. Everything hurt, especially when she breathed deeply or tried to talk. She didn't know why she was in such pain, but she wanted it to stop.

As they stabilized her inside the wagon, the horse shifted from side to side, which made the wagon list slightly like a boat in splashing water. Melanie grasped the sides of the narrow plank.

"Don't worry," one of the men offered. "We won't let you fall."

Melanie loosened her grip.

"Are you feeling any better now?"

"I'm warmer, but I'm in a lot of pain."

Then the men climbed out, and the doctor who had taken such good care of her stepped up into the wagon and grasped Melanie's hand. She took a quick look at him, but that just made her miss Justin terribly.

"Thank you," she whispered, as she felt the wagon lurch as each man jumped up into the seat in front. Then she heard the whip snap, and the horse started walking slowly. "Oh," she said.

"They won't go too fast," Thomas said. "They know you're in pain. You'll be fine, though. We'll be at the hospital soon."

"I was so cold," Melanie said. She realized the ambulance attendants had wrapped several blankets around her.

Thomas placed his hand on Melanie's shoulder." "You still don't remember how you got here, do you?"

"No."

"And where did you get these clothes? I've never seen anything like them."

Melanie thought for a moment. Her last memory before turning up on a bench in the middle of Copley Square was running toward the bus stop on the Upper West Side, looking forward to seeing Justin. She remembered slipping and falling, and then feeling something hit her, but after that her memories were a blur. She thought she remembered the sound of sirens pounding in her head, making the crushing pain even worse. Then voices, female and male, loud, urgent, and finally her mother's voice. She felt tears welling up in her eyes.

"No need to cry now." He wiped Melanie's face gently with a soft handkerchief that he removed from his pocket, and after daubing her eyes, he folded it back up and replaced it. "Almost there."

She looked up at the ceiling of this vehicle and realized it was made of some kind of heavy black material strung across a metal infrastructure. She had never in her life seen anything like this. For a moment she thought maybe it was a dream, that she had dreamed up this odd setting in what was a city not her own. But the pain in her ribs and head told her this was real, not a dream. Every time the horses clopped over a bump in the road, it exacerbated her discomfort, and Melanie groaned. Thomas had left his hand on Melanie's shoulder, and she was grateful his touch was gentle. She was feeling warmer, and it was comforting to have a doctor on board, even though his resemblance to Justin made her sad.

"This is an ambulance?" Melanie didn't want Thomas to think she was out of her mind, but she had to find out what was going on.

"Yes. An ambulance."

"Why is it pulled by horses?"

Thomas laughed, but not in a derisive way. "How else would you like it to be pulled? By people?" He laughed again.

Melanie decided not to answer. There was something here that didn't make sense. Not long ago, she'd been in her apartment, getting ready to go to work. But when she'd opened her eyes, she saw Trinity Church in front of her, from a freezing cold bench in Copley Square with a crowd of people gathered around her, dressed oddly and gawking at her. She knew that this man had stepped forward, a doctor who looked so much like Justin, and taken charge to get her to the hospital. But why? How had she gotten to Boston? And then, as if a flash of cognition had struck her like a bolt of lightning, she had a thought that was more frightening than enlightening. Could it possibly be? She had to ask.

"Dr. Thornwell?"

"Yes?"

"What is the date?"

"Oh my, you really have had a head injury, haven't you? It's February tenth."

"What year?" Melanie was shivering again, but not from the cold.

Thomas leaned down close, and Melanie saw that his eyes were an interesting green, with brown and gold flecks, and his hair dark brown, almost black. She was mesmerized by his eyes, but she also noticed that the doctor had a look of surprise on his face, his eyebrows arched, his mouth slightly open in an oval, the tip of his tongue placed over his bottom lip. That look worried Melanie a bit, but she just wanted an answer.

"You don't know what year it is?" It was hard to tell whether his tone was exasperated or sympathetic.

"No."

"You must have hit your head hard. It's February 10, 1886."

Chapter 3

The bumpy ride to the hospital was replaced by a bumpier ride once she was removed from the horse-drawn ambulance, which shook back and forth on its metal frame as the snorting animal lowered its head and stomped its feet.

"Whoa! Easy there, Bella!" One of the ambulance men grabbed at the reins, but it was too late to save Melanie from the jostling, which not only hurt but also made her stomach lurch. She wondered when she had eaten last and had a fleeting thought about the banana she had grabbed on her way out of her apartment. She wished she could have one now.

Once they had removed the gurney from the ambulance, they wheeled her over ramps and wooden planks that seemed to have cracks every few inches. The gurney bumped and swung from side to side. Now Melanie could grab the sides with her hands, which had thawed somewhat and seemed to be working all right. She still couldn't feel her legs, which were wrapped in coarse wool blankets up to the knees.

"How far do we have to go?" she whispered, as they trundled through what looked like an enormous portico with a high domed ceiling. "And what is this place?"

"This is Boston General," Thomas said, hurrying alongside the gurney, shouting instructions to the ambulance workers. "Have you ever been here before?" he said.

"No, I don't think so." At least not in 1886, Melanie thought, but she didn't dare say it out loud.

"It's the most modern hospital in the world," he said, excitement in his voice. "You will be warm here. We have a new central heating system. It runs on coal. Hardly anyone has that!" His voice had a smile in it.

"That's good," she said.

"They are taking you to the admissions ward, and then the other doctors and I will examine you. The doctors here are the absolute best. We'll take good care of you. We know what to do."

The last sentence felt a bit ominous. *They'll know what to do*, Melanie thought. *What will they do? What will they do when they find out I was born in 1986, a hundred years from now? That I graduated from Harvard in 2008? That I live in Manhattan and take a bus every day to my job in Connecticut?* The renewed panic made her head throb with pain even more. How would they treat a concussion in 1886? She wondered whether her cell phone had made the "trip" with her, but then realized it would do her no good now.

The room they wheeled her into had a high ceiling too, but not the massive dome that the entry had had. The lights were yellowish, and they extended from sconces on the walls, and one large fixture hung down from the middle of the ceiling. The ambulance attendants wheeled the gurney directly under that fixture, and Melanie was transfixed by the arcing of the filaments inside the clear glass of the lights. She lay there for a few minutes, while Thomas spoke to the ambulance attendants in the corner of the room. The warmth in this room was lulling her into a light sleep. Suddenly, she was exhausted, and she wanted only to close her eyes.

Sometime later, she awoke with a start, with a man she

assumed was a doctor in a long, starched, bright white coat, bending over her and poking at her. He had a handlebar mustache and a large stethoscope around his neck. He got so close to her face that she could smell strong cigar tobacco on his breath, which made her gag.

"Hello, dear girl," said the smoker, "I am Dr. MacInerney. I have to check your eyes and your throat. Is anything hurting you?"

"Yes," she said, "My head and my ribs. And my stomach feels queasy."

"I'm told they found you freezing on a bench in Copley Square. You look as though someone beat you around the head. Did someone attack you?"

Melanie didn't answer. She hoped he wouldn't ask anything about where she came from or how she got here.

"What is your name?"

"Melanie Swift."

"How old are you, dear?"

"Twenty-five."

"You don't sound as if you come from around here." It wasn't phrased like a question, but his voice rose at the end of the statement as if it was.

"I'm from New York."

"New York City?"

"Yes."

"Do you know what day this is?"

Melanie strained to remember what day of the week it was when she'd left for work in the morning. Thinking seemed to hurt her head, made the pain throb. But she recalled that she had spent the weekend working on the presentation. "Monday, I think."

The doctor had been leaning over, checking Melanie's feet, but he rose from the waist and raised an eyebrow toward Thomas, who was standing a few feet away at the foot of the bed. "No, dear. It's Wednesday."

"Oh."

"And do you know what year it is?"

Melanie was grateful that Thomas had told her in the ambulance. "1886, right? But how could it be—"

"Good. How did you arrive in Copley Square, and what happened to you?"

"Dr. MacInerney, she's had a very rough time. Don't you think we should let her rest before you start asking her questions? After she gets some sleep, you can ask these questions in the morning."

Thomas was hovering now, and if it didn't hurt her insides, Melanie would have laughed at the two of them, peering at her over the bed with their eyebrows raised, MacInerney tapping his finger along the side of his bearded chin as if that might help him find the answers he was looking for.

"Dr. Thornwell, I am concerned about the head injury. I don't want her to sleep unless we're sure she'll be all right. She also seems to be reacting to any kind of pressure on her ribs, so obviously she's been through some severe trauma, but I'm not as worried about that. It's all right to let her take short naps, but you should have the nurse wake her every hour to make sure she is all right."

"I understand, Doctor." Thomas, Melanie realized with some gratitude, had assumed the role of the protector who was going to save her from any untoward probing and get her through this ordeal. "I will be happy to sit with her overnight if need be. I was the one who found her, so I feel a little responsible. If you can spare me from my regular rounds?" Thomas put his hand on Melanie's shoulder. "And I'm sure she'd appreciate being lifted off this hard examination table onto a more comfortable bed, wouldn't you Melanie?"

"Yes, I guess so."

Her mind was starting to clear a little, now that her body was no longer a block of ice. But with the clarity came increased anxiety. How would she explain to these people where she came from and what had happened? How could she figure that out herself? *Have I lost my mind?*

Melanie didn't know whether she had spoken or thought

those words, but she felt herself drifting off.

"I am taken aback by the sutures in her head wound. Did you see them?" MacInerney pushed back Melanie's hair and pointed to the sutures that were neatly lined up vertically along the hairline at her left temple.

Thomas bent over closer to take a look and shrugged.

"I've never seen anything like that. They're green, and I can't determine by sight what the material is, but it is certainly not silk or silver," MacInerney said, now with his finger tapping the side of his nose.

"I agree, Doctor, I felt they were rather strange as well."

"Yes, quite unusual to say the least. I shall write my findings in her record, but in all honesty, I have no idea what to say about those."

"Will you be checking in tomorrow morning, Doctor MacInerney?"

"Yes, Doctor. I have rounds quite early, and I'll be back after that. I must say, this is the most interesting case we've seen in quite some time. You're sure you don't mind staying with her overnight?"

"No, I don't mind at all."

"All right, then, I'll make sure your other patients are covered. Will you be comfortable sleeping in here? Would you like the attendants to roll in a cot of some sort?"

"Not necessary, Doctor. I can nap in a chair while she sleeps. The night nurses will wake her as needs be. I'm happy to do this for her. She's been through a difficult time. She is somewhat confused."

"I'm sure she'll thank you, Doctor."

"As you know, I'm very interested in diseases of the brain and trauma, so it will be good for me as well to become familiar with her case."

"That makes sense, Doctor. Would you please look more closely at those sutures, and try to urge the patient to let us know where she received them. I would like to write a letter to that hospital and ask them for all the details." He shook his head back and forth slowly, as if that might help him figure out the mystery of the sutures. "This is all quite mysterious, I must say. Oh, and make sure you remind the nurses to keep her feet warm. Her feet seem to be regaining their normal color again. I just want you to monitor that overnight. Rubbing her feet will help to get the circulation back to normal."

Thomas removed his hand from Melanie's shoulder. She opened her eyes and watched as the two doctors walked to the far end of the cavernous room and huddled in conversation. She wished she could hear them, but the room was too big, and they were speaking in quiet whispers.

"Do you think we should contact McLain's?" MacInerney said, confident he was out of Melanie's earshot.

"My feeling is no, Doctor," said Thomas, "At least not yet. There's no indication that she's demented or insane. Despite her injuries and exposure, she seems perfectly lucid to me. Just a bit befuddled, but I don't consider that insane."

"But her appearance, Dr. Thornwell, and her clothing, and the fact that she insists she has no idea how she traveled here from New York, or at least she doesn't remember doing so. Added to that, she didn't know what day it was. What do you make of all of that?"

"I think it's much too early to tell, Doctor. She needs some time to recover. She is not insane. I would stake my life on it."

"All right. I trust you. Your intuition about people is excellent, so I will go along with your analysis for now. But you know, if we don't get more answers, we may have to consult with the alienists. McLain's is a modern facility, and they're up on all the latest research about mental disorders."

"I'd rather wait and see how she recuperates, Doctor, before making any such drastic decisions."

"Yes, yes. I'll contact the rest of the medical staff and bring them up to date. It's very interesting, for sure. In the meantime, I leave her in your capable hands. Take good care of her."

"Thank you, Dr. MacInerney, I shall."

"Good. Then I'll see you on my morning rounds. Hopefully we'll know more. You try to get some rest as well."

"Good night, Doctor."

Chapter 4

Melanie's room was on the west side of the hospital, and the setting sun was pouring into the small window on the wall next to her bed. She could see the red of the sunset through her closed eyelids. That made her feel warmer. She couldn't seem to get enough warmth.

"Do you need anything, Melanie?" Thomas was back at the bed, looking down at her. "Are you hungry?"

"I think I'd like to try to get some sleep."

"We need to make sure you're all right. I'm sorry we have to wake you so frequently." Two nurses in starched, white uniforms with ruffled shoulder straps entered the room with a warm gown and a pot of steaming water. "These nurses will give you a sponge bath and get you into more appropriate clothing. I'm going to step out of the room until they're finished, all right?"

He left the room, closing the door behind him, and the two women went to work removing the clothing Melanie had been wearing, carefully working from the bottom up so that they didn't hurt her head any more than it already was.

"If you feel uncomfortable overnight, or if you need more blankets, let Dr. Thornwell know, and we'll bring more in for you. We will be checking in hourly."

"Thank you."

Within moments, they had slipped Melanie's hospital gown off and replaced it with the long, heavy, buttoned-up garment. As they did, something fell out of the pocket of the gown and clattered to the floor. One of the nurses bent down to pick it up, but it had rolled under the bed, and she didn't go after it. Instead, she concentrated on getting Melanie comfortable.

The new gown was a bit itchy, but it was warm, with long sleeves, buttons up to her neck, and a hem that went down below her ankles. After the nurses left, Thomas returned, and Melanie was already sleeping. Thomas tried to nap, but his thoughts were so jumbled and excited, he couldn't fall sleep. He sat in the chair watching Melanie, wondering over and over again about how this had all happened, closing his eyes but staying fully awake, a slave to his own wonder. Every few minutes, he rose and walked over to check Melanie's breathing. She was sleeping so deeply, he had to bend over her to make sure she was breathing.

Thomas stared at Melanie's face. Fine features, peaceful now for the first time despite the bruises, naturally red lips, a small nose, prominent cheekbones. A beauty, Thomas thought, as long as those sutures didn't leave a bad scar. But even with Melanie's eyes closed, Thomas noted that her face exuded a kind of unusual intelligence, although he couldn't explain how he knew. He rubbed Melanie's feet lightly, so he wouldn't wake her, as the doctor had requested, and he laughed to himself about the fact that her toenails were painted a bright, robin's egg blue. He had never seen anything like that, and it just compounded the growing mystery surrounding this woman.

What else would he learn about her to confuse him more? Then he walked back to the head of her bed and leaned down over her again.

He was only a young "house assistant" who had recently graduated from Harvard Medical School after attending

Harvard College. He marveled at how lucky he was to get a case like this to study. It didn't hurt, he thought, that she was such a beauty.

Thomas thought about his father Edward, also a doctor, who had volunteered as a medic in the Civil War on the Union side. Edward Thornwell had returned badly wounded, with mental and physical scars that would never leave him, and had died when Thomas was a small child. The worst of the elder Thornwell's injuries was a terrible blow to the head, which he had received from the butt of a Rebel's rifle as he bent down, tending to a wounded soldier. He had never quite recuperated from that head wound, despite all the modern medicine that had been applied.

Thomas Thornwell had lived his life knowing he would honor his father's memory by becoming a physician as well, and he was determined to be the best physician in the world, spending days and nights in the hospital learning everything he could. He was especially interested in diseases affecting the brain, head injuries, stroke, and other traumas. So the case of a young woman who had entered the hospital in such a strange way interested him very much. He was grateful that veteran doctors like MacInerney respected him and relied on him as much for what they considered his modern training as his dedication.

Thomas brushed a strand of hair off Melanie's face, and she awoke feeling groggy but a bit more rested. When she saw him, she was startled again by his resemblance to Justin. She couldn't help notice that the tall, well-built doctor was very handsome—the shock of thick, dark hair that framed his strong face and chin, the well-trimmed, reddish brown beard, the full, expressive lips, the piercing green eyes, and broad shoulders apparent even under his white coat, were hard to avoid. She tried to pull away from those eyes, but it was impossible. They were such an unusual green, she couldn't help thinking that Justin's eyes were exactly the same color, and she had never seen eyes like that on anyone else.

"Are you all right?" Thomas said it with such care, that Melanie couldn't think of anything to say. "You seemed alarmed when you woke up."

Melanie opened her eyes wide and then blinked as if she was having trouble getting accustomed to the yellowish light. She opened her mouth slightly, as if she was trying to speak, but at first, no words came out. "Oh, it's just that you remind me of someone," she said, finally.

"I see." His eyes were twinkling, even in this semi-dark room. He had pulled down the shades, and the only visible light was the yellow light in the corner, the filaments dancing in the bulb. "A special person?"

"I don't know. Maybe. I miss him, though. I think he might be worrying about me."

"I'm sorry to wake you, you were sleeping so peacefully. But I'm afraid I have to ask you some more questions. Do you feel up to talking a little?" He bent down, even closer to her face. "It's important that we find out about what happened to you. I'm very curious about the sutures along your hairline? Can you tell me how you were injured?"

There was that question again, the question Melanie couldn't really answer without these people believing she was mentally ill. She made a sound as if someone had surprised her with very bad news, a choking noise that caused Thomas to lose his smile and wrinkle his forehead with worry.

Melanie tried to sit up, but she groaned with pain as she did, and she fell back onto the pillows.

"What is the last thing you remember before you were freezing on that bench?"

"I was going to work. Running toward—" She hesitated, wondering whether they would know what a bus was.

"Running toward what?"

"Going to work. I was late, and the streets were icy, and I think my heel broke and I fell, and something hit me. That is the last thing I remember. I think I was dreaming that I was in an ambulance. I did hear my mother's voice, and people I thought were doctors talking about my condition and how it was very serious. I just don't know if that was really a dream or if it actually happened. Then I was somehow freezing in Copley Square, and you found me and saved me. I'm finally a little warmer, and I was able to sleep, but I have no idea how I got here."

Now Melanie was staring at Thomas, and he was looking back at her. Their eyes had locked in a gaze that seemed nothing, if not magnetic. Thomas questioned his own motives, wondered whether his attraction to her was because he had saved her life, or because something organic was happening to him. He felt it was inappropriate, but he couldn't help himself.

"Melanie, I want to know everything about you."

"Dr. Thornwell—"

"Why don't you call me Thomas?" he said. "I'm not that much older than you, and perhaps it would make you feel more comfortable."

"Thomas," she said, "I am trying my hardest to help with this." She wanted to cry, but she fought it and made a semi-successful attempt at a smile.

"I have to find out, where did you get these green sutures?"

"Green sutures?"

"Yes. They're in your head. You obviously had a terrible gash, and someone put very neat, regular sutures in it, but I've never seen suture material like that before." He reached up and again brushed her hair away from the stitches, gently, hardly even touching her skin. His touch made her skin tingle.

"I don't know."

"Do they hurt?"

"My head hurts, inside and out."

One of the nurses entered the room, but Thomas didn't notice, he was so intent on his patient.

"Doctor, I need to take her vitals now. Dr. MacInerney said we had to make sure she is all right, after she almost froze." She waved Thomas away from the bed, and he turned his back and rubbed his eyes. "How are you doing, young lady?" The nurse picked up Melanie's hand and began to take her pulse.

"Better," Melanie said.

"That's good, dear." She finished her work and beckoned for Thomas to walk with her to the corner of the room. "She seems fine, everything normal," the nurse said. "Are you all right, Doctor? You look a bit distracted. Would you like to take some time and walk around for a few minutes? Perhaps you have other patients who might need a visit? Miss Swift is doing well. She'll be fine here if you want to take a break. Then perhaps she can get some sleep."

"No, I'm fine. I don't know what came over me," he said.

"Please don't leave," Melanie was whispering, but she said each word distinctly. "My pain is better when you're here."

"I don't want to leave you alone," said Thomas, "But I do have other patients. You need to get more rest, and I will come back after I visit the others."

"All right," she said, but she felt like crying. "I just feel very homesick."

"I'll be back soon," he said. "I think it's best I leave for a while."

"Come, Dr. Thornwell, I'll be here. I'll stay. If there's any problem, I'll come after you." The nurse—her starched, white hat with the little black dome at the top—sounded like a schoolmarm, scolding a misbehaving student.

"Yes, of course, Nurse," he said. "Melanie, I will be back soon, I promise." As he walked out of the room, he turned his head to look at her until he was completely gone.

"Miss Swift, you must get more rest," the nurse said after Thomas had gone. She plumped up the pillows, straightened the blankets, made sure that Melanie's hands and arms were covered. "The doctor will be back soon."

Melanie turned her head to the side and closed her eyes.

"He reminds me so much of someone at home," she said, feeling tears well up.

"Yes, he's a very good doctor for someone so young," the nurse agreed, ignoring Melanie's statement and her tears.

Melanie sighed. "I miss..."

The nurse had no response. There were rumors circulating in the hospital about this patient, and she couldn't tell whether Melanie was delirious from her injuries or just not in her right mind.

It wouldn't help if Dr. Thornwell allowed his obvious attraction to her to cloud his judgment. The nurse pulled the chair under the window and sat down. After Melanie fell back asleep and her breathing became regular, the nurse tiptoed out of the room. When Melanie woke up, Thomas had returned and was sitting beside the bed.

"Good morning," he said. "Nice to see you."

"It's morning already?"

Thomas nodded.

"I had some dreams."

"Dreams?"

"I dreamed that I was in my own house, in my own bed, and that none of this ever happened."

"I'm sorry. I wish I could help you."

"What time is it?" Melanie could see that it was still semi-dark outside, no real sign of the sunrise yet.

"Six o'clock."

"Oh."

"Dr. MacInerney should be making his rounds soon, and I'm happy to report to him that you're doing well." But he couldn't turn off the thoughts that had been plaguing him all night, especially the strong pull she had on him.

"Good morning, Dr. Thornwell, Miss Swift." Dr. MacInerney was standing in the doorway, several medical students trailing behind him. "Is our patient doing well?"

"She had a deep, restful sleep. Her vitals seem to be normal this morning, and her feet are pink and warmer."

"That's good news, indeed." He approached the bed, and

the students stayed several feet behind him. "Miss Swift, how are you feeling?"

"A little warmer, thank you."

He picked up her hand and, a large pocket watch in his other hand, took her pulse. "Are you hungry?"

"I guess so. I haven't been thinking much about food."

"Dr. Thornwell, would you please have the nurse go and fetch a tray for Miss Swift? A hearty breakfast would be a good start to help her recover."

Thomas Thornwell never replied—he continued to stare at Melanie, tried to convince himself that her bruises were clearing up, but he wasn't sure.

"Dr. Thornwell?" MacInerney had a black fountain pen, and he was tapping it on the sheaf of papers he was holding.

Thomas jumped. "Oh, I'm sorry. I will go right now and ask the nurse." He left the room, still looking back at Melanie.

"You slept, Miss Swift. That's very good. Do you remember anything more about what happened to you?"

Melanie shook her head no. "I wish." She frowned a little. With a shudder, she remembered that it was 1886, and then she wondered whether she had brought her cell phone, and then she shuddered again. "Where am I again?"

"Boston General Hospital."

"Oh, right. My head has been a little foggy."

"You got quite a bump." As he talked he examined her, beckoning to the students to look at the sutures. Some of them gasped, some smiled. "And we don't know how or where or when. But I'm happy to say, it looks as if you are mending. You'll be here in the hospital a while. But I'm optimistic. You need sleep and to eat healthy food, and I think you'll be good as new. Any questions?"

Melanie shrugged, and the students did the same.

"All right, then. I'll be moving along on my rounds. If you need anything, please discuss it with Dr. Thornwell."

"Thank you, I will."

coco

"I don't know what's come over me, but I feel as if I've known you forever. I want to be with you, want to take care of you. I want to make you happy," Thomas said when he returned.

Melanie laughed, and Thomas marveled at the musical lilt of her laughter. "Ouch, it hurts my head to laugh. But that was so sweet of you to say. I feel almost guilty wishing I could go home."

"Sweet, but not very professional—not very doctorly. I must do an examination and ask you all of those annoying questions once more."

"I'd like to know about you, too. I feel as if you're my only friend here."

As he probed and tapped her reflexes, Thomas began to explain what had happened to his father in the Civil War, but halfway through the story, watching the surprise on Melanie's face, he stopped. "Oh my goodness, I'm supposed to be here examining you, not telling you the story of my life."

Melanie laughed again, this time a soft chuckle so that she would protect her sore head and ribs. "No, please tell me everything," she said.

"Fine, but first things first. Do you remember anything more about how you got here?"

"Not really. You are interested in diseases of the brain, Thomas, correct?"

He nodded in agreement, his hand now reaching further up her arm, stroking it as if he wanted to calm her. She pulled away a little bit.

"Do you think I'm insane?"

"No, Miss Swift, from everything I've observed, I think you are as sane as I am."

"Do you promise you won't haul me off in a straitjacket if I am perfectly honest with you?"

"I promise with my life."

"Because what I'm about to tell you might make you change your mind."

"I am all ears." Thomas removed his hand from her arm, and she thought she saw a shadow come over his face.

"Dr. Thornwell?"

"Yes, please come in."

A nurse in a starched white uniform and cape with that small round cap with the see-through, black dome walked in. Her white button shoes squeaked a little on the shiny floor.

"You are supposed to be at morning rounds, Doctor. Is there a problem with this patient?"

"Oh, no, Nurse, she's fine. I'm just coming now." He rose from Melanie's bed, straightening out his long white coat and adjusting the stethoscope. "Will you be all right until I return? I do want to hear your story." As he followed the nurse to the door, he never stopped looking back at the mystery woman who had captivated his mind.

"Yes, Doctor," she said. Then she fell back asleep and dreamed about Justin. In the dream, she told Justin she loved him, and he said he loved her too.

Chapter 5

When the tray of food finally arrived and Melanie was still sleeping, the attendant, in a white dress, cleared her throat to wake her.

She touched Melanie on the shoulder. "Miss Swift? Your breakfast is here. Dr. MacInerney wanted me to make sure you woke to eat it."

"Oh, I'm not sure I have an appetite," Melanie said.

"Well, at least try, please. We don't want Dr. MacInerney to be angry, do we?"

"I suppose so," Melanie said. "Can this bed be raised?" She thought of modern hospitals and how all you had to do was to push a button to raise or lower the head and the foot of the bed.

"Of course, but I'm afraid you'll have to sit up so that I can work the lever in the back. I hope it's not too uncomfortable for you, sitting straight up."

Melanie sat up and stretched, but a searing pain coursed through her head. "Oh!" she cried.

"What, miss? Do I need to call the nurse?"

"I have to take it easy, I guess, until I recuperate from all of this. Is there somewhere I can go to the bathroom?"

"The bathroom?"

"You know, is there a toilet here?"

"Oh, yes, of course. Let me help you. Do you think you can walk?" The woman guided Melanie up and out of the bed, her considerable expertise apparent. "Can you ambulate by yourself?"

"Yes, I think so. I'm a little shaky, but now that I'm warm I can do this."

The attendant moved over and held out her arm. "I'll walk you, and then I'll come back for you in a few minutes. The water closet is on the ward."

"Thank you." The trip to the toilet took a while, because every step caused pounding in her head and pain in her ribs. As they walked, Melanie wondered if she could ever accustom herself to this "new" age. She thought again about her cell phone. She decided she would ask the nurse or Thomas to bend down and look for it under the bed. She knew she couldn't use it, but just having it in her hand would make her feel as if she had some connection to her "real" life. Perhaps that would convince them she wasn't insane when she told them she lived in a different century. Melanie felt a bit apprehensive. She hadn't yet spoken to anyone about when and from where she had come. Would they want to send her to an asylum?

"Miss Swift? Are you finished?" The woman was standing outside the water closet door.

"Yes, thank you. Is there a place where I can wash my hands?" There was no sink in this small room.

"Why don't I bring you back to your room and give you a sponge bath? The bed is in an upright position now, so you can sit up. It'll make you feel much better. Then you can eat."

They made their way back to the room, and Melanie sat up in the bed while the attendant sponged her with warm water and medicinal smelling soap. "Thank you so much," she said when it was over and the woman moved the tray of food closer to her. The food was cold, but Melanie did her best to take a few bites.

"Is there anything else you need before I go?"

"Do you know when Dr. Thornwell will be back?"

"I think he'll be here as soon as his rounds are over."

"All right," Melanie smiled, "If you see him, would you please let him know I want to talk to him?" She peeled the orange on her tray and was surprised how flavorful it was. Fruit didn't taste that good at home. She finished it and pushed the tray away. She couldn't remember when she had eaten last, and thought again about the banana she had taken to work with her. The gash in her head was feeling a little less sore, and she dozed off, sitting up, her head turned toward the pillow. As soon as she fell asleep, she started dreaming again.

Melanie's dream was about New York—she was in the middle of a large avenue, although she couldn't tell which one. The cars, the taxis, the buses—they were all going by fast, back and forth. They were too noisy, horns honking at her like angry reprimands. In the dream she was afraid of these vehicles, but she couldn't move out of the road, even though the vehicles were coming at her from all angles. Her arms and legs and all of her muscles were paralyzed, no matter how hard she tried to move. The frustration and fear made her cry out.

"Oh dear, you're having a nightmare. Come on, it's all right. I'm here with you."

Melanie's eyes popped open wide, although her head felt fuzzy, and she was staring into Thomas's face. His furrowed brow told her right away that he was concerned. He had one hand on her shoulder, and the other holding her hand.

She felt herself shaking. "Oh, God," she said, "It was so real."

"What was real?" Now the hand on her shoulder moved up to her face, and he brushed the tears away from her eyes.

"I was back home—back in New York—and I was in the middle of the road. I couldn't move, Thomas, I couldn't move. They were all rushing around me, and I was scared I'd be hit."

"Who was rushing around you?"

Melanie snapped awake. She noticed that Thomas had brought a big pad with him, which he'd laid down on the bed. "We have to talk."

"Yes, no doubt we must talk," he said. "I know absolutely nothing about you." He turned his gaze away from her eyes, and stared downward. "Why don't I start with your history?"

Melanie felt herself gulp. "You have to promise you'll believe I'm not crazy."

"I don't think you're crazy, Melanie."

She squeezed his hand. "Wait until you hear my story, and then promise me you'll tell me that again. Okay?"

"I promise."

"Where do you want me to start?"

"What is your full name?" He raised the pad to his lap and pulled a black fountain pen with a mother-of-pearl tip out of this white coat.

"Melanie Rose Swift."

"That's a beautiful name." He wrote the name down.

Melanie giggled.

"What is your date of birth?"

"November 16, 1986." Melanie felt her jaw tensing as Thomas's head jerked up to meet her gaze.

"What?"

"You heard me." He tried to look into her eyes, but she couldn't give him the eye contact he wanted. She looked down, away, anywhere but into those piercing green eyes.

For a few moments, Thomas didn't say anything. He put his pad back down on the bed, holding the fountain pen away from the sheets with one hand. He rubbed his other hand across his forehead, and Melanie could see some beads of perspiration forming at the bridge of his nose.

"This is February, 1886."

"Yes, that's what I am told."

More silence, more perspiration. "I'm trying hard to make myself believe that you're not insane."

"Thomas, you promised me!" She felt tears of frustration forming in the corners of her eyes. "I have no idea how I got here, but you have to believe me. I am as sane as you are, and as confused. The last thing I remember, I was on my way to work, running to catch a bus."

"Bus? You talked about a bus before."

"It was a Monday, and it was 2016. I had an important presentation I had to give to the top managers of my corporation. The advancement of my career depended on it. I was nervous, and I was late. I was rushing. I tripped on an icy sidewalk, and my heel broke. Then I fell, and I think a large vehicle hit me, and that's the last thing I remember clearly. I have some vague memories about being brought to the hospital by ambulance and hearing people's voices. I was frustrated, because I could hear them, but I couldn't see, couldn't move, and couldn't respond. I remember hearing Justin's voice and my mother's voice, and she was distraught. I wanted to comfort her, but I heard someone say I was unconscious and needed a CT scan."

"CT scan? And who's Justin?"

"That's a test they can run on a person so that they can see what's happening in your brain and inside your body."

"Oh, my! How do they do that?"

Melanie couldn't tell whether Thomas was skeptical or hungry for information. She decided not to pay attention to the skepticism, if that's what it was, and to plunge ahead with her story. "I don't know. They roll you into a big machine, and then it takes pictures of your insides, but I have no idea how it works."

"I never heard of anything like that—"

"I know. This is 1886."

"Do you know who the president is?"

"Are you testing my sanity or my knowledge of American history? I'm embarrassed to say that I'm not sure who was—is—president in 1886."

"Grover Cleveland."

"Oh, right, and what I can tell you is that he will lose the next election, but he'll come back four years after that and win. That's a piece of presidential history that's always stuck in my mind."

Now Thomas sat staring at her, his mouth agape.

"And I can tell you that in 2016, the President of the United States is a black man, and I worked on his campaign."

"My father fought for emancipation of the slaves and was a medic in the Civil War. But a black man elected president? I can hardly believe it. How sad that neither Father nor I will ever see it. I wish my father were still alive so I could tell him!"

Despite what he said, his wide-eyed look told her he might be questioning her sanity—humoring her. She was determined to convince him. "And we have cars on the streets, no more horses. And buses that have electric motors. And no one has an outhouse anymore, everyone has indoor plumbing, and there are jet planes that fly all over the world all the time."

"You're taking my breath away, Melanie. But this still doesn't explain how you got here and whether you're sane or just a psychotic blathering gibberish. And who is Justin?"

Melanie laughed. "I know I'm not crazy, Thomas, but I have no idea how I got here. Justin is a man I know." She took a deep breath. "He works with me, and I—like him."

Thomas raised his eyebrows, a question there that remained unasked. "Perhaps this is still a dream? Perhaps I'm not really here?"

"No, you're here. I'm sure of that. Both of us couldn't be having the exact same dream. You're not going to send me to the asylum, are you? To McLain's?" Melanie made a frightened face, but then she burst into nervous laughter, and so did Thomas.

"How do I know this is true? Can you prove to me that you landed here from the future?"

Melanie thought for a moment. "Well, what I had on when I ended up on that bench was the hospital clothing they use in 2016. Did anyone look at it? There might be a date on the label." She hesitated to mention the phone, concerned he would think her truly delusional if she brought it up.

"I'm not sure what happened to those clothes. The nurses were talking about them most of the night. They couldn't figure out where they came from. I think they put them in the laundry."

"Well, when they come back from laundry, check the label. It will probably say 'Made in China.' Would that convince you?"

"Made in China? How could your clothing be made in China? Have you been to China?"

"No, never. But I'd like to go."

"How on earth would you get there?"

"By airplane. I'd fly."

"You're making my head spin."

"You should come back with me to 2016, and then you could see all of this for yourself."

"Now I'm really beginning to think you're dotty. How in the world could I go back with you? How in the world could you go back—uh—forward?"

For the first time, Melanie realized that what he was saying was logical. She had no idea how she'd gotten here, and even less of a clue how she might get back. That scared her, not to be able to see her apartment, her mother, her friends—Justin—ever again.

"You're trembling, Melanie." Thomas bent over and steadied her with his strong arms.

She hadn't noticed before, but she loved his smell. It was sweet but masculine, and she just wanted to breathe him in. She felt as if she were betraying Justin, so she tried to put the attraction to Thomas out of her mind.

"This is very difficult, I know, but maybe I should say that you seem to be doing a great deal better this morning."

She nodded. "I feel a little better, at least physically."

"Do you want to go on with your tale?"

"It's the truth, not a tale."

"I'm sorry, it's just difficult to believe."

"As difficult for me to believe I'm actually here as for you to believe I live—lived—in 2016.

"For now, I'm trying to figure out how to explain to the hospital staff that you are a visitor from the twenty-first century."

"Why do you have to?"

"I'm sure questions will be asked," he said. "Someone in strange clothing marked 'Made in China' doesn't just appear here. When I found you, you looked as if you'd been in a very bad altercation. They may feel you should be transferred to a mental ward, that you're daft."

The smile melted off Melanie's face. "But, Thomas, you believe me, don't you? And I'm not *daft*." She imitated his inflection, but he didn't seem to notice.

"I believe you." He hesitated, which made Melanie clench her teeth. What if he didn't really believe her? "But put yourself in my shoes. If I had appeared in the middle of your world in—2016, right?—telling everyone I had arrived from 1886, how do you think I would have been regarded? Would people not think I'd lost my mind?"

Melanie had to admit it would have been very disconcerting to have someone dressed like this, with that old fashioned way of speaking, appear out of nowhere saying he was from the 1880s. A harsh knock on the door caused them both to jump. "Come in," he said.

A nurse in a crisp white uniform and cape with one of those starched hats that all the nurses wore, entered the room. "I have to take Miss Swift's pulse and temperature, Doctor. Also, I have this clothing, which was laundered." Melanie looked around, and she saw the hospital gown neatly folded, in the nurse's hands."

"Oh, thank goodness," she said, hopeful the label would back up her story.

The nurse laid the neat pile at the foot of the bed. "Doctor, would you like to leave the room until I've completed my examination?"

Thomas glanced at Melanie, who made a slight movement with her head as if to say, *don't leave me*. She needed him there, needed his support. These nurses were a little gruff.

"That's all right, Nurse, I'll just turn my back."

The nurse went about her business without another word, gripping Melanie's wrist a bit too hard, which made Melanie wince. The nurse then pulled a thermometer out of a small container. Melanie opened her mouth and let the nurse slide it under her tongue, wondering how they sterilized medical equipment in 1886. She would ask Thomas later, but right now, she didn't want to make a fuss. No need to have this nurse leave the room and talk about the "madwoman" in the ward. Finally, the nurse came close to Melanie and looked at the sutures along her hairline.

"All right, Doctor. Everything seems normal," the nurse had pulled the thermometer from Melanie's mouth and was shaking it down. "I think those sutures are healing well."

"Thank you, Nurse," he said.

"Aren't you off duty now, Doctor?"

"Yes, I'm just doing some more work with this patient."

As the nurse turned her back on them to leave the room, Thomas pivoted around, facing Melanie, and shrugged.

As soon as the door shut with a convincing click, Melanie felt her body relax. "That was tense," she said. "She was pretty bossy."

"These nurses take themselves very seriously, and you are apparently a great subject of conversation around here."

"Great," she sighed, "I miss my life."

"I wish I could help you get back there," he said, "But to be honest, a part of me is quite happy you're here. Is that a terrible thing to say?"

"No." Melanie felt her own voice tremble. "If I had to be found by anyone, I'm glad it was you. At least you're making an effort to believe me. Oh, would you please hand me those clothes? I want to check the label to see if they are made in China."

Thomas picked up the neat stack and handed it to Melanie, but when she looked at the label, either this laundering or previous launderings had bleached out any information that might have been there. The label was now just a small, rectangular, fraying piece of attached material with no print visible.

"Damn," she said, "They must use strong soap here." She held it up for him to see, and he shook his head slowly.

Moments later there was another knock at the door, and the janitor entered with a bucket and a mop, and behind him another nurse with bed linens. The janitor began his floor cleaning, and Melanie almost gagged from the strong ammonia smell rising from the bucket.

"Would you like me to help Miss Swift out of bed and on to the chair so that you can do your work?" Thomas asked the nurse who was now at Melanie's bedside.

"I'm perfectly able to change the sheets around her. Perhaps she's had enough exercise for one day."

Thomas gave a dismissive wave of his hand, and the nurse didn't pursue her question. Melanie wanted to say, *I'm here, please address me, and don't talk about me as if I'm not right in front of you.* But she held her tongue. Instead she struggled to sit up. "No, I'd actually prefer to get up. This bed isn't very comfortable."

Thomas rushed over and held out his arm, which she grabbed. He was slim but well-built and muscular, with broad shoulders. She felt his arm could have supported her in a tornado. She had never touched Justin's arm, and she closed her eyes and fantasized that this was Justin, helping her. Thomas guided her to the chair, and she sat down. It felt good to be out of bed. "I think some activity will be very good for me anyway."

"You don't want to rush to do something too fast," the nurse mumbled as she changed the sheets and the pillowcases. "You've been through something."

"But I feel better," Melanie said. "And moving around will make me feel even better."

"She is progressing very well," Thomas added, as if to underscore Melanie's statement. "I think we'll be able to remove those sutures very soon. And the ecchymosis around her eyes is fading."

"All right, then," said the nurse, whipping the old linens into a pile, which she hung over her arm. After she left, the janitor maneuvered his mop under the bed, and there was a small, clattering noise. He bent down to look, and came up with the cell phone Melanie had dropped.

"Is this yours, miss?" The janitor stood several feet away from the chair where Melanie was sitting, as if he was afraid to approach.

Thomas took the phone away from him, and stared at it, turning it around in his hand before he looked over at Melanie, his eyebrow raised again. The janitor left the room, pushing his bucket in front of him.

"Oh, thank heavens," she said, whispering. "I almost forgot about that."

"You can close the door," Thomas called after the janitor, who did as he was told. "He's gone. What is this thing?" Thomas inspected the iPhone, running his fingers around the edge as if it was made of glass. "What are these buttons and holes?" He tapped the buttons, his touch very light. "What do you use this for?"

He looked so confused that it made Melanie feel sorry for him.

"That is a telephone. They call it a smart phone. It's my way of convincing you I'm not crazy," she said.

"A telephone? That doesn't look like any telephone I've ever seen."

"Turn it over and look at the back."

"It looks like a drawing of an apple with a bite taken out of it. What does that mean?"

"It's just a brand called Apple."

"Apple? Why?"

"I'm not sure. It just is, and that company's been in business probably since the 1980s or so."

Thomas looked between Melanie and the phone. "This is scaring me a little bit."

"You don't have to be scared. What about me? Suddenly I get plunked down into 1886. I think I have the harder adjustment here, don't you?"

"Maybe."

"Let me have that. I want to show you something. I hope the battery isn't dead."

Thomas laughed as he handed her the phone. "What do you mean battery? This thing is tiny. You couldn't fit a battery in there."

"You know about batteries?"

"Yes. They're very big."

"Not anymore," she said. "I mean, not in 2016." She pressed the button on the phone, and the indicator showed that the battery was still charged. "Thank goodness," she said. "Now, look at this." She pressed the calendar icon, and it opened to February, 2016. "See how I have a meeting scheduled for February eight at ten? Obviously, I missed that." She sighed. "Do you believe me now?"

Thomas stared at the small calendar and then looked up at her without moving his head. His forehead had contracted into deep horizontal lines, and his mouth was slightly open, but he said nothing.

"Turn the phone over and see what it says on the back. Under the picture of the apple."

He did as she asked and then squinted at the tiny imprint. "It says 'Designed by Apple in California,' and 'Assembled in China.' Here we go again with the China thing. I still don't understand."

"It's because labor costs are much lower in China, and that's why a lot of companies pay to have their merchandise manufactured there. It's cheaper to do that than to have the stuff made in the United States, where labor costs are way too high."

"What about the people in this country? Doesn't that take work away from them?"

"We do other work now, but frequently manufacturing is outsourced to other countries."

"How do they get there? How do they communicate with China? That's a long boat trip."

"Yes, it would have been. But in 2016, ships are very fast, and we fly around the world in even faster airplanes. We call them jets, and you can get from Boston to New York in forty-five minutes, and to Los Angeles in six hours. We use telephones to communicate with anyone in the world, and I won't start to tell you about computers, networks, and email. I don't want to kill you with all this information."

"Whoa, whoa!" he said. "My head is spinning." He backed up and sat down on the edge of the bed, holding a hand across his forehead as if he was in pain. "This is too much to take in all at once."

"So, we're in the same boat, right? Both of us struggling with how to believe everything that's happened."

"I have been following the progress of development in flight, Melanie. I'm fascinated by it. The fact that such airships will exist makes me excited and jealous at the same time, because I'm not sure whether I'll ever see such a thing. Do people fly to China?"

"Everywhere. And believe me, there's every chance you will live to see it. When you do, remember I told you so."

"And they can talk to people around the world?"

"Yup."

"How do they do that?"

"You wouldn't believe the technology we have." She paused to make sure he was all right. "I'm sorry. I didn't mean to shock you."

"What else do you have? Tell me everything!"

Melanie took her phone back and turned it off, and gave it to him to put on the table beside her bed. Then she laughed again. "Where do you want me to start?"

"What kind of medical technology do you have?"

"Wow. Okay. We have these drugs called antibiotics. They fight bacterial infections like strep. You know, like a strep throat?"

Thomas raised his eyebrows. "Streptococcus?"

She nodded. "I guess those infections kill a lot of people now, right? Well, we can treat them so that people get better. The problem is that antibiotics have been overused, so the germs are becoming resistant to the drugs. So research is going on constantly to develop new ones."

"My God."

"We have CT scans and MRIs, so that a machine can look inside someone's body and diagnose things like tumors without invading the body."

"MRI?"

"It stands for magnetic resonance imaging, so it's done with magnets. You can actually see the inside of someone's body, in three dimensions."

He breathed in, a deep, loud breath. "What else?" Now he'd stood up and was pacing between the bed and the chair. "I'm hungry for all of this, as hard as it is to believe. I feel short of breath. If only—"

"Thomas, please sit down. You're breathing so fast, I'm worried you'll hyperventilate."

"No, please tell me more, Melanie." He grabbed her hand.

She moved it so that it was touching his chest. She tried to massage him to calm him down, but he pushed her hand off. "I need to know everything."

"I'm not a doctor, Thomas! I only know what I hear about on television and read in the papers."

"What is television?"

"You're breathing too hard. Don't you want to sit down? Please?"

Thomas put his hand up to his head and sat back down on the bed. She noticed that all the color had drained out of his face. His situation almost made her forget about hers.

"Come on, Melanie, please. What else can you tell me?"

"Are you angry with me? You sound angry."

"No, just envious. You're not making up these stories, are you? Honestly, it would be easier to think you're *non compos mentis.*"

"No, I'm not making it up. How could I make up stories like this? You saw my phone. You need to trust me. I don't want to end up in an asylum."

"Please, just tell me everything."

"We don't use horses anymore. Well, some policemen patrol crowded parts of the city on horses, because it's easier to move through large masses of people with them. But now, people ride horses for recreation." She tilted her head back and closed her eyes, as if she was thinking hard. "Policemen also use motorcycles."

"Motorcycles? You mean like the motorized bicycles? I've seen some of those in expositions."

"Yes, the modern ones can go faster than cars."

"Cars?"

"Do they call them horseless carriages now? Automobiles? Do they have any yet in Boston? In my world, most people drive gasoline-powered cars, but some of the cars are electric now. There are problems with the emissions from gasoline engines. The emissions are destroying the earth's atmosphere, changing its climate."

"Wait, wait—I am more confused by the minute."

She ignored him. "They can go very fast, and sometimes drivers have accidents that hurt people. Maybe—" Melanie had a flutter of a memory of falling in the street and seeing that truck coming. She shuddered.

"Maybe what?"

"Maybe that's what happened to me. I'm not sure whether I dreamed it, or it really happened."

"You think you were hit by one of these electric cars?"

"No, a truck. They're not electric. I'm not sure, but I think it was a truck."

"If you were struck by a fast-moving vehicle, that could

explain your injuries. From the way you describe these carriages, I think you may be lucky to be alive." He stood up again and wiped his brow.

Melanie tried hard to remember what had happened before she arrived here, but the memories were fleeting and short-lived. She couldn't wrap her brain around anything certain, and it frustrated her. She clenched her fists without realizing she had done it, and Thomas noticed it.

"Let's just relax now, okay?" he said. "No need to get you so frustrated it makes you sicker."

"I feel better with you here. But..."

"Yes?"

"You worked all night, and now you're here with me. Shouldn't you go home and get some sleep?"

"I don't want to leave you. I feel as if you have so much to tell me."

"I don't want you to go either, but maybe we should both get some rest. I'm feeling exhausted again."

He stood up. "There is a room in the hospital where doctors on duty can nap. I will sleep a few hours if you promise to do the same."

"Won't your family worry about you?"

"I live with my sisters and an old footman, and they are used to my unpredictable hours. It's all part of being a doctor. But, Melanie?"

"Yes?"

"I don't even know anything about you. Where are you from?"

"I told you, New York City."

"What do you do there?"

"I have a junior position in a financial services corporation. I graduated from college two years ago, and I was very lucky to get this job. I can't imagine what they're thinking about me now."

"I'm afraid they're not thinking anything about you. It's 1886. What do you mean by a financial services corporation?"

"Large institutions give us money, and we invest it in various commodities. The idea is for their money to grow exponentially. We constantly analyze the markets and do research tweaking our algorithms as necessary."

"Algorithms?"

"It's hard to explain. Are you sure you want to have this conversation now?"

"I don't know what I want. Are you in this institution with men?"

"And other women too," she said.

"Do many women do this work?"

"Many, although it's still rather skewed toward males."

"Where do you learn how to do it?"

"Well, you go to college and learn micro- and macro-economics, but then you learn on the job, mostly."

"You went to college?"

"Yes."

"Where?"

"Harvard."

Thomas jumped backward, banging his hand on the side of the bed. He shook it to alleviate the pain. "Do you mean Harvard Annex?"

"I don't think I know what that is."

Thomas stood with his head slightly back, his hand stroking his chin. He narrowed his eyes. "You realize that Harvard doesn't admit women."

"That changed a long time ago. First there was Radcliffe College, considered the women's college of Harvard, and then the two colleges merged. Now men and women go to college together, live together in dormitories, and receive the same diploma."

Thomas sucked in his breath. "By now, you mean 2016, right?'

She shook her head yes. "Oops, I keep forgetting." She felt a shadow pass over her, and she shuddered. "Neither of us is quite sure of what's going on here, but it's all true. Women go to college just like men, go to law school and medical school, vote, own property, fight in wars, run companies—what else do you want to know?"

As if someone had punched him in the stomach, Thomas reeled and backed up, falling onto the bed again. "Let's not tell anyone else about this yet, all right?"

"Are you worried they won't believe me? You can convince them to, can't you?"

Thomas didn't answer. He put his hand over his eyes.

"Can't you?"

"It's all just very hard to believe, Melanie, very hard to digest."

"This *is* all very hard to believe, Thomas, but for some reason I'm here and we're together, and I have to believe there's a reason for that. It's not just random."

Thomas regained his composure. "All right," he said, "We'll deal with all of this, you and I. I can't wait until you're healed and out of here and I can show you absolutely everything."

"Me too, but has it occurred to you that when I get out of here, I have no place to go? I don't know anyone in 1886 except you and Dr. MacInerney. That's a problem. No family to return to or contact. They're not even born yet."

At that point, the two of them started to laugh, Thomas almost uncontrollably. "The situation is so absurd, it's funny," he said. "We will figure something out. I promise you."

Chapter 6

Neither Thomas nor Melanie noticed Dr. MacInerney enter the room. Thomas was still slumped on the edge of the bed, his head in his hands, while Melanie was sitting in the chair, staring into space, her face still animated by the laughter.

"Well, you two, looks like the patient is improving?" He approached Melanie and pulled out his stethoscope. "Are you comfortable on the chair?"

She nodded, trying to look serious.

"Would you please breathe normally, Miss Swift?" He examined her leaning over to look at the sutures at her temple. "Anything new, Dr. Thornwell? I see the color is returning to normal and the swelling has gone down somewhat." He hesitated. "Dr. Thornwell, are you all right?"

"Yes, sir." Thomas sprang up and stood behind his superior. He was at least a head taller and half the girth of Dr. MacInerney, but the older doctor projected such an air of *gravitas*, it was obvious Thomas was the student. "Nothing new but her miraculous improvement," Thomas said, his hands behind his back, standing a couple of paces behind his chief. "She is definitely feeling better. She is a strong young woman."

"I trust you took all the information?"

"I did, sir."

"And, have her family been contacted?"

"Uh…" Thomas shot a worried look at Melanie, a flash of panic crossing his face.

"I'm in the room, Dr. MacInerney," she said, "You can ask me these questions. I can talk."

"Oh right, I'm so sorry." MacInerney's tone softened, and he touched Melanie's arm lightly. "I get so used to barking orders at my students. Do you have a place to go after you're released from this hospital? You may not be sick enough to be hospitalized, but you will need some aftercare. Will your family be traveling here?"

Melanie shot what she thought was a furtive glance at Thomas, who gestured, glaring, from behind Dr. MacInerney that she should be quiet. Thomas's mouth was drawn thin, his eyes small slits.

"A long trip back to New York might not be advisable until you're much stronger." The older doctor raised his eyebrows, as if he was aware the two were trying to communicate something.

"My family is not able to make the trip," she said, looking down at her lap.

"Ah, I see." MacInerney placed his finger over his lips, tapping them lightly.

"Excuse me, Doctor," Thomas said, his words soft and fast, "I've offered to have her move in with us until she's fully recuperated."

MacInerney wheeled around, his mouth open as if he couldn't control it. "*What*?"

"I have invited her to move into my house. My sisters spend much of their time alone there, and they could use a woman to guide them while I'm at the hospital."

"So are you saying, Miss Swift will be their governess?"

"No, not exactly, sir. They are both adults, but I'm afraid they are floundering without my mother's presence in the house. Jane's been hit very hard by our mother's death and could use Miss Swift's happy disposition to cheer her."

"Hmmm...I see." MacInerney shifted his gaze from Melanie back to Thomas and then back again. Melanie was still not looking at him.

"Jane is a nursing student, and she can see to all of Miss Swift's medical needs until she's able to return to New York," Thomas continued. "My other sister, Athena, takes care of the house, and I know she would love to have another female companion. Honestly—" His voice had become quick and staccato. "—Jane could use the influence of a confident young woman in the house."

"Slow down, doctor, you're talking so fast I can hardly understand you."

"I'm sorry, Dr. MacInerney."

"Dr. Thornwell, this is quite noble of you, but highly irregular. You are not acquainted with this woman, nor she with you, and as far as I know, neither of you is married, certainly not to each other—her family might object."

He raised one eyebrow as he stared at Thomas, who was now looking straight down at his feet. Melanie tried not to giggle, but she noticed that the color had drained out of Thomas's face, as if someone had given him very bad news. She hoped he could figure out some excuse. One way or the other, she was moving in with Thomas, not only because there was no other place to go, but also because he was the only one who knew anything about her. She would deal with his obvious attraction to her in her own way on her own time.

"I'm not sure what other options we have, Doctor."

"Perhaps there is a ladies' residence where she can go? The YWCA? Or perhaps a family could take her in for the time being. That appears a more seemly choice, do you not agree? I believe there are such families in Beacon Hill. It's a charity type of thing, and the well-to-do participate. But a doctor should not take such a personal interest in his patients. Especially when the patient is an...um...attractive young lady without a husband or any family in the area."

Thomas would not look at MacInerney, but he looked up at Melanie, now with his mouth turned down as if in defeat. Melanie realized she would have to be the one to take over the conversation. "Maybe Dr. Thornwell could check on other possibilities for me, Dr. MacInerney? And we'll make the right decision. After all, his is a family too. You don't need to worry."

"You are quite a determined young lady," MacInerney said, "For someone who has been through such trauma."

"I try," she said, her hand over her mouth.

"What's that?"

"I said, it will all work out." She glanced over at Thomas, whose face had relaxed back into its normal good humor, the color returning and the lines smoothed out. It was funny to her that he was relying on her to deal with his boss, but she didn't mind.

"Well, medically, anyway, I'm delighted with her progress, Doctor," MacInerney said, snapping his stethoscope back around his neck. "And her attitude is very good. Keep up the good work, young lady. You are young and strong. Another week or so, and you will be ready to be released from the hospital. Dr. Thornwell, your shift is certainly over, is it not? You can feel free to go home."

"Thank you, Doctor," Thomas said, his voice light with relief. "I will do that."

With a small wave behind his head, Dr. MacInerney left the room, not looking back. His footsteps echoed on the concrete floors as he made his way down the ward. Neither Melanie nor Thomas spoke until they were sure he was out of earshot.

"Do you have to go home now?" Melanie sounded so sad that Thomas chuckled.

"I really should go home and discuss this plan with my sisters, don't you think? I don't want to shock them. Do you need me to stay?"

"I do feel awful that you haven't had any real sleep."

"Would you like me to help you back to bed? Once you

fall asleep, you won't notice my being gone, and I'll be back before you know it."

Thomas approached her and held out his hands to her. She grabbed them, and he pulled her up slowly, but she was already quite steady on her feet. As she got back into bed, he wouldn't let go of her, so she gently removed her hands from his, despite his resistance.

"I will work on you until you feel about me the way I feel about you," he said.

Melanie sighed. "It's too soon for me," she said. "My Justin is still in my heart."

"But you may never see him again." Thomas stamped his foot, like a little boy who'd been denied candy.

"It's just too soon," she said again, and folded her hands across her lap.

Thomas leaned down and brushed the hair away from her wound, inspecting it closely.

"I want so much to kiss you," he said. "I want to change your mind."

"Too soon." She turned her head away. "Too soon."

"I wish you could accept being in my world."

He tried to pick up her hand, but she tucked her hands under the covers.

Thomas moved away from the bed, stopping at the window, where he turned his back on her. He sighed.

"Are you angry at me?" she pouted.

"I just don't know what to think, Melanie. You appear here, with your smart phone, as you called it, something I have no concept of at all, with the date sometime in the year 2016. I hardly believe it myself, but I think I'm falling in love with you. It started happening the moment I laid eyes on you when you were a block of ice on that bench. It hurts me when you keep taunting me with this Justin fellow. I'm confused—about everything."

"I'm sorry, Thomas. I don't want to make you feel bad, but I think I'm in love with him."

"I don't know how you think you're going to get back to

him. And I think you need to accept that you're here to stay. To move on."

"I don't even know how I got here in the first place. Maybe I'll go back the same way. It's just too early. For everything, Thomas. I'm sorry, but that's just the way it is."

"You frustrate me, Melanie."

"So you are angry with me, then? I don't want you to be angry with me."

"Just please try to understand, all right? I'll do the same. But you may have to meet me in the middle."

"I'm trying not to think about that part, you know? What's the point? If I do, it hurts my head even more than my head hurts on its own."

"Is your head hurting more?" He approached her again, his concerned doctor face peering down at her.

"No, it's mostly just the pain of confusion."

"I have that too."

"But it could be worse. What if you hadn't found me?"

"Indeed, it could be much worse."

"But I miss my old life, even so. When I think about it, I just want to cry."

"I promise you I will spend mine trying to make you happy. I never thought this would happen to me, not in a million years, but then something sent you to me. No matter how confusing it is, I'm falling in love with you, and I can't wait until you're happy here with me. Even without this." He reached over and picked up the cell phone that was lying beside her pillow.

"You need to be patient."

"But I'm impatient."

"I know what's going to happen. Did that ever occur to you? I can tell you how the world is going to evolve, who is going to go to war with whom, who will win those wars, what the shape of the world is going to be. I told you that in 2016, the President of the United States is a black man."

Thomas sat down on edge of the bed with a thud. The bed bounced a little, several times. "I know. That's unbelievable. A black man." He said the words slowly, as if he was chewing them a little, trying them out in his mouth, as if they didn't fit very well.

"Well, half black. His mother was white. His father was born in Kenya."

"So black people can vote?"

Melanie laughed. "Just like women, yes. It's been a long, hard haul for African Americans, believe me. It still is—will be—in 2016. But we have a black president, and he was reelected to a second term."

"You will tell me everything, everything. And I will do the same for you."

"Will your sisters be appalled that I'm moving in with you?"

"I'm not sure. But I am confident they will quickly learn to like you as much as I do, and it will be so good for them to have another woman in the house. My sister Jane was young when we lost our parents, and it affected her profoundly. She is a lovely, bright young woman, but she has never really gotten over losing them, especially our mother. She's sad much of the time. She never goes out with friends or shows any interest in the nice young men who call on her."

"I'd love to try and help her. Maybe we can bond over the fact that I have lost a parent, too. I can't wait to meet her."

Chapter 7

Melanie's recuperation continued to astound Dr. MacInerney, who wanted to keep her at Boston General a while longer to make sure she was all right, but she worked on him every time she saw him, telling him she felt up to leaving the hospital.

"What will I wear?" she asked Thomas on a Wednesday, after having been given a tentative go-ahead by MacInerney to be discharged the next day. "All I had on when I got here was the hospital gown from New York."

"Oh, my!" Thomas looked stricken, as if she had assigned him the most impossible task. "It didn't even occur to me. I'm not sure we can get something made for you by tomorrow."

"There are no places where you can buy ready-made clothing?"

"Perhaps, but my sister Athena is such a wizard with a sewing needle, she sews all of Jane's dresses and her own."

"Maybe I could borrow something from one of them? Do you think they'd mind?"

Thomas looked at her, squinting his eyes. "I don't think they'd mind, but I'm not sure you're all the same size. Jane is shorter than you and Athena taller."

"It doesn't have to be perfect. Just good enough to get

me out of here. Maybe a pair of her shoes as well?"

"Oh." He looked down at her feet and got the most per-plexed expression on his face.

"When you go home tonight, just ask them, okay? As soon as I get to your house, we can figure out what else we have to do to get me some kind of wardrobe. I wish I could be reunited with my blue jeans, that's all."

"Blue jeans? Do you mean bloomers? Jane might have a pair of bloomers you can borrow."

Melanie giggled. "Never mind! We'll work it all out."

The day proved a flurry of activity, nurses monitoring her every couple of hours, especially checking that the scar along her hairline wasn't infected or hurting. The stitches had come out easily, the doctors still marveling at what they were made of. Melanie hadn't been able to provide any in-formation, but a steady stream of medical professionals had looked them over, handled them carefully, put them back into the metal tray afterward. Melanie tried not to think about it. She was so ready to get out of here and go "home" to Thomas's house, where she could make some attempt to be herself, that she let herself be poked and prodded, ques-tioned over and over again. None of it mattered, as long as she could leave soon.

At about four that afternoon, Thomas appeared with a long garment bag, which he unbuttoned with care. He re-moved a beautiful pink organdy dress, hand embroidered with flowers all along the bodice, with buttons down the back and a deep pink silk ribbon around the waist. "It's Jane's," he said.

Melanie gasped when he brought it over to her. "Oh, goodness! That dress is beautiful. It looks like a ball gown. Are you sure she's okay with lending it to me?"

Thomas looked as if he was about to cry. "I convinced her," he said, under his breath.

"Oh, I hope she's not angry. You didn't have to bring her best dress to me for a trip from the hospital to the house."

"Don't worry about it. I'm sure you won't ruin it."

"I'll be careful, but I hate to think she's unhappy with me already."

Thomas shrugged. Melanie was so ready to leave that she didn't think much about the dress. "I'm so ready," she said, slipping the dress over her head. It fit pretty well, perfect on the top but a little short. She turned around for Thomas to button the back, and then she tied the ribbon tightly. Thomas's hands hesitated on her back, lingering a little with each button.

"I would like to take you in my arms," he said.

"You need to be patient," she said. "I like you, but not that way."

"I will work my hardest to change your mind." His voice was so low that she had to strain to hear. "Look, I want to give you something, to show you my affection is real."

"That's not necessary, really. You've given me enough." Melanie felt tears streaming down her face again. That was happening too frequently, and she wondered whether it had anything to do with the head trauma she had experienced as much as with the roller coaster of emotions she was feeling. "What if your sisters hate me?" She looked up at him through the tears.

"Jane and Athena will both adore you. I'm sure of it."

"How do you know that? They've had you all to themselves, now here I come, and I'll be taking your attention away from them."

"But you'll be there for them. They need someone like you, especially Jane—a confident young woman to help them get through their troubles. Jane needs to get over her shyness. Athena's not shy, but she spends all her time working in the house. Heaven knows, I don't know what to do about it."

"What if they resent me?"

"Melanie, where is this coming from? I thought we agreed this is the best solution for all of us."

"I know. I guess I'm getting cold feet."

"That's an odd expression," he said, "Particularly after the way I found you."

Melanie laughed through her tears.

"What other solution is there?" he said.

"I know you're right. But you have to promise me that if you decide it isn't working out, or if the girls hate me, we will think of another solution. I don't want to be somewhere if I'm not wanted."

"Melanie, there is no question in my mind. Something threw us together, and there has to be a reason for that. I know it. Everything happens for a reason."

Melanie sighed. "Don't hate me for having doubts and for pining away for Justin."

"We will make a new family, Melanie. I promise you that. I can't wait to show you Boston. I'll take you on the swan boats, we'll stroll through Harvard Yard, and go watch the Boston Beaneaters play baseball, even though they're pretty lousy."

"Boston Beaneaters?" She restrained herself from laughing, because he looked so serious when he said their name, even reverent. She couldn't even think of telling him about the Red Sox and how they had won the World Series three times after losing for decades. Then, he'd have no idea what the World Series was.

"Yes, I love baseball." He didn't notice that her eyes were laughing, and she averted his gaze. "Do you like the symphony? The Boston Symphony plays at the Boston Music Hall. My family has always had season tickets. Our seats are tenth row, center orchestra. Do you like the symphony?"

"We used to go as college students and get the half-price tickets an hour before each concert. We sat way up in the balcony of Symphony Hall."

"Symphony Hall?"

"Another thing I get to tell you about before it actually happens. You're going to be the smartest person in Boston, and people will come for miles around to have you predict the future." The tears were gone, and Melanie was laughing now.

"That is if they don't cart *me* off to McLean's. Maybe you should watch what you tell me."

"But seriously, Thomas, what if Athena hates me so much that she tries to poison my food?" The smile changed to a slight downturn of her mouth, and Thomas shook his head, slowly back and forth.

"Are you losing your mind?"

"There's a famous movie called 'Gaslight.'"

"Movie?"

"Right, never mind. But it's only crazy and funny a little bit. There's some truth to my fears. You have to admit this situation is not at all normal."

"Do we have to go over the facts again?" He pulled his hands away and held on to the edge of her bed, as if he was afraid the bed might slide away.

"No, no. I know these circumstances are strange. I understand I need a place to go. Of course I'm going home with you, but I can't help being a little apprehensive of what might happen next."

"We will weather it together." He looked into her eyes, but she thought his gaze was far-away. She couldn't get him to look straight at her.

"Yes, I know."

"I just want you to be content."

"For someone who had a terrible accident and ended up in a different city in the century before last, I guess I'm as content as I possibly could be. Just a little nervous. And homesick. But I don't want to argue with you."

"Nor I with you." He drew his lips in and furrowed his brow.

"But I tend to be someone who likes to plan things out, you know? I make my little 'pros and cons' lists, think about things, consider the 'if, then, elses' of life before I make decisions. This is all uncomfortably spontaneous for me."

"You might not believe it, but I am the same way, mostly. This time, though, it feels so right, I hate the thought of wasting time. I just have to convince you to feel the same way." Thomas brushed his hair back with his hand, and Melanie noticed it was the exact same thing she'd seen Justin do when he was concentrating hard on something.

"I can't promise anything," she said. "You just need to try to be a little patient with me."

"Whoever put in those sutures did a wonderful job," he said, changing the subject, drawing in close to her, and touching the pale pink line, one inch at a time, that was left along the side of her cheek where the stitches had been removed. "There will be hardly any scar. And even if there is, you will still be the most beautiful girl I've ever seen."

"I'm not really worried about the scar," Melanie said. "What I am worried about is your sisters."

Thomas put his hands in his pockets. He remembered the conversation he'd had with his sister Jane the day before…

∞∞∞

"Tom?" she had said, "what if I don't like her?"

When he got home from the hospital, he'd found her sitting on the window seat in the big bay window at the front of their house, the damask drapes framing her small torso like a shawl, just staring out onto the snowy street. It was twilight, and the lamplighter was making his way up Commonwealth Avenue, lighting the gaslights.

When he reached her, he said, "What are you doing there?"

"Just looking at the horses and watching the lights go on. This is my favorite time of day. Almost dark but not quite. Did you need something? How was your day?"

He had closed in on her, his tall frame dwarfing her slight body, and bent down to put a hand lightly on her shoulder. She lowered her head to the side, lingering a moment on his large hand. Her hair was light brown, long, and soft—almost blonde. It tickled his hand. "I do need another favor."

"Did you have a good day? Did you cure lots of people?" She looked up now, and her eyes were almost twinkling in the half light.

"I cured everyone!"

"My brother, the medical genius."

Thomas laughed. "May I borrow your coat?"

"My coat? Why?"

"I told you, Melanie is coming home tomorrow, and it's so cold outside."

Jane had looked out the window again, tearing her gaze from his face. "But she already has my dress. Why does she need that coat? I like it, and I don't fancy lending it out."

"Jane, she will use it only long enough to come home from the hospital. You're not lending it out." His words came out crisp with exasperation.

Jane had sighed, long and deep. "I just don't...I just don't think I'll like her."

"You will adore her! She can't wait to meet you."

Jane had looked up at him, and he thought he saw a tear forming at the corner of her eye. "This has been a terrible winter. I miss the warmth of the summertime."

"You two are about the same size."

"So now it's my coat and my dress? What will she want next?" Jane was terrified about Melanie's moving in with them. She had tried to figure out a way to make him change his mind about it, these few weeks since Thomas had first mentioned this strange woman who had appeared out of nowhere, talking about how she lived in the year 2016. She was either crazy as a loon, or a liar, and yet she seemed to have taken over Thomas's heart. Jane had precious little time with him anyway, and now this new person was going to be living with them, taking him away from her even more.

"Just for the day, Janie."

"When is she coming?"

"I told you, tomorrow, and don't worry, Melanie will take very good care of your things."

Jane pushed herself up off the window seat, as if it was difficult even to move. She shrugged, and then she disappeared up the stairs. Thomas walked to the back of the house, looking for his sister Athena. When Jane reached her room, she threw herself down on the bed and sobbed.

Chapter 8

They left the hospital, Thomas steering Melanie by the elbow, she taking small steps, not her usual preference, but she was still tentative about falling, even though the floors of the hospital were clean but not slippery. She felt uncomfortable in Jane's party dress and button shoes, which were a little too narrow for her feet. Jane's coat was a little short too, but Melanie pulled it up to her chin. As Thomas opened the tall, heavy door, a blast of cold air almost blew her over.

"Oh, I'm still not that steady on my feet." Her voice was soft, as if talking loudly might make her weaker.

"I'm sorry!" He moved closer, circling her waist with his strong arm. "It's freezing out. Maybe I can help you."

"I wish it were summer."

"Funny, Jane said the same thing yesterday."

"I remember last summer. I biked all over the city, down at the edge of the Hudson River, it was breezy and wonderful. That wind wasn't cold like this wind."

He heard the catch in her voice, held her tighter and stood a little in front of her to shield her from the frigid air. "What else did you do last summer?"

"Well," she said, her voice a little stronger, "We went to the ball park a lot, you know? I love baseball too."

"As soon as spring comes, we will go to the ballpark! Perhaps you will bring our team better luck." He looked down, loosened his grip, and then looked away.

"I don't care if they're bad, I just love the game."

"I know. There's nothing like it on a hot summer day."

"Sometimes my friends and I had picnics on the beach. The water was cold, but I love jumping the waves. And the sand was smooth, like flour."

"I've never seen sand like that. The beaches here have rocky soil, and the water is so cold, it's almost impossible to swim." He coaxed her through the door, pulling the collar of his sister's heavy coat up around Melanie's face. "I'd love to see your beaches." He sighed. "Are your hands warm enough?"

Melanie dug her hands deeper into the pockets of the coat. She squeezed her hands into tight fists. The coat had a pleasant soft floral aroma, but when she breathed in the air, the cold hurt her lungs.

"I forgot how much colder it is in Boston than in New York."

"I've never been to New York," he said, a little sadness in his voice. "What is it like?"

"Well, in summer it's hot and muggy, but I love that feeling. You don't have to wear much—you know, cut-offs and a tank top. You can go sit on the roof of your building with a good book, and if you drift off to sleep, it's fine, as long as you have a good sunscreen."

He was happy she'd forgotten how cold she was. "What else do you do in the summer? And what are cut-offs? And sunscreen?"

Melanie laughed and watched her breath make curls of vapor in the cold air. "I'll draw you a picture when we get to your house, okay? Do you have a drawing pad and some pens?"

"Of course. Jane loves to draw. Sometimes she sits for hours by the window, drawing the trees and the horses and the street lamps. She likes to draw ice skaters," He sighed. "Sometimes I wish she'd do more things with other people and not spend so much time alone drawing and reading."

"Does she like ice skating?"

"Like it? She is an extraordinary ice skater. When she's on the ice, she transforms into a translucent angel." He threw his head back and closed his eyes for a moment, conjuring up the image.

"I'll go ice skating with her. I can't wait to see her skate."

They had reached the corner now, and Melanie knew they must be getting close. "Is the house far from here, Thomas? I'm a little tired, and these shoes are uncomfortable."

"Should I have arranged to have our carriage meet us at the hospital?" His voice was hushed, concerned.

"No, I'm glad for the walk. I've been in that hospital bed forever. I need to get my strength back. I can make it if we walk slowly. It's just cold."

"It's just a few more blocks to Commonwealth Avenue, and then one block from there to the house. I can't wait for you to see it!"

Melanie looked up to see a horse and carriage trotting by, kicking up the light snow that had fallen the night before. The horse's hooves made a ringing, metallic sound on the cobblestones. "This looks like a scene out of Currier and Ives," she said.

"You know about them?"

"Sure. They've made it into a lot of art appreciation courses. This is just the live version of them." She took a deep breath. "The sound is wonderful. Do the horses ever slip when it's snowing?"

"I guess they do sometimes. I never much thought about it. Having four legs helps when it's slippery."

"Currier and Ives are popular now?"

He laughed. "Sure. We have one of their prints in our parlor. It's a picture of the skating pond in Central Park in New York. Jane actually loves that one. She nagged mother to buy it until mother couldn't disappoint her anymore."

"That's a pretty famous print, Thomas. Someday it will be worth a lot of money. Take care of it." She looked so serious as she lectured him, that he laughed.

"You'll have to look at it and let me know if it's preserved properly. You can be my art expert. I have no idea what anything's worth. It's just stuff that my parents accumulated." He gave her a little squeeze around the waist. "Are you warm enough?"

"I'll be okay," she said. "Do you like to go ice skating too?"

"Sure. Jane and I used to go to the Frog Pond to skate when we were little children. The nanny would take us. Since I've been so busy with medical school and the hospital, I haven't really gone, and believe me, I was no expert. I spent more time on my rear than up on my skates."

"I used to go to the Wollman Rink when I was a teenager. We'd ride in from Princeton by bus and spend the day in Central Park. Sometimes we'd go to the rink at Rockefeller Center."

"Rockefeller Center?"

"Right. I'm going to spend a lot of time explaining things to you that are ordinary to me but don't exist for you."

"I'm sorry."

"There's a man named John D. Rockefeller. Have you heard of him?"

"He is the tycoon who founded Standard Oil, isn't he?"

"Yes, that's the one."

"A very rich man."

"Right. Well, one of his sons, John D., Junior, is probably a little child now, but he will grow up to spend a lot of those millions on philanthropy, including a famous medical research university in New York. He will also develop a huge area in New York City as an entertainment mecca. I'm not sure about the details, but Rockefeller Center is a huge complex of television studios, restaurants, retail stores, corporate space, and a beautiful ice skating rink." She sighed.

"Television again. You whet my appetite for this stuff, but it's exhausting for you, isn't it? All this explaining. It's exhausting for me too."

"It's so strange that we are probably only five years apart in age, but I might as well be a hundred and fifty years older than you."

"There's the house!" He pointed toward a large, two-story brick house set far from the street behind a high, wrought-iron gate.

For the first time, Melanie allowed herself to look up and down Commonwealth Avenue. "Oh, my goodness," she said, and she sank into Thomas'd\s grasp.

"What? Are you all right?"

"Yes, I'm fine, but I'm just astounded by this street. There's really not very much here." She looked up and down the wide avenue, and the divider between the north and south sides was lined with small, young trees. Nothing like the broad, tall magnolia trees she was used to. Most of the land was undeveloped, and there was a direct line of sight almost from the Common to Massachusetts Avenue at the other end.

"There's been so much building going on since they back-filled the bay, though. It looks much more inhabited to me since we built our house and moved here."

Melanie stared at the house, which stood out for its massive size and grandeur. "It's so big!" She stopped, staring up at the roofs and chimneys. "So many chimneys!"

"You need a lot of fireplaces to heat a big house like this."

"Ah, no central heating?"

"How could a residence possibly be able to have central heating? We have coal stoves, and the house stays very warm."

"I see," she said. "Now everyone has a furnace in their basement, and we just use fireplaces for romance." She laughed. He shook his head slowly, raising one eyebrow as he steered her through the gate and up the walk. "I don't mean to be insulting, Thomas." He had been so excited to show her his house, and now he'd become quiet. "The house is beautiful. When was it built?"

"My father wanted to come home from the war to build his new house here, on this reclaimed land. But after he returned, I don't think he was ever able to appreciate it, and he didn't have the energy to participate in its construction the way he had wanted to. He was never the same after the war, and then he died."

"I'm so sorry."

"We moved here in 1868. We were just little children, Jane two and I nine and Athena ten. It was a big, new house that we could run around in. But father just spent the rest of his days sitting in a chair and looking out the front window."

"And you said you had a nanny?"

"Yes. My mother wasn't really up to nursing a sick husband and dealing with two active little children at the same time. It all affected her mind and her body, and she needed the help."

"She had the money to pay for a nanny?"

"Luckily, both families had money, and then after my father died in 1870, my mother was able to get a death pension because of my father's service in the war. And he was a doctor, so it was easier for us to get the pension than for many other families. In that way, we were lucky. But my mother would have given up all her money and the house and everything else if she could have had my father back healthy and whole."

"What was the matter with him?"

"Well, he'd had some physical injuries, but I'm pretty sure that's not what killed him. He was never the same mentally after the war. I'm sure he saw things that human beings are never meant to see—young men with their limbs blown off, their heads blown apart. Even doctors aren't always immune to those things, you know? And even more, I now realize that, as a doctor, when you lose a patient, it takes a great deal out of you. Losing patients is inevitable, but my father couldn't help so many of the soldiers he treated on the battlefield. He had terrible nightmares and flashbacks that he wasn't able to control, couldn't sleep, wouldn't eat, spent his days and nights sitting on that chair. My mother cried all the time. Then in the middle of one winter night in 1870, my father just walked outside and lay down in a snowdrift. My mother came downstairs the next morning, and when she saw he wasn't in his chair, she ran out the door and found his body not fifty feet from the house. He had committed suicide, frozen to death. I don't like to think about it. He never got to enjoy his new house, never got to see his children grow up. It all affected my mother profoundly. She couldn't get over the fact that she should have been able to help him. She died four years ago."

Melanie reached her arm around him and held tight. "In my time, we have a name for the condition your father had."

"What is that?"

"PTSD."

"PTSD?"

"Yes. That stands for post-traumatic stress disorder. It's a big deal for soldiers coming home from wars. Some people never get it, but others suffer with it for years, sometimes forever."

"So your world still fights wars."

Melanie made a choking noise. "I'm afraid so, many wars. And now the weapons and the way they deploy them are so much more advanced, they can kill thousands of people much faster than ever."

"I'm so sorry to hear that."

"Now I've depressed you, and I don't want to do that. Let's talk about happy things. We have so much to talk about, to learn about each other."

As Thomas fumbled for his key, the ornate front door flew open, and there, in the foyer, stood two people. On the left, a tall, young, cafe-au-lait-colored black woman. She was dressed in a high-necked uniform with a ruffle-trimmed apron that reached from her shoulders to her ankles. On the right, a stooped man Melanie thought must be in his seventies, balding at the top with wisps of gray hair lining the sides of his face. He was dressed in cracked leather boots, jodhpurs, and a cutaway jacket; he held a top hat in his hand. Melanie released her arm from Thomas's waist.

"Hello, miss," the young woman said, "Pleased to meet you. I'm Athena. Is it true you come here from a different century?" Her voice was throbbing with anticipation, her mouth slightly open, her dark brown eyes wide and sparkling.

Melanie regained her composure and stuck her hand out. Athena grabbed it and held on tight. The two women smiled at each other, and then Melanie to turned to Thomas, her eyebrows arched in a question.

"Oh, Melanie Swift, I'd like you to meet Athena Thornwell and Mr. Archibald Nelson, our stable man for decades."

Archibald clicked his boot heels and touched Melanie's hand. "Pleased to meet you, miss," he said.

"So this is Athena," Melanie said, reaching out her hand. She marveled at the young woman's beautiful, intelligent face and light brown skin. Athena picked up Melanie's hand, curtseying. "Yes, it's all true, Athena. So Thomas told you. I've somehow arrived here from the twenty-first century. I have no idea how, but I have to believe it happened for a reason. It's been…interesting." Athena's forehead rose into shallow, horizontal lines as she raised her eyebrows. "Really," Melanie continued. "I know it's hard to believe. I keep telling everyone I'm not crazy."

Athena smiled and pulled lightly on Melanie's hand, motioning with her other arm for them to enter. "You must be tired from your walk," she said. "Come in out of the cold, both of you," she said. "Tommy has assured me you're anything but crazy. Janie, do you want to come and say hello to our new sister?"

Athena beckoned toward the parlor, where Jane was sit-

ting on the window seat. Melanie walked across the marble
threshold into a spacious, two-story foyer, decorated with
dark, gilt-flocked wallpaper and several ornate gaslights
installed along the walls. A huge candelabra hung from the
ceiling, but Melanie wondered how you could light the can-
dles without climbing up on a tall ladder and risking your
life.

"I'll be getting back to the carriage house," the older
man said, "Very pleased to meet you, miss, please feel free
to contact me if you need assistance with anything." Then
he disappeared out the door and into the darkness.

"May I take your things?" Athena reached over to Melanie, who removed the coat. Athena took it over her arm and
walked away.

"Why is Athena wearing a maid's uniform?" Melanie's
voice was a whisper. "She's a member of the family, isn't
she?"

"She and her mother were sent up through the under-
ground railroad before the end of the war. Her mother was a
household slave in Georgia, and the plantation owner
abused her, physically and sexually, impregnated her. She
was a brave woman, managed to hide her pregnancy until
the end, and she made plans to escape the plantation after
giving birth to her baby. There were sympathetic white people who helped with those escapes, you know?"

Melanie nodded. "I've read about that."

"The day after Athena was born, they managed to get her
out with her baby. They made their way up north until they
reached a safe house here in Boston, but Athena's mother
had been so ill after the birth that she died shortly afterward,
leaving a tiny, orphaned infant. My mother was active in the
abolitionist movement here in Boston, and she and my father had not yet had any children. She fell in love with the
pretty little orphan baby, and she and my father took her in."

"What about her name?"

"Her mother had named her Athena. She said she had
high hopes that her baby would be able to read and write, so

she wanted to name her Athena after the Greek goddess of wisdom."

"But has your family always used her as a servant?" Melanie didn't mean for that to sound judgmental, but she knew it did. Thomas didn't seem to notice.

"She was educated with us. When we were very young, the nanny taught us all the same way, so Athena reads and writes as well as Jane and I do. I went to Boston Latin School before Harvard, and I brought all of my schoolwork home and taught her Latin and Greek. She devoured all the lessons, learned a great deal on her own. She's every bit as smart as we are. Maybe smarter."

"Yes, Thomas, but what about the maid's uniform?"

Thomas looked at her, and she thought he seemed perplexed, but she couldn't help being annoyed that this young half-black woman, knowledgeable in Latin and Greek, was being used as a domestic. "Well, she takes care of us. She doesn't mind."

"Really? Do you pay her?"

"She gets room and board, and if she needs anything, she just asks me and I give her the money. She seems very happy."

"So she's kind of an indentured servant. Doesn't that make you feel uncomfortable?"

"Not until this minute." He had walked into the columned foyer and slumped against the tall, white column as if he couldn't stand on his own. "I just don't know what you're getting at."

"I thought she was part of the family."

"Yes. She is. I think of her as my sister."

"Do you dress your sister Jane in a maid's uniform and give her an allowance?"

"Melanie, you're scaring me. I don't know what this conversation is about."

Melanie felt a flush starting at her neck and traveling all the way up to her forehead. Was this the beginning of the end of this new relationship? Would they ever be able to find a confluence of cultures between them? She knew she would be able to adapt to no automobiles, to riding in a horse-drawn carriage or walking when she wanted to go places, to having her clothing handmade, God forbid to no cell phones—but would it be possible to change his thinking about something so basic as human rights? She felt a slight bit guilty, having had the advantage of a century and a half of evolution on her side, but she couldn't—wouldn't—live with someone who didn't get this. She determined to change his attitude, but she worried it wouldn't happen any time soon.

"Okay, look, do you promise to let me share my feelings about this? To try to open your mind? I won't do it now. We have too much to do. But I'm determined to make you understand how I feel." And, she thought, to change him for the better. "And I want Athena out of that outfit as soon as possible."

"I'm not sure what you're saying, but yes, of course. If I'm doing something wrong, I want to know. You frightened me a little."

"I can tell. Your voice sounds a little shaky."

"I promise I'll listen to whatever you have to say."

"Okay. But I want you to be able to talk to Athena and understand her feelings as well."

"Melanie, you are the new lady of the house. You may do what you want to do. I'm not your lord and master. Not anything like it."

"I thought you were!" She walked toward Thomas and held out her hands in a kind of peace gesture, which he grabbed and started to bend down to kiss, but she pulled away. "How about Archibald?"

"Archie? He was my father's footman for as long as I can remember. My father took him with him to the war. He will never leave us. He takes care of the horses and the carriage, and he's like an old uncle or grandfather. But he refuses to live in the house. Doesn't feel it's appropriate."

"So he lives in the carriage house?"

"Yes."

"He has heat in there?"

"He has a coal stove and an ice box and a very comfortable bed. Plus, he can take meals with us whenever he wants to. Besides, he and the horse are best friends."

"All right. As long as he's happy."

"I can't imagine him happy anywhere else."

While they stood there in the massive foyer, Melanie still trying to take in the extent of this massive house, silent, Jane got up from the window seat in the front parlor, and on slippered feet, tiptoed up the stairs without making a sound. Melanie caught a glimpse of Jane's sylphlike figure gliding upwards.

"Jane?" Melanie walked around the corner of the room and looked toward the window seat where Jane had been sitting. The window seat was empty. "Where did she go? I feel bad that I made her uncomfortable, Thomas."

"Jane has been so sad since our mother died. I have done everything I know to try and help her, without much success. I hope you can figure out what to do with her. I admire your...self-confidence. I'm quite embarrassed by her behavior, and I have no idea how you've been able to handle all of this with such optimism."

"Well, I'm not sure I'd call it optimism," she said, her gaze sweeping across the room. "But If I hadn't met you, I'm not sure what would have become of me, so I'm willing to try. Should I go after Jane? I want to let her know I'm here to be her friend."

"Yes, go. But please be gentle with her."

"I will. I just want her to know I'm not her adversary."

"I'll check on Athena and see what she's preparing for dinner."

"She cooks too?"

Thomas looked down at his feet. Melanie had trouble catching his eye. "We can't change everything in one day, Melanie."

"I know, I'm sorry. I didn't mean to sound so harsh. It's

just that—" She looked around, turned around in a complete circle trying to absorb the enormity of the house. "There are a lot of changes to be made. I promise I won't try to do it in the first week, okay? It's just that once I get something into my head—"

"If anyone can turn this family around, you can. My main concern is Jane."

"I don't want to get your hopes up. You hardly know me, and I still have to get used to life the way it is here."

"I feel as if I've known you forever, Miss Swift, felt that way the first time I laid eyes on you. I have high hopes."

"Okay," she said, "So do I have *carte blanche* about taking Jane's problems into my own hands?" And, she thought, about lightening up this dark house, but first things first.

Thomas looked away. "I just want Jane to be happy," he said, a small catch in his voice.

"I don't mean to be insulting, but this place is dark and dismal. That must add to your sister's depression. Everything is dark brown and dark purple, heavy velvet drapes pulled shut, so dark that no light can get in. Everyone living in this house is young. I would love to lighten everything up."

"My mother decorated this house."

"All right, we'll take this slow. I don't want to sully your mother's memory. That wasn't my intent."

"Thank you," Thomas said, but Melanie noticed him rubbing his hands together as if he were in discomfort.

"Really, I won't mention it again, not until you're ready." Melanie turned her back to him and walked from room to room. "Every room is darker than the last one..." she said, her voice trailing off. Thomas stood, slouching against the column, curling into a ball more with each criticism she made. Then she walked into the kitchen and was dazzled by the white—white tile floor, white tile walls, a huge white wood stove, and an ice box that stood in one corner, with spigots on each side. "Oh, I love the kitchen! It's so...quaint."

Thomas stood up and followed her into the large room. He looked around at everything in there. He realized he had never really looked carefully at the kitchen before. It was bright in here, a large window rising up behind the white porcelain sink. Everything was new and modern. "Quaint?"

"Yes. It's like something out of a history book."

"Oh." He looked down again.

"No, Thomas, here I go, offending you again. It's a beautiful kitchen. Is that an icebox?" The icebox had a cherry-wood door with a long metal handle.

"Of course."

"No electric refrigeration yet."

"I guess that's coming, then?"

She walked to him and reached up and put a hand on his shoulder. "I'm going to make an effort to stop talking about what's coming, okay? I think I'm making you sad, and I didn't want to do that. Besides, suddenly I'm exhausted. Maybe I should take a little rest before I start changing the world?"

"Melanie, I'm sorry. Of course you're exhausted. You've been through so much. Let me take you up to your room, and you can lie down for a while."

"Yes, that sounds like a good idea."

They walked up the grand, curving staircase, his arm tightly around her waist as he supported her along the way.

Chapter 9

The next few days were a whirlwind of activity. While Melanie felt stronger and stronger each day, there was so much to get used to that her aching head was always in a state of muddle and confusion. She was determined to fit in here so that she could help Jane as soon as possible, which was what Thomas wanted. Jane didn't seem to agree with the program.

"Was she always like this, Thomas?" Melanie and Thomas were sitting at the big, metal table in the kitchen, drinking tea. It was after midnight. She had waited up for him to get home from the hospital so that she could discuss it with him. They spoke in hushed tones, in case Jane was lurking somewhere, listening.

"Like what?"

"You know she hates me—"

"I don't know why you say that, Melanie. You keep telling me she hates you, but Jane doesn't have a bitter bone in her body, I know her very well."

Melanie sucked her breath in. "I don't know how I can convince you. She is lovely to you, but to me she breathes fire! She just does things."

"What things?"

"Athena was making me a skirt. I don't want to have to

borrow Jane's clothing all the time, you know? I know that doesn't make her happy. And after I tried on the skirt and Athena finished it, I took it up to my room and left it on the bed. When I went back up there later, it had a large rip in the back. Poor Athena had to do almost as much work to fix it as she had making it."

"And why do you think Jane did that?"

Melanie pounded her fist on the table. "Thomas! Do you think I did it?"

Thomas buried his head in his hands. "I'm very tired, Melanie. It's been a long day. I don't have the energy to argue with you about this."

"I don't mean to be hateful toward your sister. I want to like her, and heaven knows I want her to like me, but it's hard living with her hostility. Earlier today after she criticized me for something, for making her sandwich wrong, I ran up to my room and sat on the bed and cried, and she burst in and snickered at me—called me a weakling. Can you imagine? She's relentless, I don't care what you say. I'm going to bed now." She pushed the chair away from the table, supporting her weight with her hands. The chair clattered backwards onto the floor.

Thomas grabbed her hand and looked at her. Their eyes were locked in some kind of emotion Melanie didn't understand. "I think—thought—I was falling in love with you, Melanie." He sighed.

"Don't do that, Thomas!" She pulled her hand out of his grasp, something she was doing frequently these days. "I just don't know whether I can love you back. I told you, there is someone else."

"Look, I promise I'll talk to her, okay? I'm sure she doesn't mean anything by it. She's just worried she'll lose me. God knows, she's lost everyone else."

"Promises," she said. "In my world, we say, 'put your money where your mouth is.'"

"That's an interesting idiom."

"Idiom is an interesting word." She threw her head back, arching her back. "Not many people I know throw the word idiom casually into their conversations."

"Melanie, stop teasing me! Are we done talking about my sister?"

"I guess so, but I think we should be allies here, not antagonists. She has to know that we're both on her side, and she has to know that you support me."

"Of course I support you."

"Well, Jane needs to know that. And it's important that you don't get defensive every time I talk about this with you. I'm on your side. What choice do I have? I've tried hard, but she frustrates me at every turn."

"When you talk like that, I worry. I want you to be here because you want to be."

"I want to help your sisters. I just hope they want my help. At least that Jane does. Athena and I get along great."

"Is it all right if we call a truce now? We'll talk more tomorrow, I promise. I think we should get some sleep now." He raised his eyebrows. "I was hoping you might change your mind about...um...getting closer to me. I've been honest about my feelings for you."

She averted her eyes. "I'm still not ready. I'm sorry."

"When I found you, I thought I'd found my true love. You, however, are making me live without you, even though I cured you and have to look at your beautiful face and body whenever I'm home. It makes me want to stay longer at the hospital."

"Listen, Dr. Holier-Than-Thou, I could go to that women's residence Dr. MacInerney mentioned. Perhaps I should? It would make Jane very happy, and then you wouldn't have to lust after me all the time."

Thomas sighed. "I'm sorry. I want you here. I keep hoping you might feel about me the way I feel about you."

"Why did Jane quit nursing school, anyway?" Melanie

changed the subject. She started for the stairs, and Thomas followed her.

"She said she couldn't concentrate on her studies, that she was still too upset about our mother's death."

"Do you believe her?"

"I never thought of not believing her." He was behind Melanie and had one hand gently on her back. "I'm disappointed, of course, but why wouldn't I believe her?"

"Didn't your mother die over four years ago?"

"Yes, but—"

"I hope I can help her. But if she continues to destroy my clothing, I'm going to have a hard time liking her. I'm tired of her acting out. She's an adult, not a child."

"I'm so tired of this, Melanie. I think you are exaggerating."

"No, Thomas. You are in denial."

"You are a hard case, Miss Swift. You look so charmingly adorable when you get angry. It makes me want to take you in my arms, but you smash all my hopes."

Melanie shrugged. "Just trying to protect your reputation, Dr. Thornwell. We are, after all, not married."

"Who would even know?"

Melanie shrugged her shoulders. "The walls have ears."

"These walls are very respectful of our privacy."

Melanie laughed. "Then we should act respectably so as not to embarrass them." On the landing, she craned her head and looked around to try to see the top of the staircase, in case one of the sisters was lurking there. But the wall blocked her view.

"What makes you think anyone here is interested in what we do behind closed doors?"

"Hah! You are living in a fool's paradise."

"I believe that phrase comes from *Romeo and Juliet*, does it not?" he asked.

"You are a shameless show-off, sir. Whatever the source, it fits the occasion."

"Perhaps we are like the two star-crossed lovers."

"Well, someone in this house who shall remain nameless would love to instigate a blood feud. Of that, I have no doubt."

"Miss Capulet, I feel you are stronger and cleverer than any feud."

"Time will tell, Mr. Montague, time will tell."

"By the way, do you think only married people make love?"

"If your culture were like ours, then the answer would be no. I hate to keep bringing this up, Thomas, but I am in love with a man from my time. His name is Justin. Even if I were inclined to, I feel I would be a terrible person if I made love to you."

"We go over and over this," he said, "But there's no resolution. You are here now. You may never see this man again. Can't you love me?" His voice sounded so pathetic that she laughed.

As they reached the top of the staircase, she touched his hand lightly. "You are a very attractive man." She sighed. "You so remind me of him, it's uncanny."

He clasped her hand gently and brought it to his lips.

"But anything more than friendship is impossible, at least for now. At least until I can get into Jane's good graces, and until I'm sure I won't be going back home." She extracted her hand from his. "I'm sorry, but it's the best I can do for now."

"I won't lose hope—I refuse to lose hope. And I won't stop trying."

"Suit yourself."

"I will make you love me, if it's the last thing I do." He stamped his foot on the carpeted step, and she laughed again.

As they walked toward their bedrooms, Melanie thought she heard a noise coming from behind Jane's door. She put her finger across her lips and pointed down the hall, whispering. "See? She's been eavesdropping."

Thomas shook his head.

Melanie opened her bedroom door and, as she entered, Thomas stood at the door, a sentry, tall and handsome. She looked back at him. "You know, I'd like to show you how this phone works. Would you let me take a selfie of us?" She reached for her iPhone, which was placed neatly on the bedside table. "The battery will be dead very soon, and I want to make some sort of record of our friendship."

"What in God's name is a selfie?"

She beckoned for him to come into the room, and then positioned him under the Currier and Ives print of a sleigh with two horses on a snowy street. Then she adjusted her position and held the phone in front of the two of them, and clicked the button.

After the flash, he stayed there, as if he needed her to release him before he could move. The phone would be useless soon, but it was such a habit to take pictures, and even if she could never look at them after the battery died, she wanted to preserve the moment this way.

"See, how cute we are! This is a selfie! It's a picture we took of ourselves. And I managed to get the print in there, as well as the beautiful headboard. The wood on my bed is so intricately carved."

He stared at the picture on the phone, shaking his head. "Rosewood, imported from Brazil. I think my grandfather had it imported."

"I've never seen anything like it."

"Neither have I," he said, turning the phone around in his hand, as if its mysteries might be revealed by looking at the back. "That is truly unbelievable. How does it work?"

"I have no idea, but it does, and we look adorable, don't we?"

He leaned down and ruffled her hair. "This was my bedroom when I was a child. It gives me all kinds of warm feelings to know that you're sleeping in my bed."

"Incorrigible!"

Thomas walked back to the door and started removing his tie and unbuttoning his shirt. "I assume you'll be sleeping when I leave tomorrow. What are you going to be doing with your time?"

"I'm going to look at all the fabrics that Athena had delivered. And Athena said she'd be happy to sew me some dresses. I need clothes badly and we both know what a wizard she is with a sewing needle."

"That she is," he said. "That girl can do most anything."

"Do you think the world would be shocked if I asked her to sew me some trousers?"

"*What?*" His color drained out, and the only way Melanie could describe his face was that it looked grim, his lips pulled in to a narrow slit.

"George Sand wore pants."

"Yes, but she was French, and you're not."

Melanie giggled. "Don't worry, I won't shock the world that way. But I have to say, pants are much warmer on these cold days than the skirts that let the wind blow up, you know, and I still feel a little cold."

"There are some extra feather quilts somewhere," he said. "Athena will know where to find those too."

"Well, I'm going to have her make some nice frocks for herself, Thomas. I don't think it's right for your sister to have to wear a maid's uniform all the time."

"Did you ask her how she felt about that?"

"Why? Don't you think she'll be happy to feel like a family member and not a servant?" Melanie could feel her voice becoming strident.

"Here we go again. Is there anything you like about us? Or does everything we do annoy you? Perhaps I *should* have found you a women's residence instead of taking you in." His shoulders sagged, and he stood there, his shirt half unbuttoned, his hair mussed, his face drawn.

"I'm sorry, I can't help myself. I guess I've got the advantage of a century and a half of progress. I don't mean to cut you down at every turn. I just want things to be fair. For Jane too, although I'll have to figure out a way to convince her I mean that."

"I am going to go to bed and try to sleep. My mind is churning with so many complications, about you, about us, about this family. I just hope we can work them all out."

"I'm an optimist," Melanie said.

Thomas picked up her hand and brought his lips down to it. He kissed it gently. "I am pretending it's your lips," he said. "I think you should have some dresses made soon. Our friends the Gardners have invited us to a salon at their house week after next. I think she's having a soirée for John Sargent, the painter. Something about a scandal with a portrait he painted."

Melanie sat up, ramrod straight. "John Singer Sargent?"

He nodded. "You've heard of him?"

Melanie laughed. "Yes, Tom, he was—is—a famous artist."

"Oh."

"And the Gardners?"

"Yes, Jack and Isabella. They live over on Beacon Street. I think you'll love them. Our families have been close for years and years. After they moved to Boston from New York, they had us over all the time. When Father came back from the war, Aunt Isabella used to take us sometimes in the afternoons, to give Mother and Father some time alone, you know? She fed us warm cookies and milk, and she let us draw on very large drawing pads with long pieces of charcoal. Never got angry if we rubbed the black off on our clothing. Wonderful people. They lost their own child. It was very hard on her."

"Aunt Isabella?"

"Yes. We called her 'Aunt,' because 'Mrs. Gardner' just seemed too formal, and of course we weren't allowed to call her just by her first name. She's not really our aunt."

"Isabella *Stewart* Gardner?" Melanie had fallen backward onto the bed. She felt herself breathing hard.

"I think so. Are you all right?"

"I know I promised to stop doing this, Thomas, but I have to tell you, that woman, your Aunt Isabella, is going to be known as one of the great art collectors of all time. She will build a beautiful museum here in Boston to house her collection, and there will be a horrible art theft..." Her voice trailed off, and she buried her head in the pillow. *Aunt Isabella*! She hoped Thomas didn't hear the last part. She wished there were some way she could alter history, but she was fairly sure that was impossible.

"What did you say?" He was still hovering over her.

"I said, she is a great art collector."

"Yes, she is. After her little son died at the age of two, Jack tried to raise her spirits by taking her out of the country. They traveled all over Europe and started collecting art from France and Italy—all over. I imagine part of the reason she's having this salon for Sargent is because she wants one of his paintings. You'll understand when you see their house. The walls are full of paintings. I don't claim to understand them all, but—"

"John Singer Sargent, the artist."

"Yes, that's what I said."

"I know. I can hardly believe it."

"Melanie?"

"She and her collection are very famous. At least in my world. So is Sargent."

"So you mentioned." He wheeled around and stared at her. "Of course. You would know, you little art historian."

"I'm worried I'll be tongue-tied when I meet them."

"You? Tongue-tied?" He laughed. "I doubt that. Isabella is very easy to talk to, and smart and delightful, I might add. A bit dotty like you. She's always determined to get her own way, and she generally prevails. Her husband adores her."

"Dotty?"

"*Avant garde.*"

Melanie laughed. "Seriously, you don't understand. I think I'm hyperventilating. It's like...reading a history book, and then being able to go into the pages and talk to the people."

Thomas leaned over her, his eyebrows up in concern. "Are you sure you're all right? Do I have to worry that you'll faint?"

"I'll be okay. It's just that all of this is so hard to understand, you know? What if I said to you, 'Come on, Dr. Thornwell, let me introduce you to this artist I know. His name is Goya. He's over at my neighbor's house.'"

He shrugged. "I can't help it if we know these people. To me, they're just our old friends."

Then he was gone, down the hall and into his room. Melanie lay back on the bed and tried not to cry. She missed home, missed Justin, wondered what he was doing and whether he was thinking about her. If only she had been more forthcoming about her feelings toward him. She thought about how much Thomas resembled Justin and about how she had rebuffed Thomas so many times since she had been here. She was troubled that Jane hated her and that Athena was treated like a maid. She wished there were some way to share all of this with Justin, but she knew that was impossible. He wouldn't be born for a hundred years. There were no solutions, at least not immediate ones. The tears came despite her best efforts to avoid them.

Melanie lay down on the featherbed and tried to sleep. Her thoughts played like a movie with one scene fading into another, starting with home and the little she remembered about the accident. Moving to the ride in the ambulance where she could hear everything but respond to nothing—Justin's voice hovering there, worried, anxious, calling her "honey" and "dear." Next Thomas's frustration with her and the difficulties with Jane.

Finally, she couldn't stand it anymore and sat up in bed. There was a candle in a holder on the nightstand. She picked it up and lit it. The dim light it created wouldn't show outside the door. She walked toward the window but stopped at the desk, a heavy, wooden structure with a roll top. This had been Thomas's room when he was a growing up.

She opened the roll top, and it creaked as if it hadn't been opened in a long time. She pulled the wooden chair away and sat down. Under the roll top was a box of pencils and a stack of paper. She noticed, as she brought the candle closer, that the paper was a heavy stock, light beige with some kind of lighter colored flecks, and at the top of each page, an ornate, gilded monogram—TT—Thomas Thornwell. Melanie picked up one of the pencils and pulled a piece of the stationery off the pile. She had a sudden urge to write a letter to Justin, although she had no idea whether he would ever get it. But why not? If she couldn't tell him in person how she felt, at least she could write down her thoughts. Maybe if she got them down on paper, it would clear her mind. How to start? "My Love"? "Dearest Justin"? "My Darling Justin"? She decided to keep it simple.

> *Dear Justin, my heart aches for you. If I could only hold you in my arms and tell you how I feel about you—how I have felt about you but never had the courage to let you know—it would make me the happiest woman in the world. I know you were there for me on that awful day. My memories are still hazy, and perhaps I'll never have a distinct memory of what happened, but I do recall lying in the street and being picked up and put in that ambulance, and you came with me. I remember your voice, worried, comforting me, asking the ambulance attendants constantly for an update on my condition. I realized then that my*

*feelings for you were love, and my frustration was
that I couldn't tell you, as much as I tried. I couldn't
move, couldn't talk, couldn't give you any sign, but I
loved you then and I love you now. I only hope you
love me too. I don't know how or why, but I am in
Boston now, with a family who took me in, and, yes I
know this sounds crazy, it is 1886. You are not born
yet, not a glimmer in anyone's eye, except for mine.
The world is very different here. I'm living in a huge
house with Dr. Thomas Thornwell, who rescued me
from a park bench, and his two sisters, one of whom
hates me. It's too much to write now, but someday I
hope I can tell you the whole story.*

*The house is like a huge mausoleum, with dark
walls, heavy dark drapes, dark wood floors, and
heavy moldings. I try not to think about that. I would
love to take a brush and paint everything white! Justin, I don't even know why I'm writing this to you, because it is all so futile. My only hope is that somehow,
some way, we will be reunited, and then I will not
hold back with my love for you. For now, I will stop
and try to sleep, hopefully to dream of being in your
arms and making the dearest, most passionate love to
you. I love you, Melanie.*

Melanie picked up the page, written on both sides in tiny
letters, and held it up to the light of the candle. She sighed.
She wondered what Justin was doing, whom he was with,
and then caught herself when she realized that Justin didn't
even exist yet. Tears flowed, falling down her face, stinging
a little where the sutures had been. She brushed them out of
her eyes and touched the paper on which she had written her
first love letter. Some of the words smudged.

"Damn," she said, "What's the point?"

And then with a resigned laugh, she crumpled up the
page with both hands, until it was the size of a golf ball, and
dropped it onto the desk.

Chapter 10

"Is Jane up?" Thomas walked first into the kitchen, craning his neck to see if his sister was there.

Athena hung her head. "No, Tom. She wouldn't get up again. I tried, but I'm sorry, I failed."

"Not your fault, Athena." Melanie gave the other woman a hug. She had come downstairs very early, having slept fitfully most of the night. "Thank you for making this incredible breakfast again."

"I'm surprised to see you here," Thomas said, his voice tinged with a smile. "I thought you'd still be in bed by the time I left."

Melanie shrugged. "Too much to think about," she said.

"I'm hungry," he said to Athena, "What do we have today?"

"I thought you might like some flapjacks. I made some bacon to go with them, with maple syrup that came all the way from New Hampshire." Athena poured each of them a mug of coffee and pushed a pitcher of cream toward them.

Melanie took a sip of the hot, black coffee and closed her eyes in satisfaction. She would need it to help herself stay awake this morning. "I'm going to get fat from your cooking, Athena," she said, slipping into a chair at the white metal kitchen table. The legs scraped along the floor as she slid the chair in. Thomas was already digging into a stack of syrup-laden pancakes, licking the sweet goo off his mustache. "It's hard to get used to this amazing cooking," Melanie said.

"I enjoy it," Athena said, "And it is heartening to see Thomas looking happy."

"We need to talk today, Athena," Melanie said, her words a little garbled from the food in her mouth. She was happy they took most of their meals in this bright kitchen, not in the gloomy, cavernous formal dining room, with its long, rectangular dark-wood table and chairs.

"Do you have a problem with me, Melanie?" Athena pulled another stack of pancakes off the stove and placed them in front of Thomas. Her smile had devolved into a slight frown.

"Oh, no, not at all. That's not it. I just want to find out what you really want to do with your life." She took another bite. "Somehow, even though you're damn good at all of it, I don't think your aspiration is being a domestic servant forever." Thomas shot Melanie a veiled-eyed glance, a fork full of pancakes stopped in mid-transfer from plate to mouth.

Athena turned toward Melanie, and Melanie noticed what she thought were tears forming in the corners of Athena's eyes. "What makes you think that?" Athena said, her words distinct and slow. Melanie marveled at the smoothness of her mocha brown skin, the brightness of her eyes.

"You're an intelligent, extremely capable woman. I think I realized that the first day I met you. There's more for you than this, even though you're so good at this." She pointed at her fork, full of food. "God knows, you're a fantastic cook. Your dressmaking skills are amazing as well. But I can't believe it's enough for you, Athena. Am I wrong?"

Athena sat down opposite the two of them. Melanie wondered whether Athena had eaten already or whether she was waiting for them to finish. She would help Athena clean up the breakfast mess. The past two days, Athena had cooked and cleaned and done everything to keep the house

running. Melanie was determined to change that. She needed not only to get through to Jane but to figure out how to
guide Athena toward a satisfying future. She wasn't sure
which goal would be harder to accomplish.

Thomas, changing the subject, said, "I thought this
weekend we could do some things. I have a day off on Saturday. We can take a walk to the Common and do some ice
skating. Does that sound like fun?"

"It sounds like wonderful fun," Melanie said. "Where
will I get ice skates?"

"You can use mine, if they fit you," Athena offered.

"What will you use, Athena?" Melanie asked. She
looked at Thomas—who, she thought, looked uncomfortable again and was rubbing his chin. "Athena, do you want to
go with us?" she asked. "Yes, of course you do. She and
Jane will go with us. We'll all go. We'll figure it out."

Thomas pushed his plate away. "All right, if that's what
you want."

"That's what I want, and I'm the lady of the house,
right? You told me I was." Melanie shot a quick glance at
Athena, who looked down at her hands.

"You are indeed the lady of the house, if that's what you
want to be."

"Well, then."

"So now I must get to work, or I'll just sit here eating
and enjoying your company all day. Thank you, Athena. As
usual, the breakfast was delicious."

"My pleasure, Tom."

Thomas jumped up and strode out of the kitchen toward
the front door. Melanie trotted behind him, trying to keep up
with him. "You're not angry with me, are you, Dr. Thornwell?" she said, as she helped him with his coat and scarf.

"No, of course not. I'm not angry with you at all. I feel
relieved that you're taking all of these issues out of my
hands. I'm grateful. I can't believe my good fortune. I just
wish…" He leaned down as if he was about to kiss her on
the mouth, but she turned her head, and his kiss landed on

the hair just behind her ear. "I won't give up," he said.

"Tommy! Wait!" Jane's voice reached them from the staircase landing. "Don't go yet. There's something you have to see."

She almost skipped down the stairs, her step lighter than Melanie had seen it since she had arrived. As Jane reached the foyer, she held one hand behind her back.

"What do you want me to see, Janie? I have to get to the hospital."

"Oh, this is worth waiting for." With a broad smile on her face, she thrust her hand out toward him, and Melanie saw right away what it was. It was the balled up love letter she had written to Justin, opened up and smoothed out, its creases reflecting the sun from the doorway. Melanie tried to reach for it, but Jane snatched it away and put it into Thomas's hands. "There, that's what this ungrateful girl is doing in our house! Look at that."

Melanie felt welded to the floor. Her mouth was open, and Jane never stopped grinning at her. Melanie thought that, if venom could come from a human's mouth, it would be dripping out of Jane's.

Thomas stared at the letter, turning it over several times, looking from the letter to his sister to Melanie. Then he folded it and put it in his pocket. Melanie wanted to sink down into a corner, to hide behind something, but she couldn't move. "You have no right to go into her room without her permission, Jane." He pulled his lips taut, the edges turned downward. "How dare you? I would never go into your room, and you don't have the right to do it either."

"That used to be *your* room," Jane said, stamping her foot. Melanie felt a little better. Jane was acting like a two-year-old. Melanie stood up a little straighter, still silent. "She doesn't have any right—"

"But it is Melanie's room now," he said, dismissing her with a wave of his free hand, his tone not softening at all.

"I thought you'd be happy to see what she's doing be-hind your back. Why are you angry at *me*?"

"I don't have time for this, Jane, and you know better. You need to start treating Melanie better. She is not leaving. She can help you with many things, and all you do is try to sabotage her."

"Damn you!" Jane had gotten close to Melanie's face and screamed the words at her. Then she turned around and ran back up the stairs, pounding each one as she ran, slamming her door when she got to her bedroom.

"I am so sorry," Melanie said, looking down. "I didn't mean to be so ungrateful for everything you've done for me. I know that letter was foolish. I told you I had some unfinished business before I left. I thought maybe writing down those things would clear my mind. I certainly didn't want to make you sad, when you have been so nice to me."

Thomas put his finger up to her lips. "Shhh—let's not talk about this now, all right? You told me about your old life."

"I'm sorry to frustrate you," Melanie said. "But—"

"But," he said without hesitation, "There is that man waiting for you at home." He frowned, ran his hand across his mouth. "In 2016?"

"That's the problem. I don't know if he'll be waiting for me. I don't even know for sure whether he had feelings for me. I don't know if it will ever be 2016 again. It's just too confusing. I'm sorry. I need more time."

"I'm a patient man," he said, a tight smile on his face. "A very patient man." He removed the letter from his pocket and handed it to her. Then he turned and walked out the door, closing it securely behind him. She crumpled it back into a ball and threw it into the fireplace.

By the time Melanie went back to the kitchen, Athena had already cleared the table and was up to her elbows in soapy water, washing the dishes. "Let me help you with that, Athena," Melanie said.

Athena looked up with a half-frown. "You don't have to do that, miss," she said.

"Melanie."

"I'm sorry."

"Athena, this family takes advantage of you!" Melanie grabbed a towel and started drying the dishes Athena had stacked to the side of the sink. "You have to push back, demand better treatment."

"This family took me in when I was an infant," she said, staring down at the suds, which were dissipating. "Without them, heaven knows what would have happened to me."

Melanie thought she saw a small shudder pass over Athena's shoulders. "Yes, but they did that because they wanted to. Obviously, they had the means to. Look at this place! Look at what an amazing person you turned out to be."

"I know, but it's been very difficult here for Tom and Jane since our parents passed away."

"I'm sure it's been hard for you too, hasn't it?"

"I'm a strong person. I'm stronger than Jane."

"What about before Mrs. Thornwell passed away? And did you call her Mrs. Thornwell?"

"Yes."

Melanie put down the towel and the bowl she was drying. She looked at Athena, who was still busy scrubbing the griddle with a rough dish cloth. "Why?"

"I never thought about it, really."

"That's ridiculous. You were raised as one of her children, weren't you?"

"I guess so. Yes."

"You are never to call me 'miss' again. Is that clear? And Jane and I will help you with the dishes and the cleaning. This house is immense. I can't believe you take care of it all by yourself. Not to mention the sewing."

"It's not really a hardship, Melanie."

"I've seen you with your books and your studies. That's what you really love, isn't it Athena?"

Athena dropped the cloth into the sink and looked over at Melanie. Her dark brown eyes sparkled, and she broke into a full smile. "That is what I love," she said. "I love reading about everything, science, history, literature, everything. Mostly science. It fascinates me."

"That's what you're going to do from now on, as much as you want to," Melanie said, thrusting her head down for emphasis. "In my opinion, you are brilliant, Miss Athena. No way should you be wasting your life slaving over a food-encrusted pan."

"But, who…" Her voice trailed off.

"We will all pitch in, and if that's not enough, Thomas will hire someone to come in here and do the household chores. He'll do it if I ask him to. I suspect it just never occurred to him."

"I am glad we're talking, Melanie. I believe he loves you very much. I can tell just by the way he gazes at you. He can't take his eyes off you."

"Love is a fantastic thing, Athena. I hope you experience it someday. But the problem is, I'm not able to love Thomas back the way he loves me. At least not now. I worry that I'm taking advantage of his feelings. I couldn't sleep last night. There is a young man where I came from, and I think I love him. But I don't know whether I'll ever see him again. And—" Melanie put down the towel and put her head in her hands. She couldn't stop the barrage of tears that flowed, as if she was finally crying for everything that had happened to her. The sobbing made her gasp for breath. Athena approached her, arms out. The two embraced and stood there hugging for several moments. When Melanie finally regained control of herself, she realized that Athena was crying too.

"What do you think you're doing?"

They jumped apart, startled by Jane's silent approach and her angry greeting.

"Are we going to try a new start?" Melanie went to Jane, who had walked to the table but was standing there, her hand resting on one of the chairs. "How are you? It's a beautiful day."

Jane looked down, and Melanie put a hand on her shoulder, pulled out the chair for her. Jane shook Melanie's hand off.

"I can't believe my brother is letting you stay here."

"Your brother and I have been very honest with each other," Melanie said, rubbing her hand. "He knows all about my other life."

Jane shrugged, made a sound that Melanie thought sounded like a snort.

"I'd like to make breakfast for you, Jane. Athena has studying to do upstairs. What would you like me to make? Go, Athena!" She shooed Athena away, pointing her head toward the stairs.

"Are you sure?" Athena cast a sidelong glance at Jane and took one step toward Melanie.

"I promise we'll be fine. Go read. Jane, what do you want for breakfast?"

"I'm not hungry," Jane said, her voice hardly louder than a whisper. Athena started backing out of the kitchen tentatively, as if she thought Melanie might change her mind. Melanie shooed her off again with a hand gesture.

"You are going to fade away if you don't eat something. How about some coffee and a piece of bread and butter?" And to Athena, "See, I won't even mess up your stove."

"Why are you doing this?" Jane said. "I can take care of myself."

"There's some fresh strawberry jam in the ice box, Melanie. Do you want me to get it?" Athena made a move toward the other side of the kitchen.

"I don't want to hear another word out of your mouth, Miss Thornwell, until you can recite everything in your chemistry textbook to me. Now be off with you. I'll manage the jam and the butter and the bread. I promise!" Melanie stood, hands on her hips, tapping one foot impatiently on the tile floor, until Athena had disappeared around a corner. "And don't be standing there with your ear to the molding. I mean it." Athena's footsteps up the stairs made Melanie smile. "Now, Jane, is that with jam or without?"

"I don't have a preference."

"Great. Then I'll make the decision." Melanie went about her business, refilling her own coffee cup and filling one for Jane. "What do you take in your coffee?" She pushed the creamer over to Thomas's sister, who dutifully poured some into the cup. "Sugar?"

"No. Why don't you leave me alone?"

Melanie cut a thick slab of the rich, dark bread Athena had baked, and slathered it with a dollop of butter and a large spoonful of jam. She pushed it in front of Jane, who sat, touching it and moving it from one side of the plate to the other.

"What can I do to make you understand that I want to be your friend?"

"Well, I don't want to be yours." Jane had raised her voice, and now she started to cry, at first expelling soft, gasping sobs. Melanie walked over to her and put both of her hands on Jane's shoulders, but Jane just slipped out from under Melanie's grasp, stood up quickly, and flung her chair out from the table. The metal legs hit Melanie's shins as if Jane had aimed perfectly. Melanie let out a little gasp, the pain registering seconds after impact.

"Damn it, Jane, what am I supposed to do? I don't want to be here either."

But Jane was already halfway up the stairs. Melanie sat down at the table and rubbed her legs. *In my world*, she thought, *they'd write a prescription for Zoloft or something and tell her to start talk therapy.* In this world, this girl— young woman—was depressed and out of control. Her threat of a reign of terror just made the people around her do whatever she wanted them to. Melanie did have compassion for Thomas's sister. But she wanted to be able to commiserate on an equal level. Melanie had lost her father too, perhaps not as violently as Jane had, because of the after effects of a terrible war. Nevertheless, her father was gone as well, and it was difficult and painful. Thomas had asked her to try to help his sister, but as long as Jane had this pent-up anger coupled with a violent and vindictive streak, Melanie didn't know whether it would be possible.

The sound of Jane's door slamming on the second floor brought Athena back downstairs. "Is everything all right? I'm afraid her door will come off the hinges, she slams it so hard."

Melanie was still at the table. The plate of bread and jam she had prepared for Jane was still sitting untouched. Melanie shook her head and sighed. "Nothing is all right."

"Do you want me to bring Jane her food upstairs?"

"No!" Melanie pounded her fist on the table. "You have to stop enabling her. She'll never change."

"Enabling? I'm sorry, I don't understand."

"She's acting like a tyrant, and everyone just tiptoes around her. If her bad behavior doesn't get good results, she'll change the behavior." Melanie wasn't even sure this was the case, but she knew that acting the same way they had been wasn't helping, so she tried to feel confident about her statement. "I don't think anyone ever starved themselves to death voluntarily," Melanie said. "When she's hungry enough, she'll come downstairs to eat."

"But the bread will be stale and hard."

"Good! Let her see how much she likes stale bread. The next time she'll eat when she's supposed to."

"I thought you wanted to help her?"

"Damn it, Athena, I do, but she's making sure that I don't!" Melanie's outburst made Athena recoil. "I'm sorry, I didn't mean to explode at you. This isn't your fault. But I'm frustrated, and she acts like a damn brat." Melanie stamped her foot.

That image made Athena laugh. Melanie stood up and hugged her. "At least someone here appreciates me," she said.

"I would say that two people here appreciate you," Athena said.

Melanie rolled her eyes. "I would say you're right."

Chapter 11

S he's still in bed. I can't tell whether she's sleeping or just pretending to sleep to avoid me."

"Yes, she does that often. It doesn't seem to get better, and since you've been here, well…"

After Melanie had finished cleaning up the kitchen, she went upstairs to see if Jane might be willing to talk. When Jane was unresponsive she went to Athena's room down the hall and tapped lightly at the door. Athena allowed her in, smiling broadly as Melanie approached her work desk, which was pushed up to the large bay window.

"I have to find a way to help her." Melanie leaned over Athena's shoulder, looking at the books on the desk. "But I can't help feeling angry and frustrated. And I don't think Thomas understands."

"I know. I feel so sorry for her. When we were kids, she was a happy, vibrant, intelligent person. I just think the loss of our parents was too much for her. It just sucked the life out of her. Now she sees you, and you're beautiful and smart and fun, and she's eaten up by jealousy."

"As a result, we spend our time thinking and talking only about her, Athena. So, what about you? What are you doing there?" Melanie bent over Athena, putting a hand on her back and brushing Athena's copious curls out of the way so she could see. On the desk was a massive book, lying open. Melanie turned it so that she could see the title: *Fourteen Weeks in Chemistry*, by J. Dorman Steele. She opened back up to the page that Athena had been studying. "Ahh—some light reading, I see?" She smiled, but Athena was very serious.

"It's absolutely wonderful, Melanie. I'm enjoying it immensely."

"A chemistry text book?"

"Yes. This was one of Thomas's books that he brought from college. I didn't let him get rid of any of them." She pointed to a bookshelf crammed with rows of text books. Melanie walked over and scanned the titles: *Gray's Anatomy, New American from the Tenth English Edition*; *Textbook of Physiology* by M. Foster; and many others, from Obstetrics and Gynecology to Ophthalmology, from physics and mathematics books to poetry books to history books to books on American and English literature.

"So, I was right when I said I didn't think you wanted to spend the rest of your life washing dishes and tidying up the house?"

Athena laughed, a pure, bell-like sound that Melanie found delightful, but then she stopped abruptly. "What can I do, Melanie?" She had turned around and was staring intently into Melanie's face, small wrinkles rising at the bridge of her nose. Melanie again noted Athena's clear, flashing eyes, brimming now with an intensity that seemed on the verge of anger. "I'm a woman, and a mulatto woman at that, the daughter of a former slave. I've had great advantages, I realize that. I've had the best education in the world, because I grew up in a house where I was allowed to learn whatever I wanted. But it's not enough." She tore her gaze away from Melanie and lay her head down on the open book. "I need to do something with it."

"What is it that you want to do? Do you know?"

Athena's head popped up again, the long curls flying outward from her temples. This time, her eyes were closed, her lips pursed, and her voice very soft. "I do know."

"Okay, girlfriend, spill it!" Melanie said. "What's your dream?"

"I want to be a doctor," Athena whispered. "A doctor," slightly louder. She shrank farther away from Melanie, as if she expected to be ridiculed. Her eyes remained closed tight, her face scrunched up as if she was waiting for a blow. She opened a desk drawer and pulled out a book, which she handed up to Melanie.

"*A Book of Medical Discourses* by Rebecca Lee Crumpler, M.D." Melanie flipped around the pages. "What is this?"

"Dr. Crumpler is the first Negro woman doctor in this entire country," Athena said. "You see? It's possible."

"That all makes so much sense. Your brother is a doctor, your adopted father was a doctor, his father was a doctor. Your sister went to nursing school. This house oozes medicine from its pores."

"I'm sorry," she added. "Do you think I'm a fool?"

"Anything but a fool," Melanie put the book down gently on Athena's desk. "I think it's a fantastic aspiration."

"So you don't think this is impossible?"

"Impossible? No. Challenging? Of course, but medical school is always challenging. But you're brilliant, determined, ambitious—right?"

"Yes, but I'm a black woman, here only because Mrs. Thornwell had a good heart. Otherwise, who knows—"

"I think anything's possible if you work at it hard enough and don't lose hope. I will work with you to make it happen. How is that?"

"Do you mean that, Melanie? Because I have no idea how to proceed." Athena breathed in, a loud, choked breath.

"I mean that with all my heart."

Athena sighed, letting the air out all at once. "I think I've died and gone to heaven."

Melanie laughed, threw her arms around Athena's shoulders from behind, and hugged. Athena leaned back into Melanie's embrace. "But do you think you have enough knowledge to do it? To pass entrance examinations? And is there a school here where you could go?"

"I've studied every one of the books on that shelf," Athena said. "Even the medical text books. I'd be willing to sit for any examination on any of them. And there is a medical school in the city that accepts women. It used to be called the New England Female Medical College. Now it's part of Boston University."

"Of course, you've done your homework."

Athena beamed.

"Does Thomas have any idea this is what you want to do?"

"Tom has been so busy with his work and with trying to keep Jane happy, I suspect he will be shocked when he finds out. Likely, such a thing never even crossed his mind."

"And you've never said a word to him about it?"

"Only that I want all of his books when he's done with them. He knows I study. I think he's just grateful because it keeps me busy and out of his way."

"Well, that has to end right now."

"That I'm out of his way?"

"No, that he has no idea what you want to do with your life. He may regret the fact that I for one have no intention of getting out of his way. Also that he's going to lose the best cook and housekeeper he'll ever have, but he will get over that."

"I'm scared to even hope."

"Athena, you just keep studying the way you do, and let me take care of the rest of it. Are we agreed?"

"Yes, of course. And Melanie?"

"Yes?"

"I know you need some more clothing made. Can we take a look at the rest of the fabrics that arrived here? I want to get started on all of this. I want to make you happy so you'll stay here."

"Athena, you don't have to worry. Where would I go?"

Downstairs again, Athena led Melanie back to the large utility room behind the kitchen, where at least twenty bolts of fabric had been delivered and were stacked up, awaiting Melanie's approval. The women spent the next two hours deciding which ones Melanie wanted turned into dresses and intimate apparel.

"I'm getting confused," Melanie said. "I don't usually get confused, but there is so much here. What do you think?"

"Well, if you ask me," Athena offered, squinting at each of the fabrics by itself, "I think the aqua looks beautiful lined with the white. Look at that! It suits your lovely blonde hair and your skin tone." She laid the blue raw silk over the *charmeuse*, and Melanie agreed. This new life was starting to become very real. Then, laying the fabrics down carefully on the table, her hands on her hips, she continued, "Melanie, I'm sorry if I'm speaking out of turn, but do you think there's a chance you might marry my brother at some point? He loves you, I know he does. And he's a wonderful person."

Melanie sighed. This conversation again. "You know what I'm going to say, don't you? I just don't know, Athena. I'm attracted to your brother, but I'm not in love with him, and there are too many unanswered questions. I just can't say what will happen to us."

"You can believe me, he is the finest person I've ever met. He will do right by you forever. You can trust me on that!" Athena stamped her foot and bobbed her head at the same time. The mass of curls undulated like an ocean wave.

Melanie had to smile at Athena's sober sincerity and her curly, fluid mane. "Well, I do trust you, and if you say so, I believe you, but it's just too early to answer your question."

Athena stamped her foot again. "I just don't want him hurt."

"Are you worried I'm going to hurt him?" Despite herself, Melanie thought it was funny. This woman hardly knew her, and she was doing everything she could to help Athena with what had appeared to be an intractable problem.

It was still charming that Athena wanted to take such good care of Thomas. Perhaps she didn't want to relegate that job to a newcomer and thought Melanie might take away her purpose in life. It was sweet. She'd have to mention this to him.

"I'm sorry, I didn't want to insult you. It's just that we've been fending for ourselves for a long time, and we all take care of each other."

"I understand. Really. I'll have to earn your trust, and that makes total sense. I *will* earn your trust."

"Will you tell me everything about 2016?"

"What do you want to know?" They were standing in the dimly lit utility room, surrounded by bolts and bolts of bright-colored fabric, breathing in the smell of strong dyes, with windows open and the freezing cold, late February air pouring in. All of a sudden, Melanie thought it was hysterical. She started laughing uncontrollably, grabbing onto Athena's arm with one hand and the wall with the other.

Athena looked more alarmed than amused. "What's so funny?"

"It just seems so incongruous," Melanie said. "Here I am, in 1886, looking at fabrics so that you can sew me some clothing because I have none, discussing 2016 with you as if that's just an everyday thing." She sputtered with laughter, but after several minutes she felt her entire soul turn inside out. This was serious stuff. Would she ever see Justin again? Her mother?

Her thoughts went back to what kept her awake at night—the pain it caused her to think she would never have a chance to tell him she loved him or to tell her mother how grateful she was for all the support—couldn't even tell her she'd be meeting and chatting with "Aunt" Isabella Gardner next week. She wondered whether someone had been hired to replace her at work. The doormen at her building would be gossiping about what had happened to her, how she'd disappeared. They would be moving her furniture out of her apartment, marveling about what a mess she had left, and painting the walls for the next tenant. She missed her clothing, her shoes, and her pretty purses, and earrings. She longed for the deli up the street with the incredible bagels and whitefish salad. As if adding insult to injury, here she was, knowing exactly what was going to happen over the next 125 years, unable to do a thing about it, perhaps not even being able to convince anyone that it was all real. She knew now how Cassandra must have felt. She fell back onto a stack of fabric bolts they had rejected, put her head in her hands, and cried. Here she was, crying again about something over which she had no control. But she let it all out, sobbing with abandon. She was getting tired of crying all the time.

Athena had run to the kitchen and come back with a cool, damp towel, which she placed over Melanie's forehead as she patted her back. "It will be all right, Melanie, I promise." She repeated that in a soft, halting voice, as if she was trying to convince herself. Melanie cried for several minutes. She used the towel to wipe her tears away. Finally, when she had cried herself out, she looked up at Athena, who was hovering close above her.

"Thanks, Athena." Her voice was a rough gasp as she tried to catch her breath. "I don't know where that came from."

"I do, Melanie. I can't imagine what you're going through."

"I have to get a grip. I'm just lucky to have you and Tom. My new family. At least I have a family. Right?" Melanie looked up at the other woman, whose face was bent down close to hers, her bright eyes wide with concern. "If only I could convince your sister that I mean no harm."

Athena nodded her head vehemently. "You do have a family. We are your family. We will never abandon you."

Melanie looked up from her fabric throne. Somehow she had to make this all work. There was no alternative. "Athena?"

"Yes?"

"Please promise you'll help me turn Jane around. I don't know how we'll all live together if she keeps up the war she's started with me."

"I'll do my best, but I have to tell you, Jane is quite stubborn."

"Yes, I've noticed that. It seems to run in the family."

Chapter 12

By late afternoon, Melanie was bored and missing Thomas. She had been thinking that it would be nice to get this house redecorated. She thought that might be contributing in part to Jane's depression. Perhaps painting the walls a lighter color might work, having some new drapes made that weren't such heavy, dark velvet. She would talk to Thomas about it when he came home from the hospital.

Athena had disappeared somewhere. Melanie looked for her and eventually found her in her sewing room, working on her large, black, treadle sewing machine.

"Oh, I thought you were studying," Melanie said.

"I want to make you some clothing, Melanie. I do enjoy this."

"So, I had a brilliant idea," Melanie said. Athena looked up from her table, raised an eyebrow. "Yes, how about if we brighten up your bedroom and Jane's? And mine? We could paint them in some bright colors, put up some pretty curtains, maybe a new carpet? Bright pillows? Maybe that would help Jane's state of mind?"

"How will we do this?"

"I'll ask Thomas if he would hire some painters. I'm sure he must know people who do this kind of work, don't you think? This house requires some maintenance. You could pick out your colors. A good idea?"

Athena thought for a moment. "Did you ask Jane about this?"

"No, Jane avoids me at all costs. I'm not sure how to approach her with the idea."

"Well, I would like it. I don't know what colors to pick."

"I'm glad you think it's a good idea. I'll talk to Thomas tonight. Maybe I can get Jane's attention. Or I can ask him to talk to her. No, I think I'll do it myself. I have to keep trying."

Athena shrugged. "I wish I could tell you. She's just...well, she's just sad."

Melanie gave a small wave to Athena and went upstairs to Jane's room. Jane was sitting in her window seat, staring out the window. The room door was ajar, so Melanie stepped in, one foot over the threshold, one in the hallway. She looked around the room. Everything was a dark maroon color—the velvet drapes, the carpet, the flocked wallpaper, the bedspread. "Jane?" Her voice was not much more than a whisper. "Can we talk?"

Jane turned slowly, her body not moving, her head pivoting toward Melanie and then back "What do you want? Why didn't you knock? I'm busy."

Melanie sighed, and Jane reacted, hunching her shoulders forward and crossing her arms over her chest. "Is it so much to ask, that someone knock before walking into my bedroom? I think you are a very rude person."

"Jane, I just had a conversation with Athena."

"About *me*?" Now Jane had wheeled around, and although the light was dim, Melanie could see that her face was streaked with tears.

"No, no. Well, not only about you. I was thinking it might be nice to change the colors of our bedrooms. You know? Brighten them up a bit. They are all so dark.

Wouldn't it be fun to make them a little more feminine?"

Now Jane sprang up, rising to her full height, her hands on her hips. Her eyes were slits, her mouth drawn into a hard line. "How *dare* you?"

"What?" Melanie shrunk back, pulling her offending foot back out into the hallway. "What did I do?"

"My mother decorated this house." Jane's words were clipped, low, separated one from the other. "She spent many hours making everything just right." Jane sighed. "And you have the audacity to come here and try to destroy everything we have left of her memory? Who do you think you are?"

"I didn't know, I'm sorry," Melanie started to say, but Jane put her finger up to her lips.

"And you didn't bother to find out. You just came in here and started changing everything around to your own liking. How *dare* you?"

Melanie felt herself losing her composure again. Jane had the ability to turn her into a pile of mush with a sneering look or a word. "I'm sorry, Jane. I thought you might like it. Otherwise I never would have said anything."

"Well, I *don't* like it, and I don't like you. You're bossy, and all you want to do is change everything around. We like everything the way it is. You are not being fair, and my brother is so smitten with you that he doesn't even see it." Jane stamped her foot, which, Melanie noted, was a favorite action of Jane's when she was angry.

"I don't think *you're* being fair, Jane. I can't know…what I don't know. All you had to do was tell me, and I wouldn't have asked again." Now Melanie felt the tears welling up in her eyes, and she continued to back away into the hall. As she stepped back, Jane stepped forward, and somehow Melanie felt menaced by this woman who was shorter and slighter than she was.

"I don't believe you. I think you're here to make me miserable. You want to turn Tommy away from me. You are an evil woman. I don't believe you are from some other time. You just say that to intrigue my brother. Go back where you came from and stop making me miserable!"

Melanie turned around sobbing and fled down the stairs and back to Athena's sewing room, where she hurled herself down on the floor between two large bolts of cotton fabric.

"Oh, no," Athena stood up from her sewing table and knelt down beside Melanie. "What happened?"

"She hates me," Melanie said, "And I don't think there's anything I can do to make her change her mind. I'm at my wits' end. I just don't have any more ideas."

Athena put her arms around Melanie from back to front and hugged her. Melanie liked the smell of Athena's beautiful hair, and she breathed it in, as if it might take the hurt away. "I do have faith she'll get over it eventually, but I don't know how long that will take, and I don't know how to make that happen. She really is a good person, you have to believe me." Athena held Melanie, rocking her back and forth gently.

Melanie sucked in her breath, trying to stop the sobs. "I think I have to get out of here," she said.

"What do you mean?" Athena pulled back, her mouth open. "Thomas will die!"

"I mean now, right now. I think I have to go and take a long walk somewhere. Get out of this house for a little while."

"Are you up to that? I mean, you've only been out of the hospital a few days."

"Yes, I'm fine. May I borrow your coat until I have one of my own?"

"Of course. Do you want me to go with you?"

"No, Athena, thank you, but I think I'd rather go by myself. I just need some time to think things over."

"Where will you go?"

"I'll just take a walk over to Newbury Street."

"It's freezing out, Melanie."

"That's all right, Athena, I just need to clear my head. Please don't worry about me. I'll be fine."

"I *will* worry, and if Thomas comes home, he'll probably be furious with me for letting you go."

"I'll be home before Thomas, I promise you." She grabbed the coat Athena held out to her, and the wool scarf and hat and the muff. Athena had her hand across her mouth and looked so terrified that Melanie put her arms around the other woman and hugged her. "Really, try not to worry about me. I'm just going to take a walk, that's all." She broke away from Athena, who followed her to the front door.

"Do you want me to ask Archie to get the horse and carriage out? He could take you somewhere."

"No, that's all right. I just want to walk. Oh, and Athena?"

"Yes, anything..."

"Thank you. You have been a darling to me. You can't imagine how much I appreciate it. I just hope Jane doesn't take that out on you."

The wind was blustery, and Melanie felt her breath turning into ice crystals as she breathed through the scarf, which she had pulled up around her mouth. She turned left on Commonwealth Avenue, walked down to Exeter Street, and took another left onto Newbury. How different it looked than it would look a century later. Most of the businesses were offices or churches. It wasn't bustling with people that way it would later on, and there were fewer buildings there, but some of the buildings were familiar, and the city still resembled a small European town, rather than an American metropolis. She had always marveled at how different Boston was from New York, Philadelphia, or Chicago. She walked up Newbury Street toward the Public Garden, trying to figure out what to do about Jane. She'd had an annoying roommate her freshman year at college, but it was nothing like this.

The hostility and the anger—that she could understand

on some level—but this girl was twenty-two, and she should get over it.

At Arlington Street, Melanie turned left and, when she couldn't feel her toes any longer and her fingertips were starting to freeze even inside the fur muff, decided to head back to the Thornwell house. She walked carefully in the button boots, shuddering every time she got to a curb where there was a pile of ice. She had flashbacks to the accident, but she still couldn't remember exactly what had happened. Each time she had a flashback, she heard Justin's voice trying to comfort her, and that made her the saddest, because she longed for him so terribly. As she walked down Commonwealth Avenue toward the house, it started to snow again, and the cobblestones were slippery, but Melanie made it, her heart beating hard. Athena met her at the door.

"Did you have a good walk?"

"I'm freezing, and I'm glad to be home. It's snowing, and the street is slippery."

"I'm happy you said 'home.' This is your home. Thank heavens you're back safely. Now I can breathe again."

"I just have to figure out how to make Jane understand that this is my home."

Athena helped Melanie off with the coat and boots. "You need to go stand by the coal stove," she said, "Your hands are like little blocks of ice."

"My feet are too," she said, "Brrrrr…"

"I'm afraid Thomas would be angry at me for letting you go, after you just recovered from near frostbite. I'm sorry."

Melanie noted that Athena's face was drawn with worry. "I'm a grown-up, Athena, don't you worry. I was going to go, no matter what you said. I just needed some fresh air and some time to make a plan about how to deal with your sister."

"Did you make such a plan?" Athena half pushed, half pulled Melanie toward the glowing coal stove in the corner of the room, where the cast-iron furnace was radiating delicious warmth.

Melanie stood as close to it as she could, rubbing her hands in the heat. "No, I have no idea what to do. I am not giving up, though."

"Good. Now I'm going to study a bit more before I start cooking dinner. I couldn't concentrate the whole time you were gone. If anything had happened to you out there—"

"Nothing did, Athena, but thanks for your concern." Melanie turned around and hugged Athena again. "Now get yourself up to those books, before I get sick worrying about *you*!" She slapped Athena on the rear, and the two women laughed, as Athena disappeared up the stairs.

"I think I'd like a light blue on my walls," Athena called as she got to the top of the staircase, "And maybe some white curtains with blue flowers on them."

As soon as Melanie had warmed herself enough to feel comfortable, she walked upstairs to her room. Passing Jane's room, she heard nothing, but she didn't even look in. She looked around her room to see whether anything had been touched, but she couldn't tell. She thought of writing another letter to Justin, feeling sad she had burned the original one. She opened the desk and looked at the stack of stationery with TT at the top. Thomas was so nice, obviously so taken with her, but she still couldn't remove the hope of reuniting with Justin from her mind. Writing to Justin would only make her sad. She closed the desk. Perhaps she would write more letters to him, but she would never leave them out for Jane to ridicule again. She lay down on the bed under the warm, down quilt, and she fell into a deep sleep.

Melanie wasn't sure whether it was Athena's voice traveling up the stairs or the delicious smells following the voice that woke her. It was dark in her room. She had no idea how long she'd slept, and, at first, she had trouble remembering where she was. She sat up in bed and realized she was starving. She'd eaten breakfast, but nothing else today. That smell was tantalizing. She pulled herself up and stumbled out into the dark hallway.

"Coming," she called, stretching.

The cold and the long walk had made her a little sore, so she was determined to walk more and get over her stiffness.

Thomas was already sitting at the table when Melanie got downstairs. "Hello, Melanie, I'm glad you got some sleep."

"Oh, I'm embarrassed that I slept the day away." She stretched again.

"Athena told me you had a bit of an adventure."

Melanie cast a questioning glance at Athena, who had entered the dining room with a huge platter of chicken and roasted vegetables. "I thought it was going to be our secret?" she said to the other woman, who looked down and put the platter in the middle of the table.

"Athena doesn't keep secrets from me," Thomas said. He reached over and patted Melanie's arm, and she drew it away, as she didn't want to give him the idea he could touch her whenever he wanted to. She looked up at him, and his smile had disappeared.

"Are you angry?" she said.

"No, of course not. The exercise is good for you, but I don't want you to overdo it. I'm glad you came home and took a nap. It's freezing out there."

"I just couldn't get warm, so the bed and the comforter felt good. I got lulled into a deep sleep I guess."

"You needed the sleep," he said, his face softening again. "Are you hungry?"

"So hungry!" she said, scooping some of the meat and potatoes and vegetables onto her plate. As usual, it tasted like ambrosia. Athena could take a simple chicken and make it taste like a gourmet meal. All the food was somehow tastier here. She smiled at Athena, approvingly. "Thank you Athena, this is delicious. Hello Jane, how are you?"

Jane was sitting on Thomas's other side, but she hadn't

said a word, and she was pushing the food around on her plate. She offered a little grunt, never looking up at Melanie.

"I took that long walk because I had to think."

Thomas raised his eyebrows, but he didn't stop eating.

"This isn't going to work if Jane continues to wage war against me."

Jane made a disparaging noise with her tongue and teeth, threw down her fork and knife, and left the table as the utensils clattered against the china. "I'm sick of her," she screamed, as she ran up the stairs.

"I'm sorry, Tom," Melanie said, putting her silverware down much more gently than Jane had. "I just don't know what to do. I've tried to be nice, tried to talk to her. I even offered to help her redecorate her room to make it more feminine."

"I suspect that didn't go over well, did it?"

"I had forgotten you told me your mother decorated this house. The last thing I wanted to do was make Jane think I was trying to eradicate your mother's memory. I just didn't remember."

"You should talk with me before you make these sweeping offers, all right?"

Melanie looked down at her plate. "I'm sorry, I was mistaken. But I don't think her reaction was warranted. If she had simply told me, I would have backed off. It's not good for her to stay in this constant state of rage. It's not good for me either."

"I know, Melanie. I wish I could solve this, but I haven't figured out how."

They finished the meal in silence.

Chapter 13

Melanie fell asleep easily again. By the time she woke up in the morning Thomas was already gone. Even the delicious smells of Athena's breakfast hadn't awakened her. The sun was shining today, but it was a cold sunshine. Out her bedroom window Melanie saw a fine coating of snow from the day before glistening on the lawn. She walked downstairs to the sewing room. Athena was there, sewing away as if she'd never left. Two completed dresses were hanging from hangers.

"Good heavens, you're already done sewing two dresses for me? These are beautiful!" Melanie held one of the dresses up to herself. It was the pale blue silk, and Athena had trimmed it with a darker blue silk ribbon belt. She imagined herself dancing at Isabella Gardner's soiree, and that made her giggle.

"They go pretty fast. You'll have to try them on, though, in case I need to make alterations. Hemming and whatnot."

"Well, you have no idea how much I appreciate your handiwork."

"So," Athena said, looking up from the machine, "I had an idea."

"Yes?"

"What if we just go ice skating, just you, me, and Jane.

We won't take no for an answer, and if I know Jane, she won't be able to resist."

"You mean today? Just the three of us?"

"It's nice out, chilly, but the sun is shining. Perfect for skating. It will keep us warm. Then we can just come home as soon as our bones are freezing."

Melanie laughed. "But I don't have skates."

"I had an idea about that too. Mrs. Thornwell used to go skating with Jane. I put her skates away after she—"

"Do you think they might fit me?"

"It's worth a try, Melanie, don't you think?"

"Do you think Jane will be furious?"

"I'm telling you, where ice skating is concerned, Jane rather forgets everything that's ever bothered her." Athena reached behind the sewing machine and pulled out a pair of high button, black leather ice skates. They looked hardly used. "Try them on."

Melanie sat down on the chair beside Athena and slipped the skates on. "A little snug, but I think it will be fine at least for a short time. Thanks, Athena. This was a great idea. Will you tell Jane we're going? I'm afraid if I say anything, she'll just have another temper tantrum."

Athena raised her eyebrows and left the room without a word. Several minutes later, she returned, Jane trailing behind. Melanie couldn't tell what Athena's expression meant, but it was obvious she wanted Melanie to take over the project.

"Jane, so I hope you'll be going ice skating with us."

"You ice skate too?" Jane's face was set in the frown she used regularly when talking to Melanie. "Are you going to try to outdo me in that, just like everything else?"

Melanie pushed Jane's mother's ice skates behind her, hoping not to ignite another firestorm. "Actually, I was hoping you might show me how to do it. I'm a terrible ice skater. I need tutoring. I'd like to learn how to skate well enough to let go of the railing and not be afraid of falling on my backside. Everyone here says you're brilliant at it."

Jane's hard look softened for a second. Athena, who was standing beside her sister, noticed it and shot an eyebrows-up look to Melanie, who tried not to change her facial expression at all. "Will you say that even when we get to the Frog Pond?" Jane's face resumed its hard glare.

"Honestly, Jane, I am a bad ice skater. I love it, but I'm bad at it. Athena told me you are fabulous at it, so I can't wait to see you skate."

"What else did you tell her about me?" Jane said, shooting a look at Athena.

"Nothing! I told her nothing, Jane. I just bragged about how talented a skater you are."

"So now she wants to be a better skater than I am, right?"

"No, Jane. I really don't. I will never be good at it. I just want to try it again. I'd love it if you gave me some pointers, that's all. Please, will you go with us? I am not looking to outshine you on the ice rink, I promise you."

Jane turned around and left the room. Melanie felt her shoulders slacken in defeat, but Athena followed Jane. Moments later, Athena returned to the sewing room and smiled at Melanie. "Come on, Jane's getting on her coat. Hurry up, before she changes her mind."

"You're a genius," Melanie said, energized again with their small victory. She picked up the skates and handed them to Athena, who secreted them under the voluminous folds of her overcoat. "Let me get my things on."

In silence, the three left the house and reached the street, Athena and Melanie in front, Jane lagging behind, although she kept up with them. It was late afternoon, and the sun was already starting its descent in the west.

"It's a winter wonderland," Melanie said, wanting to make small talk, but feeling a little embarrassed about the cliché. "It is so pretty with the lamp light against the trees. The frost on them looks like sugar coating. We should walk more often at this hour."

When they reached the Common, the Frog Pond was glistening in the twilight, with scores of skaters of all ages and abilities gliding around in the late winter air. For the first time since Melanie had met her, Jane looked at her and smiled.

"I'm afraid to hope," Melanie whispered after Jane passed them and hurried toward the pond.

Athena sat Jane down on a bench, and, on her knees, unlaced Jane's shoes and replaced them with her skates, which Jane had strung around her neck. "Let me help you with these."

Then she walked Jane to the edge of the rink, and gave her a little shove, but it didn't take much. Melanie watched in awe as Jane transformed into a different person, a carefree angel on the ice. Athena stood, her hands on her hips, a broad smile lighting up her face, as if she had created this phenomenon all by herself.

"I had no idea," Melanie said to Athena as a circle of skaters parted, giving Jane room. "Even after you told me."

Jane skimmed the surface of the ice, doing figure-eights, jumps, spins. The lines in Jane's face smoothed, and her smile became broader as she skated. Every time she completed a new move, the other skaters, many of whom had stopped to watch her, clapped, first politely but after a while with great gusto.

"Where did she learn how to do that?"

"She's skated since she was a little girl," Athena said. "She just had the most amazing natural talent for it, and Mrs. Thornwell used to take her for lessons every winter. After Mrs. Thornwell passed away, she seemed to lose her enthusiasm for it, but I was hoping this outing might help her forget her obsession with you, at least for a while. It looks like I was right. I haven't seen her this carefree in years."

"I guess I should put the skates on, since you were nice enough to bring them? And you?"

"I try to do it, but I look like a clumsy fool on the ice, I'm afraid. Just not my sport."

"I think you have other significant talents, Athena."

"Let me help you get this on, and then you can show Jane you're not as good at it as she is."

"You can say that again," Melanie said. "At home we go skating in tight blue jeans, so I'm not sure how I'll do in a long dress and coat."

"Blue jeans?"

"You would love blue jeans! They're pants—comfortable, and they kind of mold to your shape, and you don't have to worry about getting them dirty—" She stopped talking, marveling at the amazed look on Athena's face.

Athena's eyes were so wide that Melanie could see the whites above and below their deep chocolate color. "Trousers?" Her eyes stayed wide. "On women?"

"Okay, it's all hard to describe. We wear pants. We don't have to drag around these heavy skirts all the time."

"I wish I could be there and see for myself." Athena sighed. Then, a huge round of applause pulled their attention away from clothing styles and toward the ice, where Jane had just done some kind of flashy jump—Melanie knew the names of jumps—Axel or Salchow or lutz or loop, but at this point, none of these jumps had been developed. Jane's sylphlike figure seemed to be floating above the surface of the ice, as if gravity didn't exist. The angry, sad, bent-over, wraithlike, vacant Jane transformed into a balletic beauty on ice skates. Several moments later, Melanie caught Jane's eye as Jane skimmed the perimeter of the rink, and Jane smiled at her.

This, then, was the answer for Jane. Melanie was determined to talk to Thomas about both of his sisters. He was missing the point about both of them.

Melanie hobbled onto the ice, her feet hurting from the tight skates, her ankles wobbling, her confidence nonexistent in the heavy, long clothing. She took one circle around, falling twice, pulling herself up, and breathing hard. The third time she fell, Jane skated over and reached out both hands to Melanie, who grabbed Jane's wrists. As slight as she was, Jane pulled Melanie up with a graceful motion, and then she held on and skated around the circuit with Melanie.

"Thank you," Melanie said. "I'm going to leave this ice skating to you from now on. I just don't think I have the talent for it."

Jane smiled, the second smile of Jane's Melanie had ever seen directed at her. She skated with Melanie over to the bench, where Athena was sitting, and pushed her down lightly. "I'm not done yet. I want to skate some more."

"Yes, go ahead," Melanie said. "I love watching you."

Jane's demonstration lasted about fifteen minutes longer. When she turned and walked off the ice toward them, it was to a murmur of appreciation and more restrained applause. Even in this dim light, Melanie noticed that Jane's color was better than she had seen it. Her face looked untroubled—content—her blue eyes clearly shining, full of life, as they were caught in the rays of one of the gaslights on her way to them.

"You took my breath away," Melanie said, as Jane unlaced her skates and Athena helped her back into her shoes.

"Actually, I think that wasn't me. It was your awful skating."

Athena put her hand over her mouth, but Melanie showed her with a wave of her hand that she didn't mind the comment. "Well, it was both, Jane, believe me. You're a brilliant skater. We're coming over here every day. How in the world do you do all those jumps and moves in your long skirts? Without tripping over them or falling on your butt?"

"My butt?" Jane was still smiling, her white teeth flashing.

"Your bottom."

Jane shrugged. "Can't everyone do that?" She threw the comment over her shoulder. "We should walk home. It's getting dark." Jane had a spring in her step as they walked back from the Common. Now she walked a couple of steps in front of the other two women.

Melanie exchanged a glance with Athena, who smiled

and shrugged. "We all have our callings," she said to Melanie. Melanie squeezed Athena's hand.

They finished the walk home in silence, huddled together against the biting late winter wind, until they were close to the big house, when Jane spoke so softly that Melanie had to concentrate to hear her. "Thanks for doing this, Melanie," she said.

"What?" Melanie leaned closer to Jane, but Jane turned her head away as if she didn't want to look Melanie in the eye.

"I won't tolerate your hurting my brother, however."

"I am sorry you've had such a hard time with my coming here, Jane. We don't have to be best friends, but I hope you believe me when I say I don't want to hurt anyone here, you, Athena, or your brother. It's been a shock to all of us, my arrival, but I'm trying to make the best of it, and I hope you can too."

As the three walked up the brick steps to the front door, Archie met them as they walked inside. "Miss Swift, I have a letter for you. A courier delivered it."

Melanie took the crisp, folded paper from his hand and opened it. In a scrawl that was almost illegible, she struggled to make out the words. It was from Thomas. "Thank you, Archie," she said. "Oh my, he won't be home at all tonight, has to spend the night at the hospital."

"What happened?" Athena said.

"Apparently some carriages collided, and there were so many injured people, they've been busy all day and will be busy all night. We won't see him until tomorrow."

Melanie read the note out loud, but stopped when she got to his words that he missed her terribly, and that he would be home as early the next day as he could.

She felt tears welling up but had almost instant guilt about that. Her mind and her body ached for Justin, even though this wonderful man was trying his best to make her forget the unrealized love she had left behind.

"Are you all right, Melanie?" Athena approached with both hands out.

"I'll be fine. I'm just being selfish," Melanie said. She said no more.

"I'm hungry," said Jane.

Those words lifted Melanie's mood immediately. It would be wonderful to see Jane finish a meal.

"What are we having for dinner?"

Athena removed her coat and her hat and her scarf, and bustled toward the kitchen. "How about ham sandwiches on that bread I baked yesterday?" she called back to the other two women. "I have some wonderful cheddar too."

"That sounds wonderful," Jane said. "And I'd like a big glass of tea and some of your hot potato salad."

Chapter 14

We're fine," Jane said. "We took a long walk last evening. To the Frog Pond."

"Oh? Did you ask Archie to take the carriage out? It was very cold last night, wasn't it? Your feet must have been frozen."

"Archie offered," Melanie said, a hand on Thomas's arm. "But we needed the walk. And it was wonderful. Jane skated. She is such an excellent skater."

"Oh, wonderful. She *is* an amazing skater, but she hasn't done it much lately."

"But I want to," Jane's voice was strong, her face expectant.

"I wanted to talk to you about that, Thomas." Melanie put her hand on his arm.

"Talk about what?" He had started on the plate of food, and Athena was beaming at him from the stove.

"Jane's skating."

"Oh."

"It's more than just a hobby, I am quite sure."

"What do you mean?"

"Jane and I discussed it."

Jane had put her hands over her mouth, as if she was astounded Melanie was bringing it up. Her eyes were wide, and she wasn't talking.

"Okay."

"I think she'd probably be happier pursuing her skating than finishing nursing school."

Thomas dropped his fork and knife, which clattered onto his plate. Athena jumped up to save the dish, but she wasn't in time. He looked around with his mouth partly open, a forkful of food oozing down the sides.

"No, I *know* she'd be happier pursuing her skating." Melanie looked straight at Thomas, as if she was challenging him.

"How does one pursue skating?" His face was drawn into a frown.

Melanie giggled a little, but when she realized he was serious, she stopped laughing. "Different ways, I think. Performing, or possibly teaching. Whatever she likes."

Is this true, Janie?"

Jane had flushed a deep pink. Her face and body were tense, and her back very straight. "I—I guess so," she said, but her voice was hardly audible.

"You don't want to finish nursing school?"

"I—I don't think so. No, I don't."

Thomas looked as if he was about to cry. He put his fork down on the plate. "Did Melanie urge you to say this?"

"Thomas!" Melanie pushed her chair away from the table. "How could you even think that? Besides, she's barely speaking to me."

"I'm sorry," he said. "But nursing school has been a dream for a long time."

Jane seemed to regain her strength, as if she didn't want Melanie to take the credit for this epiphany. "A dream for me? No, Tommy, a dream for you. A dream for Mother. It made me more and more depressed to see all those people who needed so much. I just wasn't cut out for it."

"Why did you never say anything?"

"I didn't want to disappoint you. I knew how excited you were about my being a nurse. You always talked about how we would work together."

"I'm sorry, Jane. I just never realized." He pushed his plate of food away. "I think we should talk more about it after I get some sleep. I'm not thinking straight right now. I don't have to go back to the hospital until tomorrow afternoon. Is it all right with you if I go to bed for a while?"

"Yes, Tom, of course." Jane's voice had become thin again, spring breeze soft.

"I'd like to talk to you about this now," Melanie said, standing up, meeting Thomas's gaze.

"That's not necessary..."

Melanie felt Thomas's annoyance, but she was determined to turn him around, and Thomas seemed to know that she was going to do what she wanted to. She followed him toward the staircase, where she stopped him at the first landing. She wasn't smiling.

"I really need to sleep, Melanie," Thomas said as they mounted the stairs.

"You can sleep in due time," Melanie said, trying to restrain her frustration. She had hoped this wouldn't have caused such consternation. Things here always ended up more complicated than she thought they should be. "This is very serious, and I won't be able to sleep unless we have it out."

"It hurts me to think that Jane won't be a nurse."

"Thomas, if she doesn't like nursing, that's not fair to her, is it? She loves skating, and she is so talented at it. Have you ever watched her skate?"

"Of course," he said, "Her entire life, Mother took her for skating lessons. She was always a prodigy."

"Well, she's still a prodigy. She came alive on that ice last night. I've never seen such a transformation. She actually smiled at me—a little. Believe it or not, she was worried I wanted to take away from her how she excels on the ice. I'm pretty sure I showed her that wouldn't be a problem."

"You skated too?"

"I did something out there, not sure it was skating."

Thomas laughed.

"Will you at least think about it? My feeling is that she wants to please you so much, I know if you are intransigent about this, she'll just cave in and attempt to finish nursing school. She'll continue to be depressed and sad. I know you want her to be happy."

"I do want her to be happy. This is such a change of everything I expected to happen, it's hard for me to readjust so quickly."

"All I ask at this point is that you consider it, all right? Please don't deny her the opportunity to explore this thing she loves. I think it will make a big difference in her life."

"What if she doesn't succeed?" he said.

"Is it worse not to succeed, or not to try and wonder for your entire life whether you would have succeeded?"

"I never thought I'd fall in love with a smart woman," Thomas said. "I thought I'd fall in love with a beautiful woman who was willing to take care of all my needs without questioning anything."

"I'm sorry I can't return your love, at least not yet."

"Melanie, I will never lose hope."

"So you will at least give it some thought?"

಄಄಄

It was Thomas's least favorite subject in the days following Melanie's assault on the *status quo*. She thought she had finally gotten to the crux of the matter when he said, "It's just so beneath our social status, ice skating," absently, sipping the coffee Athena had placed in front of him, eating a piece of crisp bacon with his hands while he read the newspaper.

Melanie bristled. Floating this trial balloon about Jane was a good way to navigate the waters of Thomas's prejudices, to figure out a way around them. In the meantime, Jane had managed to withdraw again, not saying much, not emerging from her bedroom, and not being cordial to Melanie. Melanie knew she had to continue to urge Jane to return to the Frog Pond. It was the only way to get through to her.

"How's the dress coming for Aunt Isabella's soirée?" Thomas didn't look up, and Melanie knew it was a conscious ploy to change the subject. She decided not to press him anymore now. She didn't want to make him shut down entirely.

"It's a beautiful dress," she said. "Do you want to see it?"

"No, I want to be surprised, dazzled by your beauty and your *haute couture*."

"I'm afraid you won't be dazzled much when you see me trying to walk with that bustle. Why do I have to wear one?" She knew she was whining, but she needed to get his attention, to make him extract himself from the newspaper, which helped him ignore her.

"Melanie?" Thomas pulled the right and left sides of the paper down toward his shoulders, his head popping out of the middle. One eyebrow was raised, and he had drawn his lips into a tight, upside-down U shape.

"You're making me laugh. You look like a Jack-in-the-box popping out from behind that newspaper."

"Okay, you've got my attention. You're not actually thinking of causing a stir by refusing to wear the bustle, are you? It's high fashion, and everyone will have one."

"Not everyone."

"Every woman. You know what I meant." He folded the newspaper and placed his hands in front of him on the table. The plate of bacon was empty, and Athena quickly scurried over to refill it.

"Well it's the silliest thing I ever saw. What purpose does it have? Nothing ever changes. Women have to suffer the most outrageous styles to be considered fashionable."

"Don't you want to be fashionable and have people talking about how beautiful you are?"

"I don't want people talking about me at all."

"Too late for that, my dear. Our living together like this was your choice, and I'm afraid people's tongues wag more about you than about me. At least women's tongues. The men just think I'm damn lucky."

"We have been entirely circumspect."

Thomas frowned, his mouth sinking back into a tight frown. "More's the pity."

"You're adorable when you're angry at me."

Thomas snorted and went back to his newspaper. Melanie cycled from feeling guilty that she couldn't return his adoration to the thought that he was very attractive and there was no guarantee she would ever return to her former life. Also, she knew that the next battle was Athena's, which might prove even harder than Jane's. For now, however, until Isabella's party was over, she decided not to press him. He had so much stress with his work and was so dedicated to it, she didn't want to put more pressure on him at home. But the conflict was far from over, and it wouldn't be over until she won.

A knock at the front door broke their mood. "I'll go," Athena rushed out of the kitchen and to the door. "It's the shoemaker," she called to them.

"Oh, I forgot to mention." Thomas looked up from his newspaper again. "I arranged for the shoemaker to come by and take measurements for shoes for you. So you don't have to keep borrowing shoes."

"That was so sweet of you, Thomas, but I could have walked to Tremont Street."

"I know, but it's icy out, and I wanted to do something nice for you."

"Thomas, you bowl me over with all of the nice things you do for me. I don't know where you find the time to think of me so much."

"I thought he could measure you for a pair of walking shoes, and a pair of party shoes, and—" He paused. "—anything else?"

Melanie sighed. At home she could walk a block to the nearest shoe store and have all the shoes she wanted. "And maybe a pair of ice skates?" Her voice was very soft.

Thomas raised an eyebrow again. "Ice skates?"

"No, I just wanted to see if you were paying attention."

"You are incorrigible," he said, snorting.

"How long will it take to get these shoes made?"

"I told him we were in a big hurry, so he said he'd put everything else aside and work on yours first. You should have your party shoes in time for Aunt Isabella's party."

"Is this costing you a month's salary from the hospital?"

"Don't worry about the money. We have plenty. I wouldn't even need to work if I didn't want to." Thomas finished his coffee and got up from the table. He greeted the shoemaker, whom Athena had shown into the work room. "Mr. Downey, I'd like you to meet our houseguest, Miss Swift."

Melanie stood to greet the shoemaker, a small, middle-aged, balding man with thick glasses. She hoped he could see well enough to get the measurements right. "I'll be right in," she said. She followed Thomas to the front door. "I do appreciate everything you do for me, do you know that?"

"I'm going to miss you all day, Melanie," he said.

"And I you. I wish I had a wonderful career to go to."

"Career?"

"You know what I mean. I feel useless around here. Athena takes care of everything, workmen come and do their work, shoemakers make house calls and measure my feet. I feel like a lazy, worthless moocher."

"Moocher?" he said, laughing at her.

"It's what we call people who do nothing but prey on the kindness of others."

"From what I can tell, you're taking care of my two sisters. I don't think you're preying on them, are you?"

She shook her head no, and he gave her a pat on the head.

"My party dress is a robin's egg blue."

"Then get him to make you a pair of robin's egg blue

shoes. And a pair of black ones. And a pair of ice skates."

Melanie laughed. "No ice skates in this lifetime," she said.

"What are you planning to do today, after Mr. Downey finishes his work?"

"I thought I'd take a walk with Jane and Athena?"

"To go ice skating?"

Melanie shrugged.

He sighed. "I suppose that's what makes Jane happy."

"Yes, it's about the only thing that does."

"Then, so be it. And now I have to go to work."

After he had gone, Melanie poked her head into the kitchen, where Athena was cleaning up. "Do you need any help before I go get my feet measured?" she said.

"No, why don't you just go and meet with Mr. Downey. I gave him a cup of tea. He's in the back parlor."

"Athena, we may need to change your name to Cinderella."

Athena laughed. "That's all right, Melanie," she said, "I appreciate your concerns."

"You know I still plan to talk to Thomas about your other plan, right?"

"I know you will."

"I just want to get Jane's life squared away first. He's not going to be as easy to convince as I thought he would."

"I can't imagine his agreeing wholeheartedly to my going to medical school either." She wiped her soapy hands on a dish towel and leaned up against the sink, closing her eyes slowly. "Sometimes I think I should just stop dreaming about it."

"Never!" Melanie ordered. She wanted to stamp her foot, but she realized that would work better with Thomas. At least it worked for Jane. "You keep that dream, and together we'll make it happen. I promise."

"Whatever you say, Melanie."

"I mean it."

"I know you do."

Chapter 15

As Aunt Isabella's party got closer, Melanie's nervousness was getting the better of her. It wasn't about meeting the cream of Boston society—she was more excited than nervous about that part—but more about navigating in the costume of the day and looking like she knew what she was doing. No one except Thomas knew the story of her arrival here.

"Do you like these?"

As they sat at the dinner table, she pulled out the party shoes that Mr. Downey had delivered only two days after he had measured her feet. They were made out of soft black leather, with an inset of blue watered satin on the insteps to match her dress, and he had attached dark blue lace around the ankles.

She had worried that they would feel stiff and uncomfortable, especially because she was not used to high-top, button shoes and had very little time to break them in, given that the party was in two days.

But the first time she put them on, she realized right away that they were customized to her feet, and they were as comfortable as ballet slippers.

"Are you carrying them all over the place with you?" Athena laughed. "I think they're special."

"They are lovely," said Thomas, engrossed in one of his medical journals. He never looked up.

"Yes, they're purple with orange stripes," Melanie said. She tried to be annoyed with him, but she was more amused. "They should go perfectly with my red and green plaid dress. And they're made in China."

"Wonderful, my dear," he said, still riveted by the article he was reading, "They sound exquisite."

"Thomas!" Melanie drummed her fingers on the table, and Athena hid a giggle behind the hands she had brought up to her face.

Thomas put down the journal and looked up, surprised at her tone. "What, Melanie? I said I liked them."

"You're not paying any attention to me at all," Melanie pouted. "You say you care for me, that you want to convince me to feel that way about you, but you're bored with me already. You didn't even look at my shoes. I feel like we're an old married couple, and we're not even married, and we're not even a...couple." The sad turndown of Thomas's face made her feel guilty for being so mean.

"Melanie, I am not bored with you. How could I be bored with you? You are the most complicated, inscrutable creature I've ever met in my life."

"But you ignored everything I said to you, your nose was buried in your medical journal, and you don't care about me and my shoes."

"I do care," he said. "But there's a difficult case in the hospital and I have to find out as much as I can about it."

"Maybe you could give me five minutes of your time?"

"Yes, anything. What?"

"You just said it was wonderful that I had Chinese shoes with purple and orange stripes to go with my red and green plaid dress."

"I did not!"

"Yes you did! Athena, didn't you hear him?" She looked over at Athena for female support, but Athena was looking down at her soup and laughing. "Girls have to stick together! Jane? Will you be on my side this one time?"

"I'm afraid you did, Tommy," Jane said.

Melanie's mouth opened in a big "O." Jane's agreeing with her seemed like a huge milestone. Thomas put his journal down on the floor and looked chastened.

"You always have your nose in a book or a magazine, even at dinnertime. Melanie's right. It's rude."

Melanie flashed her gratitude at Jane with a big smile and a light slap of her hand on the table. "Do you believe your sister? She doesn't lie."

Thomas shrugged.

"Now, I have brought my shoes to the dinner table because I wanted you to see them, and I thought this might be the only place to grab any attention from you at all. Do you like them?" She held up one of the shoes.

"They are still lovely, Melanie. You have lovely taste, so I never doubted they would be."

"Would you mind just having a dinnertime conversation with your family, instead of reading as we sit here?"

"I'm sorry."

"I'm worrying about the party. What if I trip over the bustle and fall on my fanny, and people think I'm silly and stupid?"

"I promise you, no one will think you're silly and stupid." Thomas shook his head, as if he had no idea how to convince her.

"How do you know?"

"Melanie, I've been living with you. I know. If someone thinks you're silly and stupid, it only means that *they* are silly and stupid."

"What in the world am I supposed to say to John Singer Sargent?"

"I'd suggest you don't call him 'John Singer Sargent.'"

"Why? That's his name, isn't it?"

"Do you call me 'Thomas Blair Adams Thornwell'?"

"Oh, I see what you mean. I didn't even realize you had all those names."

"Well, I do. But people who are acquainted with me tend to use only one of them at a time, you know?" He winked at her. "I wish you wouldn't worry so much. You'll be fine. Within five minutes of being introduced to these people, you'll be solving the problems of the world with them, and fixing things and getting in the middle of a thousand conversations, and no one will notice that you're as clumsy as an ox in the clothing." Now Thomas was laughing.

"I guess I deserved that, but you didn't have to be so mean."

"Neither did you!"

"What do they call it? A taste of one's own medicine?"

He went back to his soup. "However, it will never hurt that you are going to be the most beautiful woman in that house."

"Thomas, you are a sly operator." Melanie felt the blush rising from her neck, and all of a sudden, she felt as if she was cheating on Justin for flirting with Thomas.

Thomas winced, but he didn't respond. "Athena, what's the main course tonight?"

⌀⌀⌀

Melanie spent the next two days having Athena make adjustments to her dress and practicing with the bustle and the shoes and the dress and the wrap and the hat. She wished she could go to the party in a pair of comfortable slacks, but that was just silly. Nevertheless, it would be so delicious to see the looks on these people's faces if she walked into their soirée in silk charmeuse slacks. But she would do the best she could in all the nineteenth century finery, and leave it in the hands of the gods. If she tripped and fell on her face, so be it.

"You are doing much better!" Athena was always Melanie's biggest supporter. "You don't even look too uncomfortable anymore."

It was the day before the party, and Melanie's self-confidence was at its lowest ebb.

"I still feel ridiculous in this getup," she said. "The crinolines are itchy, and the bustle digs into my back."

"I can't help you with the crinolines, unless we have you wear a heavier undergarment, and then you might be too hot. But I have something for the bustle," Athena said, and she pulled out a piece of lambswool. "Here, let me put it between you and the bustle." She opened about ten buttons on the back of the dress and inserted the lambswool next to Melanie's skin.

"That does feel better. Thank you, you are such a life-saver," Melanie said. "Are you sure you won't come to the party with us?"

"Oh, no, thank you. I have a lot of studying to do, and I don't really enjoy big parties anyway."

"Jane doesn't want to go either. You've both been invited. Won't Aunt Isabella be insulted?"

"Aunt Isabella will have so many guests to take care of, she'll never notice that Jane and I are missing. Anyway, you have Tom! He'll take good care of you, don't worry."

"What if I get tongue-tied and can't think of a thing to say to anyone?"

"Melanie, we've had this conversation over and over again. That won't happen, and frankly, I can't wait until this thing is done with. You're getting hard to take. I like you better when you're in my room talking about my studies."

"I feel completely worthless in this place." Melanie sank down into a crumpled ball on the platform Athena had pulled into the center of the room for her to stand on while the re-hemming was going on.

"Watch out! You're going to crease the dress, and then I'll have to press it again!"

"I'm sorry, sweetie." Melanie stood up and gave Athena a tight hug. "I love you. You are the best."

Athena put her arms out at her sides and wouldn't hug back. "The dress, Melanie, the dress!"

"After this ordeal is over, I'm going to talk to Thomas about your situation," Melanie said, pulling away from the other woman. "I've almost got him where I want him with Jane, and you are next. I'm sorry you had to wait until after this Gardner 'do.'"

"I've waited quite a long time anyway, Melanie, and besides, I don't think you'll convince Tom about me."

"Oh yes I will, Miss Athena, yes I will. He listens to me, at least when I scold him for not listening to me. And he wants to be in my good graces."

But Melanie wondered whether she would succeed. She hardly slept that night. Every time she closed her eyes, she thought about the accident in New York and her reawakening in Copley Square. About the two women who had been strangers only weeks ago but who now seemed like her own family, at least one of them. She strategized about ways to broach the subject of Athena's medical education to Thomas. For someone so brilliant and caring, she found his stubbornness difficult to deal with, but she was just as stubborn.

The morning of Isabella's party dawned gray and cold, and the air smelled like an impending snowstorm. Melanie was already in the kitchen puttering over the coal stove when Thomas came downstairs.

"You're up so early," he said, rubbing his eyes.

"I've been up most of the night," she said, turning toward him. "Do you want coffee?"

"I was dead to the world," he said, grabbing the cup she held out to him.

"I seem to be the only chronic insomniac in this house."

Pursing his lips, with one finger at the side of his nose, he said, "Are you all right, though? I worry about you when you can't sleep."

"I'll be fine, Doctor. Just a little nervous about the party tonight, you know?"

"Nothing more I can say about that," he said, "You'll

just have to go and see what it's like to be belle of the ball. If I'm lucky, you'll come home with me."

"You will be home from the hospital early, so you can change clothes?"

"I'll try, Melanie. If something keeps me there, you just have Archie bring you to Aunt Isabella's house in the carriage. I'll meet you there."

"No!" Melanie wheeled around and stared him in the face, her nose not two inches from his. "You can't do that to me!"

Now Thomas was laughing at her, sputtering as he took a sip of his coffee. "Do you know how horrified you look? You look as if you've just seen a specter that transmogrified out of the wall or the bedpost."

"Thomas, you're being mean to me."

"I don't ever want to be mean to you, dear," he said. "It's just that you're so...easy. Funny about you—sometimes you're hard as nails, and I think I've met my match, but other times you seem almost fragile."

"I don't think I'm fragile, but seriously, I'm worried about this party."

"Let's stop talking about it, all right? I think you're working yourself into a frenzy for no reason. You will be fine, I promise."

Thomas went off to the hospital, and Melanie spent her day in a whirlwind of frenetic activity.

"Do you think the hem needs a little adjustment, Athena?"

"No, I don't think so. I've adjusted it about five times. It looks perfect."

"Am I walking like a cripple on these shoes?" Melanie was wearing the corset and bustier and the shoes, walking from room to room, adjusting the undergarments, fidgeting with the laces. "It feels so tight. What if someone asks me to dance?"

"You seem to be moving pretty well right now," Athena offered. She was in the front parlor, dusting the drapes and the woodwork.

"Can you even see me?"

"You've walked by me at least ten times," Athena said.

"I wish Thomas had stayed home today. He could have helped me with all of this."

"He would have no idea what to do with any of it," Athena said, "and you would have driven each other mad."

Melanie ate nothing all day, much to Athena's displeasure. "I have absolutely no appetite, and if I forced myself to eat, I'd only vomit," Melanie said.

"I used to think you were a strong, confident woman," Athena said.

"You don't understand, you really don't," Melanie said.

"Yes I do." Athena tended not to lose her composure very much, but Melanie looked at her and saw the flashing eyes. She thought Athena might have a tantrum.

"Thanks for making me laugh," Melanie said. "I needed that. It takes my mind off how uncomfortable this corset is." She reached down and tried to adjust the undergarment, which she felt was strangling her. It wouldn't move. "Why do I have to be strangled into an eighteen-inch waist, anyway? It makes me feel like Scarlet O'Hara."

"Scarlet who?"

"No one."

"I said I understand, because I've lived my entire life trying to fit into a place where I don't really belong," Athena said.

"Oh God, now I feel about *this* big." Melanie put her thumb and forefinger together and pointed them at Athena, who had sat down with her hands and the feather duster across her lap. "You just put everything in perspective." She bent down over Athena and kissed the top of her head. "I'd sit down with you, but I'm afraid I might not be able to get up," she said. "You and I are going to take care of business—as soon as this party is done with. Now I'm more determined than ever."

Athena looked up, and there were tears in her eyes. "Someone sent you here to help me, I really believe that. Maybe it was God."

"Not sure why I'm here, but I'm definitely going to take advantage of it and do something good," Melanie said. "For now, I'm getting over myself and doing this party."

Thomas burst into the house, a flurry of excitement following him as he slammed the heavy door. "Oh, I didn't mean to do that," he said, rushing to the back of the house. "Melanie, are you ready?"

Melanie had left the kitchen, and the two almost collided as Thomas rushed in, head down.

"Here, Thomas."

"Oh my heavens," Thomas said, looking her up and down. "You are an incredible vision. You take my breath away."

"Really?" Melanie felt herself blushing.

"Really! I'm almost embarrassed to be seen with you, you're so ravishing."

Athena had gotten up from her chair and was standing in the kitchen doorway, gesticulating with both her hands at him. "Don't touch her!" she said, squeezing in between them. She'd worked hard to produce this "picture" that Melanie was, and she didn't want it messed up. "Thomas, don't you have to go up and get ready?" she said.

Thomas pulled himself away and glared at Athena, who was looking at him, her face pulled taut into a disparaging frown. "You are ravishing," he said to Melanie, "I can't wait to show you off."

Melanie smoothed out the silk dress and smiled. "I do feel complimented by that, Dr. Thornwell, but be careful. I don't want to be regarded as an object."

"I'm not sure what that means, Miss Swift, but I'm going to assume it has something to do with your evolved, superior culture."

"Assume what you like. But go get yourself ready, and

I'll be here attaching the hat and fiddling with it. I have no idea how to keep it on. It keeps falling off."

"Athena, you'll help her, won't you? I wish you and Jane were going with us."

"Of course I'll help her. I just want Melanie to have everyone's attention tonight. You just have to promise to tell us everything when you get home."

"We will tell you everything," Melanie said, "*Everything.*"

Thomas stopped staring, and then he skipped up the staircase, two stairs at a time, and disappeared into the massive second floor. Athena and Melanie struggled with the big hat.

"If you only had long hair, I could pin the hat onto your bun, but you don't have a bun."

"You don't like my hair?"

"It's not that I don't like it," Athena said. Melanie heard her sigh a little and felt guilty that Athena had given over her life this week to preparing Melanie for this entry into Boston society. "It's just that it makes my life more difficult."

"But it makes my life easier, and besides, I don't look good in long hair."

"What does that mean? You're beautiful, no matter how long or short your hair is."

"You are like the sister I never had but always wanted," Melanie said. "I don't know what I'd have done without you here."

"I feel the same way," Athena said, but she pushed Melanie away when Melanie tried to move in for a hug. "No, no more hugging and kissing. You have to stand still so that nothing is jogged out of place. We can hug when you get home and take this dress off."

"That's a promise," Melanie said, pulling her arms back and leaving them hanging at her sides. "I will follow orders, she who must be obeyed." She did a little curtsey. "Only tonight, though."

The two women laughed, and Melanie began pacing, traveling from the kitchen through the dining room into the parlor and back again. Thomas appeared at the top of the stairs.

Melanie saw him out of the corner of her eye and walked to the bottom of the stairs to look. "You said I was a vision," she said, breathless. "You look like something out of a painting. You're the most extraordinary looking man I've ever seen!"

She thought of Justin, and how she wished it were he standing at the top of the stairs. But Thomas reminded her so much of Justin, she was tempted to pretend he was. Thomas was fully dressed, his bright white shirt, shiny silver cufflinks, and white bowtie shining in contrast to the black suit, with tails and a striped silk waistcoat. He was holding his black silk top hat and a shiny black cane, with which he didn't touch the floor but held it several inches above the stair tread. His hair was brushed back, shiny, his face scrubbed, his eyes shining. He smiled down at Melanie. Athena walked over to the stairs and put her hands on her hips.

"Come down here, Tommy," Athena said. "Let me straighten your tie."

Melanie hadn't noticed that the tie was crooked. It didn't matter. The two of them made a magnificent pair. Suddenly, she couldn't wait to get into the carriage to be whisked to the ball by her handsome Prince Charming. Athena was hovering over Thomas like a mother hen, smoothing his collar, pulling at the sleeves of his jacket, brushing a rebellious strand of hair off his forehead. Melanie's eyes followed every inch of him, every move he made, and although he let Athena fuss over him, he hadn't taken his eyes off Melanie. A rap at the door told them that Archie had the brougham waiting for them in front of the house. Thomas leaned over and gave Athena a kiss on the cheek. She beamed up at him, proud that she had had something to do with the outfitting of this magnificent creature.

"Have a wonderful time!" Athena said, as Thomas glided over to Melanie and offered her his arm, which she took with her kid-gloved hand. Out of the corner of her eye, Melanie saw Jane standing at the top of the stairs, as if she didn't want them to know she was watching. Melanie didn't say anything. She would pretend she hadn't seen, but she was happy that Jane was willing to watch. It gave her some hope for her future with Jane.

Melanie felt as if she was being transported to yet another world, playing masquerade in a period play, with this delicious man in a fancy costume of his own. Archie bowed from the waist and then helped her into the carriage. She was surprised at how comfortable it was, with its luxurious purple velvet upholstery and gold satin window curtains. Thomas stepped up and sat next to her, holding the cane with both hands as the horses clopped over the cobblestones. Melanie closed her eyes and tried to sit still. They didn't say a word during the fifteen-minute ride to Aunt Isabella's Beacon Street house.

Chapter 16

They were met at the grand double door by a tall footman with shiny black high-boots, who bowed deeply as Thomas presented him with the invitation. The footman beckoned that they follow him, and Melanie felt her hand start to shake as she gripped Thomas's elbow tightly.

"Melanie, you're going to give me a terrible bruise," he said, laughing at her. "We're going to a party, not a funeral."

"I'm sorry, Thomas," she said. "This is giving me an anxiety attack."

There were people already in the grand hall, most of them holding glasses of champagne, some with long cigarette holders, all of the women dressed in long satin gowns of many different colors, with pronounced bustles and matching high, wide-brimmed hats tied around the chin with voluminous satin bows.

There were some groups of people so enswirled in cigarette smoke that Melanie couldn't make out their faces. Everyone seemed to be rapt in conversation, and Melanie caught snatches of words and phrases as they walked by.

They were ushered into the massive drawing room with twenty-foot ceilings and gold wallpaper flocked with red velvet, where another servant took over. "May we take your wrap?" he said to Melanie, who obliged, trying to be graceful as she removed the heavy shawl and floor-length evening coat.

Thomas removed his top hat and coat, and when she looked at him again in his tuxedo, she was overwhelmed by his good looks. She looked up over Thomas's shoulder, and there were garlands of purple and yellow flowers wreathed in greenery, hanging over the balustrade on the second floor, that reached almost down to the floor. It took Melanie's breath away. Everywhere she looked there were flowers—huge clusters of gladiolas, trumpet lilies in tall glass vases, actual rose of Sharon trees in five-foot tall pots, blooming with pink and white flowers—in all corners of the room. Before Thomas could lead her into one of the flower-festooned parlors, a woman came rushing toward them, resplendent in low-cut black silk, two thin strands of gold belt perfectly situated around her waist and below, her hair swept up in diamond clips.

"My darling boy, how beautiful you look!" She grabbed Thomas and pulled him close, and then pushed him away at arm's length before she stood up on her toes and kissed him on both cheeks and then again on one cheek. "It is so wonderful to see you. It's been entirely too long. And this delicious creature is your Melanie?" Isabella let go of Thomas and grabbed both of Melanie's hands and spun her around. "Let me get a good look. Oh, you did not exaggerate, Tommy. I should probably leave now, because this lustrous star outshines everyone in this house, including me!" She smiled broadly at Melanie, who was blushing and speechless.

"How do you do, Mrs. Gardner." Melanie managed to push the words out. "Lovely to meet you." She forced her tongue off the roof of her mouth, where it was stuck. "There's no way anyone here tonight is as beautiful as you."

"No, my dear, please call me Aunt Isabella. Thomas

wrote me all about you. I know everything. It's my job to convince you that he is the most worthy husband material in the world, and that you are perfect for him. You bowl me over with your youth and beauty. Spectacular."

Melanie looked up at Thomas, her eyebrows raised in a question. He hadn't told her that he'd written Isabella about her. She wondered how much this woman knew.

"I didn't tell her I'd written you, Aunt Isabella, so excuse Melanie if she's taken aback." He slipped his arm through the crook in Isabella's elbow and gave her a little squeeze.

"What exactly did he say, Aunt Isabella?"

Isabella had grabbed Thomas's hand and stood between the two of them. Then, holding his hand and with her other arm tightly around Melanie's waist, she led them into a small anteroom where she pointed them to an upholstered settee and closed the door. She pulled a chair close to their couch, facing the two of them. "I know you're not married, my dear," she said, "And that you are living together."

Melanie blushed again. "Our relationship is perfectly platonic. I feel like a glorified nanny."

"Oh my goodness, that will not do," the older woman threw her head back and laughed, a tinkling, brittle laugh. "I have known this young man his entire life, and I feel I have stepped in as a surrogate parent. I'm sorry if I come on too strong, but I want him settled with a woman he loves. All work and no play, you know?" She winked. "However, Tom was clear about not embarrassing you." Isabella stared into Melanie's wide eyes and winked. "Although it may be too late, eh?"

Melanie tried to look at Thomas out of the corner of her eye, but she thought his expression looked a little pained, and she didn't want to make it worse, although she was a bit annoyed that he had communicated with this woman at length without letting her know. "I'll deal with it," she said, but even she realized her voice held a tinge of irritation. The only good thing about this was that Melanie had forgotten about how uncomfortable the costume was, and she was ready to get on with the party. Then there was the fact that she had always considered Isabella Gardner a historical icon in the world of art. How often she had spent a life-affirming afternoon soaking up the beauty at the Gardner Museum. She wished she could tell Isabella about it, about everything she knew. But that wasn't possible, so she had to hold her tongue.

"So, my dear, I am told you come from New York?"

"Yes."

"Well, good then! New York is about a century ahead of this small town, for sure. Did you know I came from New York before I married Jack?"

"No, I didn't know."

"Well, I did, and I love to go back there as much as I can. The Metropolitan Museum is a joy."

"Yes, I agree," Melanie said, brightening.

"So, back to Boston, this boy has led a monk's life so far," she said, tapping her index finger on Thomas's knee as if it was a drum, "And he's been the sole support of those two sisters. Did you not bring them?" It was the first indication she had noticed Jane's and Athena's absence.

"No," Thomas said, "Jane has been having some...problems, and Athena wanted this evening to be Melanie's debut, so they stayed home."

"Jane's having the usual problems?" Mrs. Gardner said, looking Melanie up and down.

"I'm afraid she's had some trouble adjusting to my presence," Melanie said.

"She will get over it." Mrs. Gardner fluttered her hand in the air, as if to dismiss Jane's issues. "I assume Athena made that magnificent frock that fits you like a glove, Melanie?"

"Yes, Athena is a wizard with a sewing machine. Actually, I think she can do anything."

"That she can. Truly exceptional. But as beautiful as the dress is, you make it twice as beautiful. And I haven't seen Tommy looking so happy in years. Tommy, I wish your mother and father were here to see you." At this, she became more somber, closing her eyes for a moment, and drawing her smile into a horizontal line. "But, alas, that can't be, so I'll stand in for them as best I can and hope they are looking down at you from heaven. And now, I must get back to my other guests, but please mingle and have a wonderful time. There is so much food, it needs to be eaten, and so much champagne. John Sargent is due, and he is the most interesting conversationalist in the world. And I must introduce you to my Jack as well, but he's off smoking cigars and talking about heaven knows what with some of his men friends in one of the back rooms. I will ferret him out at some point, because he wants very much to meet you. Oh, and of course, Will Howells—have you read his wonderful book, *The Rise of Silas Lapham*? A best seller!"

Melanie shook her head. "Not yet." She had never heard of Will Howells.

"Well, my dear, you must read it. A delicious and naughty romantic triangle." She winked at the two of them. "And Will lives right down the street from us. Right here on Beacon Street. And then Arthur Whiting is coming too, and perhaps bringing some of the musicians of the BSO. His music is utterly divine. But honestly, the one I am looking most forward to is John Sargent. I have my eye on a brilliant portrait he painted, but the man is in love with that painting and won't part with it. For all I know, he's in love with the subject of the portrait too, but he'll never admit it." Isabella put her hand up to her mouth and laughed, a short giggle.

"What painting is that?" Melanie said. She was happy to have a chance to discuss art with this woman, a subject she felt able to discuss intelligently at least.

"The *Portrait of Madam X*, my dear. I believe he only painted it a couple of years ago, but it caused such a scandal in Paris that it makes the painting even more desirable."

Melanie remembered something about that painting, that it was of a rich aristocratic Parisian woman and was considered risqué, because the woman was dressed provocatively in a low-cut gown, the expression on her face considered provocative. "What kind of scandal?" she said.

"Oh, the woman who is the subject of the portrait is married to a prominent Frenchman, and there she was, her décolletage on display for the world, ensconced in a room with John painting her for weeks and months. And when her husband saw the painting, he raised the roof. Silly people! The painting is utterly gorgeous."

"I'd love to talk to him about it."

"Believe me, he will talk your ear off if you let him." Then Isabella stood up, arranged her gown around her, and walked out of the room, giving the two of them a wave and a blown kiss as she went.

"She takes my breath away," Melanie said when Isabella was out of earshot.

"She is a special lady," Thomas said. "And brilliant."

"And confident and gutsy," said Melanie, more to herself than to him.

"So, shall we go and introduce you to Boston society?"

Melanie sighed. "Now or never," she said.

Every room in the house had artworks decorating the walls, some that Melanie recognized and many that she didn't. There were tapestries, oil paintings, and beautiful ceramic vases that had to have been imported from Asia. The house itself felt like a gallery, and Melanie wondered what it was like for Isabella's boys to live here, in a virtual art museum. She hoped they appreciated this place. She herself couldn't imagine what it might be like to grow up here.

As they walked out into what looked to Melanie like a grand ballroom—two-story ceilings, opulent draperies and carpets, a magnificent crystal chandelier—a crush of people was gathering in one corner, and as they approached, Isabella was introducing John Sargent to the assembled crowd. He was easy with people, Melanie observed, quite comfortable in his own skin if not arrogant. Her knees started knocking, so she grabbed Thomas's arm and closed her eyes. Thomas leaned in, giving her support. She didn't notice Isabella approaching again, but suddenly, she was being introduced to the famous painter as Thomas's new companion, an "art *aficionada*." Sargent looked her up and down. Melanie tried to smile, and then Isabella pulled Thomas away and walked off with him. Melanie was on her own with the famous artist she had only read about, who had died decades before she was even born.

"Mrs. Gardner was telling me about the portrait she wants." Melanie cleared her throat, trying to sound as if she wasn't trembling.

He laughed, throwing his head back and putting his arm around Melanie's waist. Then he leaned so close to her that she could smell his skin, and he whispered in her ear, "Ah, she has no chance. That is one I have no desire to sell."

"She seems quite insistent about acquiring it."

"Do you like to sing?" he said, changing the subject as if he didn't want to talk about the painting anymore.

"I love to listen to singing," she said. "I have no talent in music, I'm afraid."

"Well, I love to sing," he said. "And I love to play the piano. So let's go over there and get something started. Singing is often more satisfying than talking, although truth be known, I love to talk to beautiful women." He was staring at her, she thought, as if she was nude, and she blushed. Without waiting for her to answer, tightening his arm firmly around her waist and holding tight, he half pushed, half pulled her out of the ballroom to one of the large parlors, where a concert grand piano took over almost a quarter of the room. He placed her hand up on the piano, sat down, and began to play, and Melanie was amazed that the great artist was also such a musical talent. She had never realized. A crowd of people made their way over, and all of a sudden, everyone was singing, drinking, and laughing. She joined in as well, although she didn't know any of the songs.

"How do you know him?" a middle-aged woman next to Melanie asked her above the voices.

"Oh, I don't," Melanie said. "I just met him."

"He is quite taken with you," she said.

Melanie felt the blush that was becoming so common-place rising up her neck and to her cheeks. "Oh, do you think so?" She was embarrassed, but she had to admit it was nice to be so appreciated by a famous man, let alone a famous artist.

"He keeps giving you sidelong glances. Trying to impress you with his piano playing."

"I am quite impressed, I must admit."

"Well, John Sargent has looked at you from every angle and in every possible way. Perhaps he wants to paint your portrait, but I suspect those looks are for more than his art."

Melanie laughed. "Don't worry, I'm good at protecting myself. It's quite flattering anyway, don't you think?"

The woman appeared to take Melanie's words as a joke, and she threw her head back and laughed. Then someone across the room called the woman, and she walked away, to Melanie's relief, without another word. Melanie stood there beside the piano. The concertizing went on for about a half hour, and then as abruptly as he had begun, John Sargent pushed the piano bench away and closed the cover. The crowd moved away little by little, some registering their disappointment at the end of the sing-along. He ignored them, his intense stare only for Melanie.

"I would love to have the opportunity to paint your portrait," he said, looking at her again, very close to her, his eyes narrowing with concentration. "I am in the process of moving from Paris to London now. Do you ever get there?"

She felt as if he was looking through her clothes, undressing her with his eyes, and she vacillated between wanting to cross her arms over her chest and wanting to throw off these constricting clothes. "No, not really."

"Well, you are an extraordinarily beautiful woman.

Someone will paint you, although I wish it could be me."

"No one has ever said that to me before," Melanie said.

"That is quite surprising to me," he said. "Shall we go get some champagne?"

"I would like that, Mr. Sargent. I love champagne."

He grabbed her hand and led her toward the bar, where a black-clad sommelier was dispensing wine. "Your boy-friend should be careful. Someone is going to whisk you off if he doesn't look out. Not only a raving beauty, but there is some kind of *je ne sais quois* about you. I can't put my finger on it." Melanie assumed Sargent was joking and started to laugh, but he never even smiled.

"Thank you for all the compliments, but I assume you will be going back to Europe soon?"

"Perhaps," he said, "But if you should decide to take me up on it, Isabella will know where to find me." Then he turned his back on her and took two glasses of champagne, handing her one. He clinked glasses with her, and drained his in less than a half minute.

"John, dear, please come to me!" Isabella was beckoning from the corner of the room. "Leave that poor girl alone. There are people who want to meet you." And with a slight bow, John Sargent kissed Melanie on the cheek, and then turned and walked directly to his hostess.

Melanie stood for a moment, catching her breath. How would she convince anyone at home that she had just had an intimate tête-a-tête with one of the most prominent artists of the nineteenth century? She walked around the ballroom, scanning the four corners, trying to catch a glimpse of Thomas, but either he wasn't there or there were just too many people milling around for her to pick him out. She passed a room where a string quartet was playing, and she stopped for a moment to listen to the music. It felt cleansing, and she enjoyed it, and then she walked on.

A knot of people, mostly men but with some women on the fringes, was gathered around the wide doorway deep in a heated discussion. Melanie approached, trying to be inconspicuous. She was curious about their conversation, and as soon as she got within about two feet of the two men, puffing away on cigarettes in long holders, shouting over the din, she stopped to listen.

"He is not a particularly good sculptor, you know."

"No? Then how in hell did he get the commission? That's a very prominent spot to put a colossus if you don't like the sculpture."

"Bartholdi's a snake-oil salesman is all. The Egyptians rejected a similar statue that he proposed for the mouth of the Suez Canal. So then he concentrated his attention on us. The people in this country will do anything when they are flattered by a smooth-tongued Frenchman."

"I think it's going to be magnificent. I saw the statue's head displayed at the Paris World's Fair in '78."

"I read somewhere that Bartholdi modeled the face on his own mother, as French as French can be. Some slap in the face of American freedom, don't you think?" The pro-vocateur continued his barrage of criticism.

"You must recall France was our stalwart ally in the Revolution, so it's more than appropriate."

"That's a copper statue, you know?" The other man chose to ignore the defender's logic. How long do you think it will last on the outskirts of New York Harbor, anyway? Bedloe's is quite unprotected. The first big gale to rise up the Hudson will blow it down."

"From what I hear, Bartholdi consulted with the top en-gineers and architects in Paris. There was some controversy, and there was some redesign. I think it's going to stay up."

"Time will tell, won't it? And the American people are financing that pedestal. It's a scam. I'll bet you five dollars the thing is face down in the harbor within five years."

"You're on," his nemesis said, and the two shook hands, their considerable bellies jiggling as they gripped each other, a cloud of smoke encircling each of their heads.

Melanie marveled that they were talking about the Statue of Liberty, which was apparently not assembled yet. She tried to remember dates from her history classes, and couldn't remember exactly what year the statue was constructed. She wished she could tell the one who thought it would collapse not to waste his money on a bet. *In 2016 it is still standing*, she thought, *made it through Hurricane Sandy and every other thing.* She laughed to herself at the fact that people were always the same. It was impossible to achieve any type of hundred percent consensus. She wondered if that was the same in other countries or if it was just an American cultural trait.

She moved on from the Statue of Liberty discourse and decided to look for a library if she couldn't find Thomas. She could at least look at the books, and she figured the Gardners would have many. In another room, a group of men and women was talking about *Huckleberry Finn*. She had read that it was banned shortly after its publication in the United States because of "vulgarity." One of the people discussing it said he had bought it in Canada, and a few women in the group put their hands over their mouths. *Some things never change*, she thought, trying hard to accept that Mark Twain was a current author and wondering what they would say if she told them that less than a hundred years later Mark Twain would be revered as one of the great authors in American literature, despite the fact that *Huckleberry Finn* still caused controversy.

"Melanie!"

Thomas's voice struck her like a beacon in the wilderness. She heard him, but she couldn't see him. She stopped short, hoping he would come to her. She couldn't wait to tell him about her conversation with Sargent.

She couldn't wait to tell him that the party had been better than the anticipation of it, and she hoped that would make him feel better.

He reached out his hand to her, and she grabbed it. "Melanie, I've been looking for you everywhere."

"I'm so happy to see you," she said, vowing not to sound like a gushing teenager. "You can't imagine what I've been doing. I feel giddy about my meeting with John Sargent. He left me breathless."

"I noticed," Thomas said, looking down at his hands and fiddling with his fingernails. "He couldn't take his eyes off you."

"I had no idea you were watching. You're not jealous, are you?" Melanie winked at him, and he pulled his hand away and shrugged. "You are!" She giggled. "Tom, you're jealous! That is so funny. Do you think he's going to whisk me away to Paris or London?"

Thomas grabbed at her hand again. "I'm not sure what to think," he said. "It seems you were as taken with him as he with you."

Melanie poked him in the ribs with her free hand. "Oh come on, he's a flirt. He is an artist, so he studies people with an eye toward how they would look on canvas."

"And he has an excuse to see them naked if he wants to." Now Thomas worked with one of his cufflinks, rotating it around on his shirt sleeve."

"True, again for his art, though, men and women both. But let's not talk about him anymore. I'm going home with you, not with him." She winked again. "So what have you been doing, when you weren't spying on me?"

"I was talking with Jack," he said, "He wants to meet you. Both Aunt Isabella and I have been effusive about how wonderful and beautiful you are, so he wants to see for himself. Make up his own mind!"

Melanie pulled her hand out of Thomas'. "Let's hope he isn't disappointed," she said.

"As I said before, you are the most beautiful woman in this house, and Jack will know that the moment he lays eyes on you."

"What about Mrs. Gardner? I think she is magnificently handsome, and the most fun. And her art collection!" Melanie closed her eyes and sighed.

"Aunt Isabella is a beautiful woman, but she doesn't hold a candle to you. Your beauty is spectacular and your wit sparkling. A combination not often seen."

"And you with your blarney," she said. "And you smell like a cigar."

"The best Cuban ones, that's all Jack has. I couldn't resist. Now, let's go and find the man, because if he doesn't meet you, I'll never hear the end of it."

Melanie linked her arm in his. She was getting more comfortable in her outfit, even though it still felt as if she was dressed up for Halloween, but she had mastered the skill of moving in a bustle, plumed hat, and crinolines. She was feeling almost confident when the tip of her boot caught the edge of one of the thick Oriental carpets, and she pitched forward, sending the hat careening into the air. She grabbed Thomas so hard she nearly pulled him over with her.

"Dammit!" She had spoken too loud, and as soon as the words were out, she wished she could take them back. As she stood up, a distinguished looking man with a bushy handlebar mustache rushed toward her from the other side of the room.

"Are you all right? Miss Swift?" Thomas had one of her arms, and the man had reached down and pulled up on her other elbow.

"Just embarrassed," she said, grabbing her hat from Thomas, who had retrieved it. "I am not very good at this fashion thing, I guess."

The man had twinkling eyes, and after he was sure she was stable on her feet, he let her go and grabbed her right hand, bending over from the waist to kiss it. "I'm Jack Gardner, pleased to make your acquaintance."

Melanie thought she saw his eyes looking at her from top to bottom, and she felt herself blushing. "I didn't want to meet you exactly that way, Mr. Gardner, but I'm happy to meet you anyway." She tried to restrain herself, because she thought she might cry. She was determined not to morph from a strong, twenty-first century woman into a weepy,

needy nineteenth century damsel. She would not let that
happen.

"No, no, my dear, not Mr. Gardner, never Mr. Gardner.
Jack or Uncle Jack is the best. I've heard so much about you
from my wife, I feel you have been part of the family forever. I'm sorry you tripped on that carpet. That is my fault for
not having the staff see to it beforehand." He continued to
engulf her hand up to the lace trim on her sleeve in his,
which was a little sweaty. She wondered whether it would
be rude to slip out of his grasp. She decided to let him make
the first move.

"Thank you, Jack. I hate to think I need rescuing. It isn't
a circumstance I relish."

Gardner smiled at her, a broad smile, and she stared at
his front teeth, which had a tiny gap, still not at his eyes.
"You're new to this place, I know that. When I brought Isabella here from New York, it took her a while to become
accustomed to Boston mores. And I'm sure you have intuit-
ed already that my wife does not need rescuing from anyone.
She is quite self-sufficient."

"Thank you for helping, Jack," Thomas said, "Melanie
has a lot to take in right now, and she was already kidnapped by John Sargent almost immediately after we arrived. So anyone who can survive that is a trouper." The
two men shared a look and laughed.

"Oh, he was great," Melanie said, again feeling as if she
was being treated as an object ripe for the saving. "I really
enjoyed meeting him."

"That's a relief," said Jack. "Tommy won't have to challenge him to a duel in the back yard." Jack gave Thomas a
friendly slap on the back. "So, Isabella says you are an art
lover?"

"Yes, I studied art history in—school."

"Then you and my wife will have to get together again,
frequently, because as you know, she is passionate about art.
We have collected all over the world."

"That is obvious from the beautiful pieces displayed everywhere in this house," Melanie said, grateful to be talking about something other than her honor or her appearance. "I'd love to talk to her at length, any time."

"Well, as I said, I am delighted to meet you. You are an exquisite creature, more delightful even than the reports I received, and we will be very happy to add you to our inner circle. Tom, good job finding this one."

"I wish I could take credit for finding her," Thomas said, "But in reality, she sort of found me."

"You are the most deserving man in the world," the older man said, now serious, rubbing his mustache with his thumb and index finger. "You've taken care of your sisters and the house for some time, and I hear only wonderful things about you from my doctor friends. They say you have quite a brilliant future in medicine."

"Thank you for your kind words," Thomas said, "I'm sure they exaggerate."

"I'm sure they don't," he said. "And now I must leave you two and go mingle among the other guests, because if I do not, my wife will never forgive me. She is finagling to get her hands on some Sargent portrait, and I have to sweet-talk the man. But to be honest, I think it would work better if Melanie would sweet-talk him." And he turned away with a wave, and walked out of the room chuckling to himself.

"These people are very charming," Melanie said when Jack was out of earshot. "I can see why you're so fond of them."

"I think you should take him up on his idea that you strike up a friendship with Aunt Isabella. It will give you something to do, and I know how much you love art. And you made a tremendous impression on her."

"I will do that, Tom, after I get your sisters taken care of. Then I will be thrilled to be Isabella Gardner's friend. You can't even imagine." She turned toward him and looked into his eyes.

"I hope you succeed with my sisters," he said. "It's a big project."

When they decided it was time to leave, Archie had the brougham ready for them, just outside the house on Beacon Street. He helped her up again. She was better getting into the carriage this time, pulling the long dress up so that she wouldn't trample it with her shoes. They arranged themselves for the short trip home, and Thomas said, "Did you have a good time?"

"I can see why you love her so much," Melanie said. "She is quite a woman." Melanie thought about how Isabella would be in her own world, and she had a slight pang of homesickness, which she dismissed. Isabella would love the twenty-first century. She was making the best of the nineteenth. "I love her home. The art!"

"You will sometime have to explain it all to me. It's lovely, but I have no idea what is great and what is mediocre."

"Art is as great as it evokes your own personal emotions, Tom," Melanie said, feeling sad that her intelligent benefactor had concentrated on the sciences and neglected the humanities. "So if you think a painting is great, then it is great. It doesn't make any difference what anyone else thinks."

"I still feel insecure about that. You need to help me."

"I loved how Isabella had all of those hanging flowers in her home. It made everything even more festive and colorful. I love them, the blue and purple and pink blossoms, cascading down from the second floor to the ballroom." She sighed. "I think we should have flowers like that in our house."

"Goodness, I'm going to have to work twenty-four hours a day at the hospital to pay for your whims."

"Thomas! First of all, beautifying one's living quarters is not a whim. Secondly, you keep assuring me you have plenty of money, and you don't spend it much, especially on yourself. And finally, if you are really so destitute, I can go out and get a job."

Thomas laughed. "Melanie? A job? Whatever would you do? Chambermaid in a hotel?" He laughed some more.

Melanie felt annoyed and moved away from him. "You're offending me." Her tone was cold.

Thomas became quiet. In her head, Melanie understood that they would have many more cultural mountains to climb before they could ever be sympatico. It might be impossible. "I don't know how to make you understand," he said, his voice choking.

Melanie worried he might cry. "We have so much more to figure out," she said. "I've said this before. I'm a product of my own culture, and it's extremely hard for me to snap neatly into yours. I will never be able to turn myself into a useless porcelain object for admiration. And besides, Aunt Isabella does things, doesn't she? She doesn't just hang around her house looking pretty."

"She's not as pretty as you," Thomas said.

"Thomas! You know what I meant."

"I don't want you to be angry with me," Thomas said. "I want to have a relationship based on more than your looks."

"This ride is taking longer than it should," Melanie said. "Where are we going?"

"I asked Archie to take a drive around the Common. I wanted to talk to you more about things."

"What things?"

"Melanie, I've told you this already. I think—I *know* I'm in love with you. The longer you are with me, the more deeply I feel it. I would like to ask you to be my wife." His voice cracked as he finished the sentence. He cleared his throat, moving closer to her and putting a hand around her waist. Even under the heavy cloak, she felt a kind of tingle as he touched her. She breathed in, sucking the cold air into her lungs, which made her gasp a little.

"Tom, the last thing I want to do is hurt you, but I've told you I'm just not ready." She hoped Archie wasn't listening to them, thought the street noises might be drowning out their conversation. "There is still someone in my old life, and I haven't given up on him yet."

"But that is so impractical!" Thomas almost hissed, as he turned away from her. "You're here now, and he is not. How long are you going to hold onto that fantasy?"

Melanie sighed. "I don't know. It has nothing to do with practicality, but I just...can't. Not yet. I know you're frustrated, but you need to give me more time."

Thomas slipped his arm back around her waist, and she let him get very close, although she felt tense. He kissed her on the forehead, and her body responded. As much as she needed to get things straight with him, the attraction between them was great, and she wondered how long she would be able to fight it. "I have something I'd like you to keep."

"What?"

Thomas reached into his vest and pulled out a pocket watch. The light was dim, but Melanie thought it looked gold, and it was embossed on the front with a caduceus. "This watch has been in my family for many years. My grandfather gave it to my father when father graduated from medical school. The inscription on the inside says: 'Edward Thornwell, MD, May, 1853.' After my father died, my mother gave it to me to commemorate my medical school graduation. I want you to have it as a token of my love and commitment to you, and because I want you to be part of this Thornwell family permanently."

"Tom, I couldn't possibly!" Melanie pushed his hand with the watch away. "That is something you need to cherish for your entire life. I can't take that."

"Please, I insist."

"I can't say yes to your proposal now. Does that change anything?"

"Well, I must be honest—I'm terribly disappointed. But I suppose it would be disingenuous to say I was surprised, since you are certainly a woman of your word. But please take the watch anyway. Then, when you're ready, I will exchange it for something more appropriate, a ring or a bauble worth much more."

"I can't imagine anything worth more than this watch. If you ever change your mind and want it back, please don't think you'll be offending me. I feel honored that you asked me to be its caretaker." She put her head on his shoulder, and he tightened his grip around her waist.

"I will wait for you as long as it takes," he said, "But I will not stop trying to change your mind."

Neither of them spoke again as the horse clopped along the almost deserted Commonwealth Avenue toward the Thornwell house, stopping with a whinny at the front gate.

"Thank you, Archie," Melanie said, as the old man, stooped but smiling, helped her out of the carriage. "Now you go and get some rest. You must be tired and freezing. We stayed late at that party, and you were outside in the cold waiting for us the whole time."

"Not at all, miss," Archie said, tipping his hat to her. She curtseyed back, as Thomas hopped out of the carriage onto the driveway. "My pleasure to do it. Happy to see the young master smiling all the time."

Melanie pulled her hand out of the fur muff and held Thomas's hand as they walked through the remains of the winter snow to the porch. "Isn't it about time for that poor man to retire?" she said, as they mounted the four stairs to the front door.

"I never really thought about it," Thomas said. "He seems happy. I'm not sure what he would do if we dismissed him."

"Maybe we could invite him to move in with us? This house is so huge, the four of us rattle around in there."

"You're always looking to do good works, aren't you?"

Thomas moved his head slowly from side to side as they walked through the front door. The conversation was cut short by the quick footsteps of Athena, who had been sitting in front of the fireplace in the front parlor.

"Well?" she said.

"Well?" Thomas said, winking. "What are you doing up at this hour?"

"What am I, a little child?" Athena embraced Melanie first, and then gave Thomas a little hug. "Tell me everything, or I won't be able to sleep."

Thomas laughed, as Athena helped them off with their coats. "Where's Jane?"

"In her room, hours ago," Athena said.

"Poor Thomas has to be at work early in the morning," said Melanie. "Why don't we delay this conversation until tomorrow dinner?"

Athena stamped her foot and put her hands on her hips. Even though Athena was a year older than Thomas, she reminded Melanie of a kid waiting for her parents to come home from an exciting time so that she could get all the inside dope. "You know, I am the oldest one in this house, so I think my word should be final."

"Oh," said Thomas, "We need to mind Athena, the senior member of this family."

Melanie shrugged, and Athena ushered them into the warm kitchen, where they sat down around the table. "Would you like me to make some tea?" she said, bustling around in her favorite room. She didn't wait for an answer, but busied herself with the tea kettle and the cups and the milk. "Okay, tell me everything."

Thomas started to talk, but Melanie put her hand up lightly to his mouth. "Before anyone says anything," she said, "I want to tell you that you were missed, and so was Jane. The first thing Aunt Isabella said was 'Where are Jane and Athena?'"

"Well, it was definitely Melanie's night," Thomas said. "If I hadn't been there, John Sargent would have kidnapped her to Paris without another thought. He was completely smitten."

"Oh, I wouldn't say that," Melanie said, but she felt her face reddening.

"What did he say?" Athena was back with the tea, and she had sat down next to Jane.

"Luckily," Melanie said, laughing, "Tom was keeping an eye on me, so he saved me from the jaws of the shark! No, really, we talked a little and sang a little. I had no idea John was a musician too. But there were always many, many people around. He had no opportunity to gag me and tie me up and spirit me away."

"For the entire evening," Thomas said, "Melanie was a great success. She's been invited to lunch with Aunt Isabella so that they can discuss art. Jack loved her. Everyone she met loved her. And she's on first-name basis with John Sargent!"

"I knew that would happen," Athena said, sitting down to drink her cup of tea with them. She couldn't stop smiling.

"I wish Jane had been here to greet us," Thomas said. Melanie looked down at her teacup, silent.

"I'm working on Jane," said Athena. "I think she may be coming around."

Melanie looked up, hitting the saucer with her hand. The tea sloshed out of the cup. "Oh, I'm sorry." She stood up to get a dishrag from the kitchen, but Athena waved her down and jumped up first.

"Whatever you can do to help," Thomas said.

Athena came back and tidied up the table. "Well, I'm sleepy. I think I'll retire," she said.

"Me too," said Melanie. She took her cup and Thomas's and brought them to the sink. "I can't wait until I get out of these clothes."

The three walked upstairs in silence. At Melanie's door, Thomas paused. "Good night," he said. "I'm glad you had a good time."

"Do you have the energy to have a serious discussion with me now?" Melanie had removed her shoes and was sitting on the edge of her bed.

"May I come in?" Thomas hesitated, but she beckoned him toward the chair near the fireplace across the room. Thomas hurried in and sat down.

"I thought you might change your mind," he said.

"No, I need to have this conversation with you, and there's no time like the present."

"It sounds serious," he said. "Am I going to be disappointed?" His voice was low, his words enunciated carefully.

"I hope not," Melanie said. "It's about Athena." Melanie fiddled with the buttons on her dress, but when she noticed him staring at her, she put her hands down at her sides.

"Hmmm?" Thomas said, his voice even softer now.

"Athena has a dream, and I want to make sure she is able to fulfill it." Melanie waited, but when there was no reaction, she continued. "I have been talking with her. At length. I don't know how much you really know about her, or perhaps how much you care to know."

"What do you mean? I've lived with her all my life. What more is there to know?"

"Do you agree she is a brilliant woman?" She raised an eyebrow.

"I know she's smart and capable. She can do anything."

"Exactly. Do you realize she has studied all of your text books? She has learned all of the subjects you learned, entirely on her own." Melanie thought she heard Thomas say something, but she didn't want to ask him to raise his voice. She continued. "She has a calling. She wants to go to medical school." Melanie paused, looked up at him. She heard him try to stifle a gasp. "And I want you to help her." She waited for him to respond, but when there was no answer, she stood up and took two steps toward his chair. "Thomas?" No answer. "Thomas, are you going to say something?"

"I'm trying to decide whether I heard you correctly," he said.

"You heard me," she said.

"I can't talk about this now," he said. "I'm exhausted, and I have to be at the hospital early tomorrow."

"You're not going to discourage me from pursuing this," she said, sitting back down on the bed. "I will keep bringing it up until you're so tired of me, you'll talk about it."

Thomas pulled himself up from the chair and headed toward the door. "Not now, Melanie." And he was gone.

Melanie couldn't sleep. She tossed and turned, thinking about the party, about the fun of flirting with John Gardner, about how she had blindsided Thomas, who had likely hoped she had decided to talk to him about a closer relationship between the two of them, and finally, always, about Justin and how she ached for him with every fiber of her being, how she wished she could hold him in her arms and share all of this with him.

Chapter 17

The characteristic, enticing smells emanating from Athena's kitchen woke Melanie up. She threw on her dressing gown and ran downstairs, hoping Thomas might still be there, but only Jane and Athena were in the kitchen.

"Thomas is gone already?" Her voice must have sounded desperate, because Athena jumped up and walked to her.

"Is everything all right, Melanie?" Athena put her hand on Melanie's forearm.

"I was just hoping to talk to Thomas this morning," Melanie said. "But I'm fine. Sorry I alarmed you. Jane, it's nice to see you here."

Jane shrugged, but Melanie noticed that Jane looked interested. She was making progress with Thomas's sister.

"Sit down." Athena pushed Melanie toward the table. "He had to go to the hospital early, didn't really even have much breakfast. He told us not to wake you, so we let you sleep."

"That figures," Melanie said almost to herself.

"We still want to know all about the party." Athena led Melanie to a chair and filled a cup for her with steaming coffee. "Do you want some breakfast? I saved some bacon and eggs for you."

"Thanks, Athena." Melanie was reluctant to let Athena know that she had brought up the medical school issue. She was sure Athena would try to demur, but she was not going to take no for an answer.

Athena placed the plate of eggs down in front of Melanie. "I baked some scones. Would you like one? There's fresh butter."

"I won't be able to fit into any of the clothes you've sewn for me."

"I know how to alter dresses, Melanie." Athena smiled, offering Melanie a warm scone and the butter. "So please give us more details about the party," Athena was standing, hand on her hip, pointing at Melanie. "You two were so tired when you got in last night."

Melanie laughed, sipping her coffee. "Well," she said, "I did meet a pretty famous painter. That alone was exhausting."

"Who?"

"John Singer Sargent."

Jane wrinkled her brow. "I don't think I know him," she said.

"Well, he moved to Paris, and he paints portraits of important people who pay him," Melanie said.

"Oh. Did he paint a portrait of anyone we know?"

"I'm not sure, but I don't think so."

"Did you like him?"

"I did." Melanie winked. Jane and Athena shared a glance. "He flirted with me."

"Oh," said Jane, "That wasn't very nice of you to do to Tommy."

Three steps forward and two back, Melanie thought. "Well, actually, Tom was off smoking cigars with Jack Gardner, but don't worry. He was fine. Nothing terrible happened."

Athena laughed.

"But still," Jane said, "He sounds like a blackguard. I don't think I'd like him very much. He had no right to do that to Tommy." She frowned.

"He would have thought you were lovely," Melanie said.

Jane brightened a bit, but then she went back to her frown.

"Isabella is dying to get one of his paintings, so they're having a little battle about it. He doesn't want to sell it to her."

"I think Aunt Isabella will win," Jane said. "She always gets what she wants."

Melanie didn't reply. She knew Isabella wouldn't win this battle. "So," she said, changing the subject, "We need to make a special dinner for Tom tonight. Does he have a favorite food?" Thomas seemed to eat everything with great zest, but if anyone knew what he liked best, it would be Athena and Jane.

"Lamb," Athena said, not hesitating for a moment. "Tender leg of lamb with home-made mint jelly and red potatoes baked in the pan with the lamb so that they absorb all the fat and get crispy on the outside. That's his favorite."

"Can we make it for him tonight?"

"I don't see why not. I was planning on going to the butcher shop anyway. I already have the mint jelly. I made twelve jars of it. It's in our pantry. He loves that."

"You're the best, Athena. Please see if they have any paté as well. Could you make some toast points so that we can have a little pre-dinner appetizer? Perhaps some sherry to go with it? I know he likes that."

"Yes, of course. I'll go to the greengrocer as well. I'm not sure what's available this time of year, but I'll do something delicious to go with the potatoes."

"Why are we making Tom a special dinner?" Jane said, her chin resting on her hands.

"You'll see later," Melanie said, already plotting what

she would say and how she would say it. "Do you trust me?" Jane shrugged. Melanie still hadn't won Jane over, not completely.

"Do we have a choice?" Athena's voice had an air of frustration.

Melanie ignored the sarcasm. "What's his favorite dessert?"

"Anything sweet," Athena said. "You don't give up, do you?"

"No, not on this," Melanie said. "So I'll leave it up to you. Make it delicious. And how about a good bottle of wine?"

"Archie can go down to the wine cellar and get a nice red."

"Athena, I'm so excited about this dinner. Will you have Archie take you into town to buy the food?"

"Usually I walk, Melanie."

"It's still cold and icy out. Have him take you. You're buying a lot of things, and I'll feel better knowing you don't have to lug them all." She grabbed Athena's hand and squeezed. "This is going to be a very special dinner. You really can trust me. I have my reasons. And I will be happy to help with the preparations—anything. I'll be your *sous chef*."

Jane shook her head. "I must admit, Melanie, life was never this exciting before you got here."

"I hope it's exciting in a good way, Jane?"

Jane raised her eyebrows.

"You have a beautiful smile, and I wish I could see it more."

Jane looked down again.

"Skating today?"

"Yes, I've got a student! A little girl about six years old. Her mother saw me skating the other day and asked if I would give her lessons." Jane's smile was complete and sincere.

"I hope she's paying you?"

"Yes, an exorbitant amount. She insisted. I was going to do it for free."

"You're worth every penny. Just be sure you're home in time for dinner, all right?"

"I wouldn't miss this dinner for the world," Jane said, tapping the table with her fingers. "I'm just trying to figure out why we're doing this."

"Did your brother say when he'd be home tonight?"

"He said six o'clock," Jane said.

"Wine at six-fifteen, dinner at six-thirty, sharp." Melanie stood up and pushed her chair away from the table. She would spend this day preparing for the evening. She would take a long, luxuriant bath, using the fragrant bath salts Athena had shared with her. She would wear the dress Thomas liked best, a pale green silk with buttons up the front. She would unbutton it as far down as she dared, to get him interested, although it didn't take much to get him interested. And she would do whatever *sous chef* tasks Athena wanted her to do. She worried the day would drag, because she was so excited about tonight, but she planned to fill it with taking care of things that Athena didn't have to do—Thomas's favorite throw on the davenport in front of the parlor fire place, where she planned to give him a foot massage before dinner as he drank his wine, everything neat and tidy, dusting done, to give Athena a break so that she could concentrate on the meal, the wine uncorked and breathing so it was ready for him.

By four o'clock, the dinner preparations were in full swing. "Athena, do you need any help?" Melanie had taken her bath, and was standing at the entrance to the kitchen, relaxed and dressed for the evening.

"Oh my, Melanie, you look so beautiful!" Athena had a long apron on and was holding a large wooden spoon, which she was using to stir soup that smelled delicious.

"Thanks! This house smells incredible. I'm getting hungry."

"That's because you forgot to eat lunch," Athena pointed

the spoon at her, furrowing her brow. "You shouldn't do that, it's not good for you."

"Thank you, Doctor, I'll be fine."

Athena recoiled as Melanie said the word doctor. Her surprise turned into a wry smile. "Don't make me feel bad about things that may never happen," she said, shaking the spoon at Melanie.

"Don't ever lose hope about things that have a great likelihood of happening," Melanie said, pointing a finger at the spoon. "Never underestimate me. Never underestimate the power of feminine wiles. Shall I take over from you so that you can get ready for dinner?"

"It's really all done. The lamb is in the oven. It has another hour to cook, and then it will need to be cooled and then carved. Tommy loves to carve! The soup just has to simmer. I suppose you could stir it every so often, just to make sure it doesn't burn on the bottom of the pot. Dessert is ready. I made a huckleberry trifle. I had put up some huckleberries in the summer, from the bushes behind the house. I whipped fresh cream and made a sponge cake to line the trifle bowl." She opened the icebox and beckoned to Melanie to take a look.

"Oh, that's a work of art," Melanie said. She sucked her lower lip into her teeth. "I hate that we have to cut into it!"

"Don't worry," Athena said, laughing, "Tommy won't hate to cut into it." She removed her apron and handed it to Melanie, who put it on. "I will go upstairs and get ready for the big night," she said with a wink, and she skipped out of the kitchen. "This intrigue is lots of fun, although I wish I knew what it's about," she called, as she ran up the stairs. "I feel like a co-conspirator who doesn't know what the conspiracy is." She laughed, and then her voice trailed off as she headed for her room.

She must know, Melanie thought, as she stirred the soup, looking out the kitchen window at the carriage house. *I must remember to ask Athena to invite Archie to this dinner. No one should miss this evening*. Melanie opened the heavy cast iron oven door. The aroma of the leg of lamb and rosemary found her nose, and she breathed in. *He won't be able to say no to me, not with this food. I will win.*

"Why are you sticking your head in the oven?" Jane had arrived home from the Frog Pond and was following the aroma into the kitchen. "That smells delicious. I think I'm hungry." Her blonde hair was braided and secured in a halo around her head. Her eyes sparkled. Melanie snapped to consciousness and slammed the oven door shut.

"Oops," she said, jumping away from the stove. "I was just daydreaming."

"It smells amazing in here," Jane said again. "I had a wonderful day. The little girl is doing well, and her mother has brought me another student."

"Jane, I'm so happy about that, really."

"I was awful to you, Melanie, when you first came." Jane wouldn't look Melanie in the eye.

Melanie shrugged. It was true. She wouldn't deny it.

"I thought you were my enemy, that you would take my brother from me. I had no idea you would help me find my happiest life. I really do appreciate it. I'm sorry I did such terrible things to you." She hung her head.

"You have your sister Athena to thank for letting me know what you loved. All I did was to recognize that's what you needed and give you a little push."

"You did more than that. We were floundering here. I was on the verge of despair. Tommy was working so hard, I worried he'd get ill. I hated you when you came."

Melanie raised her eyebrows. "The only one left is Athena."

Jane opened her mouth, put her hand up to her face. "Oh my goodness, is she what this fancy dinner party is about? Is it about convincing Tom that she needs to go to medical school?"

Melanie put her index finger across her lips. "You've

figured it out. Please don't say a word to Athena, all right? I don't want to worry her."

Jane nodded. "I was sort of hoping it was for you to accept his marriage proposal." Her eyes were wide.

Melanie sucked her breath in. "He told you about that?"

"He told me not to say anything."

"Will you despise me again if I tell you I'm not ready to accept him yet?"

"I just want him to be happy, Melanie."

"I do too, honestly Jane. But—"

Jane sighed. "I love my brother, Melanie, and he loves you. And I'm ready for a truce. The skating has made me so happy, I can't keep being angry at you." She held her arms out to Melanie, who rushed into them. The two women stood there, in an embrace, for several moments until Melanie pulled away.

"I hope Athena appreciates what you're doing for her too," Jane said.

"I'm just afraid she might try to talk me out of it. It makes her feel guilty that she will be leaving you all in the lurch. I don't want her to have the opportunity to think about it."

"She's wanted to go to medical school since we were kids. You can't believe how she pored over Tommy's books and overwhelmed him with questions when he was in medical school." Jane sat down at the kitchen table.

"Yes, I figured that out, but do you think he understands her passion for it?"

Jane tipped her head, tapped her fingers on the table. "I don't think he really thought about it much, honestly," she said, sitting up straight, entwining the fingers of her hands into a loose fist.

Melanie felt Jane's tension, which frustrated her. Jane, the apologist for her insensitive brother.

"He was just...too busy." Jane sighed. "Taking care of all of us. I don't think he realized how serious she was. And she does such a good job here. Did you cook this dinner?"

Melanie shook her head no. "Obviously Athena's wizardry," she said. "I'm just stirring the soup while she gets dressed."

"Do you really think you can convince him?"

Melanie turned back to the soup. "I absolutely do think I can convince him," she said, pronouncing each word distinctly, stressing the word *can*. "Athena will go, Jane, if it's the last thing I do. Just as you are progressing in your skating career. People need to be able to follow their dreams." The two women remained in uncomfortable silence until Athena came down the stairs.

"What happened here?" Athena said, as she entered the kitchen, freshly scrubbed and in her prettiest dress. "Are you two having an argument?"

"Why do you say that?" Melanie stayed facing the stove, but she turned her head toward Athena. "Oh, Athena, you look so pretty!"

"Because I don't hear any voices, and one of you is looking in one direction and the other is looking the opposite way. This is supposed to be a festive evening! I thought you two were getting on better these days."

"We were just talking about some things," Jane said. "I told Melanie that she's made a huge difference in this family in the short time she's been here. I was wrong to misjudge her."

Athena walked to Melanie and indicated that she should turn around. Melanie obeyed, and Athena untied the apron and removed it. "There," she said, "We are three beautiful women ready for a lovely dinner. Jane, go upstairs now and make yourself beautiful." She said it with such conviction that Melanie laughed and hugged her. Jane headed for the stairs, turning her head back to give Melanie a look that Melanie interpreted as unsure.

A knock at the door surprised them, and Athena went to the door. "Oh, it's Archie!" Jane said, as the elderly footman scraped his boots and walked into the house. He was dressed in his best uniform, his top hat in his hand. He made a deep bow to them as he entered.

"Good evening, ladies. I hope I'm not intruding."

"Oh heavens, no, Archie. I'm glad Athena invited you to dinner. Doesn't it smell good?"

"I'm so grateful for the invitation, miss." He bowed from the waist and rose slowly, as if it hurt. "You needn't have, though."

"Don't be silly." Melanie put her arm around Archie's waist and urged him gently into the house. "It's cold, and we have so much food, we don't want to waste it. And it will be more festive here than if we brought it out to you, don't you think?"

"I am very grateful."

"Would you like a glass of sherry while you wait?" She had ushered him into the parlor, and invited him to sit down on one of the upholstered chairs.

"That would be lovely, Miss Melanie, thank you." Athena took Archie's hat and hung it on the coat rack in the entry hall.

"Wonderful. Archie, you deserve to be part of this family. Thomas is grateful for all your years of service, and we'd like to show you some of that gratitude. I hope you like lamb?"

"I like it fine, miss," he said, "And if Miss Athena cooked it, I know it will be delicious."

"She did and it will. Please excuse me now while I finish up preparing the table."

"Yes, miss. I will be fine here." Athena handed him the aperitif, and Archie's smile lit up the parlor.

Thomas arrived exactly at six o'clock. Athena had taken the lamb out of the oven and was letting it rest while she fixed all the other dishes and started putting them on the table. Melanie ran to the front door.

"Tom, you look so tired. Was it a hard day?"

He barely looked up as he removed his boots and his coat. Melanie took the coat. When he saw her, his eyes lit up. "Oh, goodness, you look lovely." He looked her up and down. "And you smell beautiful. And so does this house."

"You smell good too," she said.

"I bathed at the hospital before I came home," he said. "It was a rather bloody day, I'm afraid. Another carriage accident. They hire young lads to drive the carriages, and those boys go too fast and have no fear."

"Well, you're coming into the parlor and having a glass of sherry with Archie, and I am going to massage your feet."

"Archie?" His smile turned serious. "Is Archie all right?"

"Oh, yes, he's fine. I just invited him to dinner. I thought he deserved it, you know?"

"That was very nice of you, my dear. Every day you surprise me with something else that you do." He followed her into the parlor, and Archie moved to stand up.

"No, no Archie. No need to stand. Sit and enjoy your drink."

"Thank you, sir." The old servant wasn't moving very easily. "I am grateful to Miss Melanie for inviting me tonight. I hope it's all right with you."

"Oh, it's fine, Archie. Anything Melanie says is fine with me. And anyway, this has all put me in a good mood."

Melanie ushered Thomas over to a sofa, where he sat and leaned back, closing his eyes. Then she brought in a tub of warm water and a brush. She got down on her knees and removed his socks, placing one foot at a time into the water bath.

"Hmmmm," Thomas said. "I have some incredible news, but you would have had no idea what it was."

"What do you mean?" She continued massaging his feet, working her way up to the calves. "Your muscles are so tight."

"I was promoted at the hospital."

He said it so simply, it made her giggle. "What do you mean?" He seemed serious, so she stood up, leaning over him and looking into his eyes. "What kind of promotion?"

"I am now an attending physician. The directors met, and

they felt I had made so much progress that I should be ele-vated to that role immediately."

"Oh, I'm so proud of you! See? It makes sense that I'm massaging your feet. Does this mean you may have more regular hours?"

"Not necessarily. I'm still a doctor."

"Well, that makes this dinner tonight even more special."

"But you never answered me. This is all amazing." He inhaled, breathing in the luscious cooking smells. "You didn't know about my promotion until now. To what do I owe all this festivity? And your amazing massage?"

"Doesn't it smell wonderful in here?"

"Divine. Obviously Athena has been busy."

"Well, it is a special dinner, just for you. Athena has prepared all of your favorite dishes."

"Lamb?"

"Yes, lamb. And you won't believe the dessert she made."

"What is it?" His face had relaxed. Melanie was now standing over him. "A surprise, that's what it is."

"If I didn't know better, I'd say you were doing this to get something from me?"

"Really?"

"Is that it?"

"Would you do something special for me?"

"Probably anything."

"Anything?"

Thomas didn't respond. Melanie walked out of the room, taking the bucket of water with her.

Chapter 18

"This was the best dinner I've had in months." Thomas stifled a burp, and Jane giggled. "Maybe in years." He was licking the serving spoon from the trifle, which they had finished down to the last huckleberry.

Melanie laughed. "If I didn't know better, I'd think you were going to pick up the trifle bowl and lick it clean." Archie had thanked them profusely and taken his leave, saying that he like to go to bed early so that he could rise with the horses and the sun, which was dawning a little earlier each day now. Athena had made him a little package of leftovers that he could have for breakfast, and he took it with gratitude. Now she was bustling around the kitchen, clearing plates with Jane's help.

Melanie reached over to Thomas and put her hand on his arm. "I need to talk to you."

"I am so content right now, you could tell me the sky was falling, and I wouldn't even care," he said.

"Good. So, this is the continuation of a conversation we had a while ago. I won't beat around the bush. I want you to promise me that you'll work on getting Athena accepted to medical school."

Thomas's face went gray, and his previous calm, relaxed expression tensed into a deep frown. He jerked his arm away from Melanie's grasp and held the edge of the table with both hands, so tight that the tops of his fingers went white. Melanie was sure she could see his hands were shaking.

"Absolutely out of the question." He said the words separately, as if it wasn't a sentence but rather a series of individual thoughts. He repeated himself, louder and more precisely. "Out. Of. The. Question. I don't want to discuss this anymore."

"Not so fast, Thomas." Melanie adopted a stern tone of her own. "I won't be put off this time. This is Athena's dream."

"Dreams are dreams, Melanie, not reality."

"She needs to be given the chance. If it doesn't work out, at least she won't go through life wondering whether she could have done it."

"What makes you think she's qualified for medical school?" He had taken his hands off the table and put them firmly in his lap. "She has no college."

"I beg to differ," Melanie shot back. "Have you ever questioned her about her knowledge? What do you think she did with all of the books you gave her? All of your college books? She's even studied all of your medical books. Did you wonder why she asked you all those questions? Didn't you pay attention?"

Thomas didn't reply. His eyes widened, and his mouth opened into a wide "O," but no words came out.

"Nothing to say to me? That woman is the smartest person in this house. Including you. All alone, without any coaching, without any guidance, she has studied those books and knows the subject matter inside and out. Did you know Boston Medical School accepts women? Women have graduated from there. And with your help, she can at least have the chance to try for admission. If you won't help her, I will." Melanie wheeled around, so that her bac facing him. She felt tears welling up, but she didn't v cry.

"Is that what this gala dinner was all about? To manipulate me so that I'd agree to this? And to think I was so elated when I got home, with my news." Thomas put his elbows on the table and placed his chin in his hands. "Did you and Athena cook this up together?"

At that moment, Athena entered the room humming, but she stopped short when she saw the two of them. It was obvious they were having an argument, and no matter what it was about, she wanted to flee, go back to the kitchen, but Thomas stopped her in her tracks.

"Is it true, Athena?" Thomas was almost enraged now, and Athena's happy face turned fearful, her eyes very wide.

"Is what true? Tommy, what's wrong? I don't know what you're talking about."

Melanie jumped up from the table and put her arm around Athena's waist. "She had nothing to do with this, Thomas. It was all my doing. So save your rage for me. Being angry at an innocent person is completely unjustified."

"What's going on?" Athena repeated her question.

"I'll tell you," Melanie stood a little bit in front of Athena, between her and Thomas, her arm still firmly around Athena's waist, as if to protect the other woman. "I just told Thomas that I want him to help you get into medical school."

Athena let out a little squeal, but Melanie couldn't tell whether it was happy or alarmed. "Melanie, you shouldn't have done that."

"Why not? You have worked so hard to be able to do this. He could help. He just doesn't want to lose his servant girl."

"Melanie, that's not fair!" Thomas shouted. "How can you insult me like that? You know I think of Athena as a sister."

"Isn't it fair? If you regard Athena as you say you do, then what is the problem? If you really cared about her or took any interest in her, other than her cooking skills, you'd be curious about what she really wants and informed as to her abilities."

Thomas rubbed his eyes, and Melanie thought she saw tears forming in the corners. She softened toward him, thought of comforting him, but she stood her ground with Athena, who was trembling and crying as well. "I care deeply about everyone in this house," he said, his voice less strident than it had been before. "I thought everyone here was happy."

"You thought Jane was happy to be a nurse, but that was not what she wanted to be. And now that she's engaged in what she loves, can't you see that she's like a different person?"

A tear rolled down Thomas's cheek, and he left it there, as if he couldn't fight it anymore. "I didn't know. Athena never said anything."

"Don't you understand how both of them look up to you? They treat you as if you were their exalted leader, even though everyone here is close in age. They never want to displease you. They do everything to make your life in this house as comfortable and easy as possible. Won't you admit to the change in Jane since she's been skating every day?"

"I have noticed. But Athena always seemed...happy."

"I am happy, Tommy. It's all right—"

"No, it's not all right. Are you going to help her get into the medical school? Are you going to visit those people and talk to them about her? Athena, would it be all right if Tom interviewed you about your knowledge? I'd like him to see for himself how much you know and how brilliant you are."

"But what will you do here if I go to school? How will we keep the house running?" Athena's voice was soft and tremulous. She had put her hands up to her face and was rubbing the tears away.

"We will hire people to do what you you've been doing. It will probably take two or three, but I don't care. I am so convinced you have the potential for an amazing career in front of you. I couldn't live with myself if we didn't help you at least try."

"Is this what you really want, Athena?" For the first time

Thomas was addressing Athena, and the angry tone was gone. His voice was serious, resigned.

Athena looked down at her feet and then slowly shook her head. She looked at him and caught his gaze. "It is. I'm sorry."

"Athena, you don't have to be sorry," Melanie said. "You should be over the moon."

"When can we talk, Athena?" Thomas was looking straight at Athena now, as if Melanie wasn't in the room. "I'd like to get a good idea of exactly how much you know."

"Any time, Tommy. I'm here. When will you have some time off from the hospital?"

"I have a day off on Thursday," he said. "Let's talk then. All right? Is that what you want?"

Athena smiled, her first one since she had walked in on them. "Yes, I'd love to discuss it all with you." She glanced out of the corner of her eye at Melanie.

"I'm very tired," Thomas said. "I have an early day tomorrow. I'm assisting in a surgery. I should go to bed." He got up slowly, pushing his chair away from the table but staying there, bent over, his eyes closed, as if he had more to say, for a moment before he stood up. Then, without another word or glance at Melanie, he left the dining room and went upstairs.

"Whew," Melanie said when Thomas was out of earshot. "I'm glad that's over."

"Why did you do that?" Athena sounded more confused than angry.

"Because you never would have. You would have lived your life wondering whether you might have been a doctor and regretting never having had the chance to try. You would have become a bitter old woman, scrubbing floors, cooking dinners, and mending dresses."

"You make it sound so unpleasant. I really do love my life in this family."

"Do you want to be a doctor? Honestly?"

"Yes! You know I do." Her voice was more animated

than it had been since she had walked into the room. As if a switch had reversed the tension, she laughed. She threw her arms around Melanie and hugged her as if she would never let go. "Melanie, I don't know how to thank you. I was afraid of him, of his reaction, so I never wanted to bring it up. I'm so grateful to this family, you know? I always thought it wasn't the right time. But at least he's willing to discuss it with me. I never thought he would agree."

"He will discuss it, and he will do as I ask. He is a reasonable man, you know? And a smart one. He knows it's wrong to keep you from your calling, and as soon as he understands your abilities, he'll get over this reaction. I think he just felt ganged up on. I'm sorry he lashed out at you. You had no idea I was going to do this tonight."

"I wondered why I was preparing this amazing dinner, though. Now I know. I'm learning some things from you." She winked.

"It's about time you learned them. Don't forget, we're not doing anything terrible here. Quite the contrary. It's in everyone's best interest that people are happy doing what they're doing."

"But I'm concerned that Tommy will be mean to you."

"Sweetie, stop worrying. He won't be mean to me. He isn't a mean man. I've landed here, and thrown a monkey wrench into what seemed like a perfect household. It took him completely by surprise."

"Thrown a monkey wrench? What's a monkey wrench?"

"Oh, I'm sorry. You know, messed up the apple cart, turned everything on its head. Made life a little more complicated around here than it used to be, especially for him."

"Yes, I understand."

"Thomas will understand too. He loves you and Jane. He doesn't want either one of you to be unhappy, and you needn't be. It will be quite easy for him to talk to those people after he finds out how knowledgeable you are. And I have every confidence you'll be accepted into the school."

"I can hardly dare to believe it."

"Believe it, I'm sure of it."

Melanie didn't rush upstairs to bed. She helped Athena finish up the kitchen chores, feeling that the other woman's emotions were so raw, they were palpable, but there was an unmistakable excitement in the air. They didn't speak, just went about their business in silence. Jane had disappeared as soon as the firestorm happened. She had trouble dealing with conflicts with her brother, and although she agreed that Athena should have the opportunity she desired, Jane detested disagreeing with Thomas. She'd lost her parents, and she didn't want to lose him. Melanie wanted to give Thomas some time to think about their conversation, because she had a deep conviction that he would consider it and eventually agree with her. But she felt she had pushed him enough tonight, and she wanted him to be the one to feel as if he had come up with the plan.

"Okay, I guess we're done here," Melanie looked around the sparkling kitchen. Only a few lingering aromas gave any hint about the banquet that had originated here tonight. "I'm going up to bed. You?"

"I think I'll stay down here for a while and read by the lamp in the parlor," Athena said. "I'm not really tired yet. I can't clear my mind."

"All right, dear." Melanie reached over and hugged Athena, who hugged her back. "Please try not to worry. It will all work out."

"I don't think I thanked you enough, Melanie," Athena said, her voice muffled as she stayed in Melanie's embrace, her face buried in Melanie's shoulder.

"I think you did, in many ways, Athena," Melanie said. Kissing Athena on the forehead, she broke free and went upstairs, taking each stair slowly. She felt tired from everything they had done today, physically and emotionally. She fell into bed and slept more soundly than she ever had since she had arrived here.

Chapter 19

The next few days dragged. Melanie and Thomas talked about everything except Athena's future. On Thursday, by the time Melanie woke up, Jane had already left for the Frog Pond. She had been worrying that once spring temperatures started to rise, she would have to wait a long time to skate again, so she was spending more time there, increasing her roster of students. Athena and Thomas had already retreated to Athena's room to talk.

I can't believe I slept this long, Melanie thought, as she made her way downstairs. The house was eerily quiet—no Athena dusting the living room, humming, no sound or smell of bacon frying in the kitchen. Athena had left breakfast on the dining room table, but Melanie was too excited to eat. She and Athena had talked the day before about the outcome of the conversation.

"Did you and Thomas make a plan for your talk tomorrow?" Melanie had said, unable to contain her curiosity any more.

"Right after breakfast. He's going to test me on all my knowledge." Athena sighed.

"Aren't you looking forward to it?"

"I'm just a little nervous, Melanie. Maybe you shouldn't have pushed for this?"

"No, this is the right thing to do. You'll be nervous, but it will be good experience for you. A little nervousness will make you perform better. I believe that. You need to build up your confidence, and he is your best friend. In his heart of hearts, he doesn't want you to fail, no matter how skeptical he seems."

"Yes, but he'll be hard on me."

"Aren't you ready for that?"

"I think so, but who knows…" Her voice trailed off.

"Just imagine, if he's going to be hard on you, what the interview at the medical school is going to be like."

"I hadn't thought much about that," Athena said, resting her chin on the broom she was holding with both hands. "I've just been trying to get through this. Now I'm really anxious." She closed her eyes for a moment. "What if it never gets to the interview at the medical school?"

Melanie knew that was a possibility. Thomas would have to be a ferocious advocate for her, and if he didn't believe in her, he would never be able to do that. He was too honest, which was mostly endearing, but sometimes inconvenient. However, revealing her doubts to Athena now would be of no benefit to anyone. "You are going to get that interview," Melanie said, feeling some color rising from her neck to her cheeks. She turned away from Athena, hoping the other woman wouldn't notice. "You are going to go to medical school." Then she paused. "If I still have a breath in my body."

Athena didn't respond. She closed her eyes and shook her head, as if she suspected Melanie was being a bit disingenuous.

⌇⌇⌇

So now the day had come, and the two principals were ensconced upstairs in Athena's bedroom—her virtual classroom. The door was closed, and Melanie couldn't hear a thing, which, she decided, was probably for the best. She was curious, and she would love to go in and cheer Athena on, to influence Thomas's impression. But she knew that was ridiculous. She was mostly ignorant about the subject matter they were discussing. On the other hand, if it wasn't going well, she wanted to delay the disappointment for as long as she could so she could continue to have hope.

Then she felt guilty for making this about herself, when she knew it should be all about Athena. Melanie tried to fill the time with something useful. She started dusting the books in Thomas's library, but her anxiety about the meeting upstairs killed any focus, and she put down the duster. She pulled a book off the shelf and tried to read, but she couldn't concentrate on that either. She read one paragraph three times without knowing what the words said. Finally she just walked into the parlor and sank down into one of the armchairs, where she pressed her face into one of the wings and tried to quiet her mind, but she couldn't stop thinking about the possible scenarios. The one thing she'd never wanted to do was undermine Athena's excitement or discourage her ambition. She hoped she had done the right thing. *No, there was no other choice. Am I just trying to convince myself?*

"Melanie!"

Melanie had almost dozed off when she thought she heard her name. She didn't respond.

"Melanie, could you please come up here?"

It was Thomas's voice, and she had no idea how to interpret his tone. Without answering, she started up the stairs, her hands sweaty and trembling on the banister.

"Yes, Tom?" The words caught in her throat. She had to pull herself together. "Do you need something?"

"We need you in here," was all he said.

As Melanie approached, he was standing in the doorway of Athena's room, one hand on the glass doorknob, one knee angled out into the hallway, as if he was holding the door open with it. When she got close enough, she saw the small smile on Thomas's face, but her doubts wouldn't let her take that as a good sign.

"Is everything all right?" Melanie tried to look in at Athena, but Thomas caught her shoulder and led her gently into the hallway away from the room.

"She needs you in there. Go," he said.

When Melanie walked into the room, Athena was sitting on the edge of her desk chair, facing away from the door, her head in her hands. As Melanie got farther into the large room, she heard the quiet sobs, and then her entire body slackened and she reached for the side wall for support. She turned around and caught Thomas's eye, her lips drawn in, her top teeth biting down hard, her eyes narrowed. Thomas was still smiling at her. He pointed toward Athena and gave Melanie a sign with his arm and outstretched finger that she should go to the other woman. Melanie took a deep breath and walked behind Athena, put her hands on Athena's shoulders, ready to comfort her.

Athena grabbed Melanie's hands and dropped them, startled. "Your hands are sweaty," she said, her words jerky, as if she'd been crying for some time. "Are you all right?"

"Am I all right? What about *you*?"

Thomas had still not said anything, but when he noted that Athena was not able to articulate words, he walked into the room and put one hand on Athena's shoulder and the other around Melanie's waist.

"Melanie, you will not believe it," he said, his eyes wide. "Athena is brilliant! We've been living in the same house forever, and I had no idea how extraordinary she is." Athena started crying again, her sobs more audible now. "I have to convince the folks at Boston University Medical School that she needs to sit for the entrance examination. The sooner she does, the sooner an extraordinary physician goes out into the world."

Athena was now weeping, her shoulders jerking with each sob. Melanie turned around and looked up at Thomas. She had suspected the opposite, but everything was going just as she had hoped. She gasped. "Is that right?"

As soon as the words were out, she realized that she sounded sarcastic, but Thomas was so enthralled with his discovery, he didn't notice.

"Yes, you have no idea. Just by coincidence, there's a meeting at the hospital tomorrow. Dr. MacInerney is introducing me and another chap as new attendings, and the dean of Boston Medical School will be there, as well as the dean of Harvard Medical School. I will speak with both of them. I know that Boston Medical School accepts women. After I talk with them tomorrow, I'm sure Athena will be invited to interview and then to sit for the entrance exams.

Melanie pulled away from Thomas's grasp. "I'm just so thrilled for Athena. What happened?"

"We talked about everything—*everything*. I couldn't get her to make a mistake. I tried. She corrected the things I threw at her that I knew were incorrect. I'm amazed at her scope of knowledge, and she did that all on her own. She will breeze through medical school." He patted Athena on the shoulder. "Don't cry, my sister. You should be laughing. You amazed me."

"I don't know what to say," Athena finally said, wiping her eyes with the handkerchief Thomas had handed her. "I'm just thunderstruck."

I'm not, Melanie thought. "So, next steps? The dean? And then what?"

"Likely the interview. And then the exam, but she will pass that without any trouble. By September, she will be a medical student. I'm convinced of it."

"Well, that gives us some time to hire someone to replace her in the house, right?"

Thomas slapped his forehead with his hand. "Oh, dear, I wasn't thinking about that. I'm not doing anything to my own benefit here."

"If you don't want me to—" Athena had turned toward both of them.

"No more of that talk," Melanie said. "I won't hear of

you not doing it. We will hire a cook and a housekeeper. You are graduating from those positions in this house. But you will have the last word about whom to hire, and you can feel free to guide them and let them know how you like things done. Does that make sense?"

Athena nodded. "Thank you," she said, looking straight at Melanie, who winked at her. "I love you."

"All I can say," Thomas said, "is I'm glad I discovered this."

Melanie grabbed Athena's hand and squeezed it. The gaze that passed between them said it all. No matter who had discovered it, Athena was on her way.

"Oh my," Athena said, her hand over her mouth, "What will I wear to the interview?"

Melanie broke into laughter, and finally everyone relaxed. "You will make yourself a new frock," Melanie said. "A beautiful one. I'll take care of the cooking for the next few days. You have to prepare."

"You don't have to—"

"Are you sure you want to do that?" Thomas looked a little stricken.

Melanie laughed again. "I know the meals won't be as good. But we can all deal with it for a few days, can't we? I'll ask Jane to help. It will be good for all of us."

"What will they ask me, Tommy?" Athena pulled on Thomas's hand.

"Nothing that I didn't ask you, dear," he said. "All you have to do is what you just did here. Try not to worry about it."

"I'll try," she said. She kissed Thomas's hand and looked up at Melanie. "I'm forever grateful to you, dear Melanie," she said.

"The pleasure is all mine, believe me," Melanie said. "Now get to work on making that dress."

Thomas and Melanie left Athena in her room, Melanie

turning around and blowing a kiss to the other woman.

"I know you did that all," Thomas said. "I wish I had. You continue to turn this house on its end, and you just got here. If I could just convince you that I'm worthy of your love."

"No, I just saw things slightly differently," she said to him, ignoring his plea. "No one needs to feel responsible for this. It's all Athena's and Jane's doing. Everyone gets into a rut sometimes, you know? Then it's hard to see something that might just be lurking around the corner." They walked toward the staircase, not moving too fast.

"Lurking?" He chuckled and then sighed. "I know you were trying to give me the credit for discovering Athena's genius. You shouldn't do that. You are the one who realized it. I was oblivious."

"But you were the one who agreed to take it to the next level for her. And now you are the one who has agreed to speak to the dean of the medical school on her behalf. So let's each claim partial responsibility, all right? I just want Athena to get what she deserves. It doesn't really matter whose idea it was."

"And so she will." He leaned over to kiss her cheek. "I want to celebrate you, my dear Melanie. Since you've been here, there are smiles on people's faces that I hadn't seen in a very long time. I wish there were some way I could convince you that you should be mine."

"I'm sorry, Tom, I wish it were different. It's nothing about you, it's me."

"Is there something you'd like to do today? I don't have to be back in the hospital until tomorrow, and the sun is shining. We should celebrate Athena's triumph. Shall we take a carriage ride somewhere? We could ride down to Beacon Street, go across the West Boston Bridge to Cambridge and stroll around Harvard Yard? I'm sure the horse would like to get some exercise, now that the weather is starting to show signs of a thaw."

"That sounds like a nice idea, Tom. I'd like that. Would you like me to make some lunch for us first? And then we can have a picnic in Harvard yard. And we could ask Athena to come as well."

"A picnic sounds nice, but I was hoping we could take our carriage ride alone. I don't feel I have enough time with you as it is, and I want some alone time where we can talk seriously."

"Should I be worried? You sound so stern."

"No, you should not be worried at all. I just want all I can get of you, and I won't give up on convincing you that I'm lovable."

"Oh, Tommy, you are definitely lovable, and sweet, and very handsome. It's just—"

He sighed. "I know, it's just that fellow at home."

"I just don't want to disappoint Athena."

At that moment, Athena came skipping down the stairs behind them, whistling. All signs of the copious tears were gone, and she got in between Melanie and Thomas and hugged them tight as she passed them.

"I'm going to take a walk to the Public Garden," she said, looking back up at the two of them as she headed for the first floor. "I want to do some thinking. I love this time of year, you know? A new start for everything. Soon the trees will be green and the tulips will be in bloom and the daffodils. I hope you get to go out and enjoy the day as well." And before they had reached the bottom of the staircase, she was pulling on her boots and buttoning her coat, wrapping the scarf she had knit herself around her neck. "If I sit around here, I'll only worry about my interview, and this way I can walk off some of my nerves. I'll start working on the dress when I return."

"Enjoy yourself!" Thomas called after her. "We're going to take a ride to Cambridge."

"Wonderful! Have fun." Athena walked out the front

door, waving at them and closing the door behind her with a resounding click.

"See? She is fine," he said to Melanie. "She doesn't even need us." He shrugged, shaking his head from side to side. "That girl will be fine forever."

Melanie busied herself in the kitchen, slicing the brown bread Athena had made the day before into four thick pieces and putting a slab of ham and cheese on each sandwich. She wrapped each sandwich in a linen napkin and put them both into a small basket. She stopped to think about her situation. If anyone had told her a month ago she wouldn't miss her iPhone, wouldn't miss television, computers, or movies if they were taken away, she would have disagreed with great passion. But she missed none of those things. Somehow, the life here was simple, pure, invigorating. She had a great family, Thomas was wonderful, Athena and she had already found a deep friendship, plus, Jane was happy and coming around to accept her after their rocky start. Melanie loved this city, looked forward to a fascinating relationship with Aunt Isabella and to watching Athena and Jane be fulfilled in the lives they had craved. The only thing that gave her terrible anguish was the loss of Justin, and never being able to tell him how she felt, that the accident and separation were the things that had informed her about her love for him. If there were just some way.

Harvard Square was bustling, but it looked so different in 1886 that Melanie hardly recognized it. "We have the Harvard Coop now," Thomas said, the pride in his voice overflowing. "They opened it in '82."

"Wow." Melanie couldn't think of anything else to say. The Coop was such an institution in Harvard Square, expanding over the years with branches at M.I.T. and the law and medical schools. To think it was just four years old blew her mind. Archie parked the carriage on the street outside the gate to Harvard Yard and helped Melanie down. The last time Melanie had been here was the day after her graduation, when she and some friends had walked around Harvard Square in cut-offs, getting weepy and nostalgic about their four years here. Now Harvard Yard looked like a sprawling, rural campus, and the magnificent mansions surrounding it seemed larger than life, because they were located on acres of cultivated land.

She wished she could take pictures of it all. She felt as if she had wandered into a dream, but then this entire experience had been like a dream.

"Are you feeling all right, my dear?" Thomas had concern in his voice.

"I'm sorry. Do I look a bit flustered? This is just all so...different. I couldn't possibly describe it without making you think I'm a lunatic. But—in my time—it had changed from this rural, farm-like town to a bustling city, and the yard had been crowded with many more buildings, and I'll just stop now." She shrank back a little.

"Would you like to go and sit down in front of Memorial Hall? There are some benches. We can look at the statue of John Harvard."

"But isn't that statue in the yard? Behind University Hall?"

"No, dear. It's on the delta. Let's go look at it. I had the honor of being at the installation ceremony in Sanders Theater four years ago."

"It's only been here for four years?"

Thomas led her by the elbow, gently, toward Memorial Hall, where Melanie had spent hours in various classes. It was such a familiar building that she felt happy to see it. It connected her to her "past" life the way most things couldn't. They sat down, getting close for warmth, on a bench facing the statue.

"Yes, and it was quite the extravaganza, the day it was installed. General Bridge was there—he actually donated most of the money to make it happen—and the sculptor, Daniel French, the president of the university, Edward Hale, and the Reverend Dr. Ellis, who have a great speech."

"How did you get to be there? Were you invited?"

"My family had donated large sums of money to the university over the decades, and that gives people some importance, you know?"

She nodded. That legacy concept had certainly made its way into the later decades as well. "Money talks."

"And then, you know, our relationship with the Gardners and their relationship with so many of the artists of the day, and whatever. Anyway, I was invited, and I was happy to go. I think he looks very distinguished, overseeing the doings of the university and the city."

"Who is Dr. Ellis? And what did he say that impressed you so much?"

"Oh, he was a Unitarian minister, and now he's a professor at the theology school. He's a brilliant man, and a great speech writer. I think he was also pretty high up in the Massachusetts Historical Society, but I think he's at least semiretired now. He's getting up there in years."

"Do you remember the speech?" The wind had suddenly roiled up into a blustery breeze, and Melanie shivered a little.

"I committed one sentence to memory, because it impressed me so deeply. At the time of his speech, my mother was in the last throes of her illness, really on her death bed, although we didn't know it, and it was very difficult, emotionally."

"Oh, Tom, I'm so sorry." She pulled her arm out of his and reached up to touch his face with her mittened hand. "I didn't realize, didn't mean to make you sad."

"No, no. It's all right." He looked up toward the sky and sighed softly. "What Dr. Ellis said about the statue that struck me so, was, 'He rests his hand on the open tome between his knees, and gazes for a moment into the future, so dim, so uncertain, yet so full of promise.'"

A chill went through Melanie like a sword, and she shuddered. "Oh."

"Are you all right? I can feel you shivering through your

things." He reached behind her and pulled her close.

"That quote just gave me the chills," she said. "It just put everything into a sharp focus, not a pleasant experience."

"In what way, Melanie?"

"How did I get here? What is this thing between us? Will I be able to forget my old life? What is my future? And yet, I do know the future. I know the future for the next hundred-and-thirty years. I know some things that you wouldn't even believe—it would horrify you."

"You can tell me anything, Melanie. I'm all ears."

"This is so strange, but in another way, is it a dream? Can I believe in it?" Melanie didn't want to, but tears welled up in her eyes and she began to cry softly. "All of a sudden, I am with you, here, in this time, in your family. You are a kind, warm, loving, intelligent man. Your sister Athena accepted me almost without question, and slowly Jane seems to be coming around to trust me as well. Your friends have made me feel utterly welcome. I live in a beautiful home, and you have given me *carte blanche* to do anything I want there. I have turned your life on its head, pushing you to allow each of your sisters to change her life's direction. How did this all happen? And how will it end?"

"Now I wish I hadn't quoted Dr. Ellis!" He looked down at her, but his eyes were twinkling, not pitying.

"Thomas! You're not taking me seriously." Her annoyance made her stop crying. "I mean this. You can't imagine how hard this is for me. I'm an analytical person, and it's frustrating not to be able to figure it all out. I feel as if I'm in a dream that won't end, but what if it does?"

"Dear, analytical Melanie, I won't let it end. Why do you worry about such things? Why not just accept it and live it and enjoy it? Why do we have to figure it out? My job is to turn you around so that you feel you might love me someday. That is my ultimate goal."

"But when I think about it all seriously, it just doesn't seem possible, doesn't seem as if it could be real."

"How can you say that? You're here with me. Cambridge is real. Harvard is real. Our horse is real. Archie is real. I am real. You have manipulated my sisters' reality in the short time you've been here. You are a dynamo. You take my breath away." He reached down and pulled several blades of grass out of the ground. "Do you see this?" He handed them to Melanie, who took them out of Thomas's hands.

"Yes, of course."

"This is real, Melanie. It's really grass, and it was just growing in the ground, and I just pulled it up. Do you see that bird?" He pointed up toward the sky, where several small birds were fluttering around. "And those squirrels chasing each other up the big elm trees?"

"Yes, I see it. All of it."

"It's real, it's possible." He tapped her on the shoulder. "Do you feel that?"

"Of course I feel it."

"It's so real. I will give you as much as you want, hopefully as much as you need. I can't get enough of you."

"I'm so sorry I can't reciprocate, at least not right now."

"I am a patient man, more than you know. I have great optimism that you will come to feel about me the way I feel about you."

"I'm just not sure," she said. She sighed. "There are some things that make me sad."

"What?" He reached over and brushed a lock of hair off her forehead. She began to cry again.

"What you just did," she said. "My mother used to do that. I often think about her, about how it was just the two of us after my father died, how whenever I felt worried or scared, she was there, and just the little things. I miss her, I can't help it."

"I'm so sorry. I miss my mother too. There is nothing like the love of a mother, is there?"

"And I worry about her, about how she is doing without me. She has her life, her work, her friends. But I know she's worried about me, frantic probably. But I can't tell her I'm all right, more than all right." Melanie left out her aching frustration for Justin.

"Why all this now?" He pushed even closer to her, his body an unmovable, constant wall of support for her to lean on as much as she needed to.

"I don't know. Maybe being here, at Harvard. Mom visited me here during my college years. We had fun discovering Cambridge together, walking around the yard—it brings back so many memories of her. She was so proud that I went here."

"Do you miss anything else?"

"You know. I've told you everything."

"I try hard not to be jealous of someone who hasn't even been born yet, but he is in your heart, and born or not, that makes me jealous."

The conversation stopped. They sat, silent, on the bench, looking up at the John Harvard statue, for some time. She hated hurting Thomas's feelings, making him worry, when he had been so kind to her. At almost the same time, they looked at each other. They knew it was time to go.

"Getting a little cold?" Thomas asked.

"More than a little."

"Let's go home. We should check in on Athena too and make sure she's okay." He stood up and beckoned to Archie, who was waiting on the street with the carriage. Melanie wondered whether Archie was cold. Archie approached and took a small bow.

"Ready to get back to Boston?" he said, smiling. "Beautiful day, isn't it?"

"Yes, and yes!" Thomas said.

"Would you like me to go by the Common and see if Miss Jane is ready to leave the Frog Pond?"

"Archie, that's a great idea," Melanie said. "We'll surprise her. I love to watch her skate, and I don't get to see it enough."

The three of them walked slowly toward the brougham, Archie walking several steps behind Melanie and Thomas.

When they had made themselves comfortable inside, Archie started the drive back across the river. Before they reached the bridge, Melanie had dozed off, and she dreamed of Justin. Jane was happy for the ride back home, and Athena was busy in her room studying.

Chapter 20

Friday a cold, early spring rain was dotting the ground with semi-frozen pellets. Melanie awoke with a start. This was Athena's day to shine, even though the sun wasn't doing the same. Melanie threw on her dressing gown and skipped down the stairs, tiptoed toward the kitchen where she saw Thomas and Athena head-to-head at the table.

Melanie stopped, hiding a little before she entered the room, so that she could listen to the two of them.

"Yes!" Thomas had a broad smile. He reached over and kissed Athena on the cheek. "You are fine. I have no worries about you. I couldn't trip you up on even one question. Just be yourself and show them how much you know. You will be invited to sit for the exam, I have absolutely no doubt."

"Are you sure, Tommy?" she said. She had her head in her hands, and Melanie thought she saw Athena's hands trembling a little. Even her curls were trembling.

"I am so sure."

"I am so worried."

"You wouldn't be human if you weren't nervous." Melanie had walked into the room and stood behind Athena, her hands on Athena's shoulders. "If Thomas says you're

ready, I believe you're ready. You've been readying yourself for this for years."

Jane was bustling around the kitchen, standing in front of
a huge, cast-iron frying pan. "Would you like some ham and
eggs, Melanie?" Jane smiled. It was still a surprise to Melanie when Jane was happy with her.

"So you're learning to cook too, Jane?" Melanie sat
down at the table next to Thomas. "I would love some ham
and eggs."

"It will be coming up in a minute," Jane said, as she fiddled with the wood stove and scraped the pan. "I'm going to
get good at this."

"We all have to support Athena," Thomas said. "Soon,
we won't see so much of her, because she'll be very busy in
medical school."

"Oooh," Athena made a gurgling sound. "I don't want to
talk about it."

"Okay," Thomas said, "Mum's the word. No more chat-
ter. You just go today and do what you have to do. Archie is
readying the carriage to take you over there and bring you
home, and I can't wait to hear what happened. Enough talk."
He got up from the table and hugged Athena. "Now I have
to get to the hospital. I will see you lovely ladies this evening, and we'll celebrate."

Melanie rose and walked him to the front door. "Do you
really think she'll be fine?" Melanie said, her voice a whisper.

"I really do. She knows everything she needs to know.
She will be more than fine."

"We'll take care of her tonight, all right? No cooking for
Athena. Jane and I will prepare a special dinner."

"If it's anything like the special dinners Athena prepares
for us, it will be superb."

"Don't get your hopes up too much, but we'll do our
best."

He was gone without another word. Athena, dressed in
the prim black dress with lace at the collar that she had

sewn for the occasion, stood up from the table, supporting herself by holding on to the edge. She hadn't touched her breakfast.

"Wish me good luck." Athena looked at the two of them.

"You didn't even eat what I prepared for you," Jane said, hugging Athena. "How can you think on an empty stomach?" Jane picked up Athena's plate and frowned, looking down at it. "Was it that my food was bad?"

"Oh no, your food was fine!" Athena reached out to her sister and squeezed her hand. "It was just that my stomach was churning and I had no appetite."

"We're expecting good news from you," Jane said, walking to the sink with the plate of food. "That's all that matters."

Athena closed her eyes and bowed her head. "A little prayer," she said.

"We'll do the same," Jane said. "Love you."

After she had left, Jane and Melanie tiptoed around the house as if they would bring bad luck on Athena if they talked. While Melanie cleaned up the breakfast dishes, Jane disappeared into her room to get ready for her skating lessons. Melanie sat in the parlor with a book, but she had trouble concentrating. She wished she had her computer or at least television to take her mind off Athena's biggest challenge. She got up and paced for a few minutes, but then there was a sharp knock at the door.

"Hello?" Melanie opened the door, and there was a man standing on the stoop, dressed in boots and a high hat, with a riding crop. Melanie didn't recognize him. His carriage and horse were parked on the street in front of the house. "May I help you?"

"Yes, Miss Swift?"

"Yes."

"I am Mrs. Gardner's employee, miss. She requested that I bring you this." He handed Melanie a pink satin-striped envelope engraved with a gold "ISG" in the corner and a gold tassel. In beautiful calligraphy, Isabella had written

"Miss Melanie Swift" on the outside of the envelope in dark brown ink.

"Oh, thank you." The man didn't move, but stood there, his back rigid, his impeccably polished boot toes pointing straight ahead. "Do you need something else?"

"Yes, miss."

"Oh, I'm sorry. What is it?"

"Mrs. Gardner would like me to stay here until you read what's in the envelope."

"Oh, certainly." Melanie pulled out the card, also beautifully printed. It said, *Mrs. Jack Gardner requests the pleasure of your company for tea this afternoon, 3:45 P.M.*

"May I give Mrs. Gardner your answer?"

Now he shuffled back and forth. Melanie determined that she needed to learn more about the customs and expectations of polite Boston culture in the 1880s.

"Yes, of course you may. Please tell Mrs. Gardner that I'd be honored to come for tea this afternoon. And thank her, would you?"

"Yes, miss, I will. Uh...do you have a card to send back to her?"

"Oh, I'm so sorry. I don't have—I am all out of cards. Would you please send Mrs. Gardner my apologies and tell her that I will be there?"

"Yes, miss. I will be back for you at three-thirty sharp." He smiled for the first time.

"Oh, you don't have to pick me up. Archie can ride me over, or I can walk."

"Mrs. Gardner requested that I come for you."

"In that case, I'll be ready at three-thirty. Thank you."

"You're most welcome, miss. I will be bringing you back home afterward as well." He bowed, clicked his boots, turned around in one swiveling motion, and walked back to his carriage. Melanie stood at the door watching him as he walked, not moving a muscle above his waist, to his carriage. She smiled. *Strange times*, she thought. Then the man leaned down and kissed his horse on the muzzle before he jumped up and picked up the reins. She smiled again. *Perhaps not so different underneath it all.* She spent most of the morning and early afternoon trying on and discarding several different outfits. Isabella had been so nice, so warm, when she met her the first time. She was grateful Isabella had given her a reason to stop obsessing about Athena.

At three-twenty-nine, the door knocker made its loud noise again. Melanie, who had been ready and waiting in the parlor for at least a half hour, jumped up and grabbed her long coat and hat. She had chosen a mauve, watered-silk dress with ivory Alençon lace around the neckline and matching mother-of-pearl buttons going from the bustline all the way down to the hem. This was one of Athena's most beautiful creations. A little dressy for afternoon, Melanie realized, but she wanted to impress Isabella, and she wanted more than anything to wear this dress. Thomas had been promising that they would go to the Boston Symphony, especially as Melanie had met its conductor, Wilhelm Gericke, at Isabella's soiree. But he hadn't been able to get enough time away from the hospital, particularly after his promotion. She had been saving the dress for that, but it looked so beautiful and felt so glamorous, she broke down and put it on.

"Ready, miss?" Isabella's footman offered his elbow for Melanie to lean on, and she took it.

"Thank you," she said. "I didn't get your name?"

"Uh," he seemed a bit uncomfortable, but he gave her the information she had asked for, "It's Ralph."

"Thank you, Ralph. This is wonderful service. I do appreciate it."

"It's my pleasure, Miss," he said, as they approached the Gardners' opulent carriage. Melanie loved riding in Thomas's carriage. She thought it was comfortable and very well appointed, but Isabella's was in another league. The seats were plush, royal blue velvet. The trimmings were gold on shiny black enamel, with gold door handles and shining wheel spokes.

"I feel like Cinderella going to the ball," she said, almost to herself.

"What's that, miss?"

"Oh, nothing, Ralph. Just commenting on how beautiful this carriage is."

"Thank you, Miss." He put one hand on her back and one under her elbow, and helped her step up without pushing too hard. She sank into the cushions and smoothed out her dress so it wouldn't wrinkle too badly. When Ralph started the horses, Melanie hardly felt the movement of the wheels. She wished the ride could last longer, or that she could convince Ralph to take the "long way" around to Isabella's house on Beacon Street. But she didn't say anything. She was excited to see Isabella anyway, and when they arrived at the Gardners' front walk, Melanie's heart was beating a little faster. Ralph helped her out as he had helped her in, and he tipped his hat to her as she began the walk up to Isabella's front door, the dress rustling under her coat. Before she even got to the porch, Isabella threw the door open and stood there, one hand on the door handle, one hand outstretched in welcome.

"Come in, come in! I'm so glad you were free today. I asked you on a whim, so thank you for being spontaneous. Some people might have been offended."

"Oh, no, thank you! I was more than free. You saved me from a day of worrying about Athena. She's at her medical school interview today, and the whole house is on edge."

"Yes, of course," she said, "I heard about her opportunity. Quite impressive."

"Aunt Isabella, you seem to hear about things before I do," Melanie said.

Isabella winked. "A certain talent of mine," she said. Then, "Come in, come in, before you freeze out here. It looks like snow again. I'm so ready for springtime."

Melanie walked into the grand house, which seemed even larger now that it wasn't full of people. A young maid in a uniform was standing just inside the door, and she helped Melanie take off her coat and took her coat and hat and left the room.

"Let me look at you!" Isabella had grabbed both of Melanie's hands and leaned back, as if she was going to start a game of "Ring around the Rosy." She winked at Melanie. "You are a breathtaking vision, my dear. You're even prettier today than you were when I saw you last. And that beautiful frock—it suits you so, so well." She sighed. "Oh, to be so young and beautiful and radiant again. My Tommy must be taking very good care of you, that's all I have to say."

Melanie laughed. Isabella was so good at making people feel comfortable. "Very good care of me, indeed," she said. "And thank you for the compliments. You are very beautiful yourself."

Isabella leaned in and kissed Melanie on one check and then the other. "Come, my darling girl, let's go sit down in the parlor. Lillie will bring out the tea, and I'll tell you why I was so anxious for you to come today." Isabella picked up a little silver bell on the coffee table and shook it several times. The maid reappeared with a large silver tray, replete with a silver tea service and a plate overflowing with small, crustless sandwiches and scones. After they had poured their tea and chosen their snacks, Isabella settled into a corner of the sofa and patted Melanie on the knee.

"So, I understand that Tom is still trying to woo you? Unsuccessfully?"

Melanie felt herself blush. "Oh my, he does speak to you about everything."

Isabella raised her hand and wagged her index finger at Melanie. "I understand you are not quite as ready as he, is that correct?"

Melanie was at a loss for words. She nodded and looked down at her lap.

"But no, that's why I asked you here, darling. I am here

to plead his case. You could not do better than Thomas Thornwell, I'm firmly convinced."

Melanie sucked her breath in. Apparently, Thomas had been working on this with Isabella. She didn't know whether to be grateful or annoyed. "Whew, this is quite a surprise," she said. "Did Thomas ask you to speak with me?"

"Oh, goodness, no. I think he would be mortified if he knew. You're not angry with me, are you?"

Isabella looked so stricken that Melanie decided to go along with it. "No, of course I appreciate your kindness, Aunt Isabella. But the heart feels what the heart feels. I adore Thomas, think he's a fine man, handsome, wonderful—"

"But you don't love him?"

"Alas, I wish I did!"

"But, Melanie, sometimes love takes a while to come. There is more to a relationship than love, you know?" Isabella was so sincere, Melanie had trouble being angry about it.

"You just have to give me time, Isabella. It's all too soon."

"I understand you and John Sargent got along quite well?" Isabella's smile dropped into a half frown.

"He is a very persuasive young man," Melanie said.

"Indeed he is," the older woman said, "And very talented."

"It was all in good fun," Melanie added.

"I think Tommy was a little jealous."

Melanie shrugged, but it was funny, this woman talking to her like a warning parent. "He needn't have been. I have no connection to John Sargent except for a little hero worship."

"What about this other young man, the one who has your heart?"

Melanie sighed. "I rather lost my chance to let him know," she said, "And I'm not sure how he feels—felt—about me. So, that is still a fantasy."

"Well, that's good, as far as I'm concerned. That gives Tom a better chance. You understand how he feels?"

"Completely," Melanie said, picking up her teacup and bringing it to her mouth, hoping it would hide her embarrassment.

They spent the rest of the afternoon discussing art, travel, love, dreams, and Thomas, every time Isabella could direct the conversation back to him. Despite the older woman's determination to turn Melanie around, they laughed and joked. Melanie decided this woman was a wonderful friend and could be a wonderful mentor. Time was flying. As the sun dropped into the western sky, Melanie realized she wanted to get home to see how Athena had made out.

"Goodness, I should be getting home. It will be dark soon," she said.

"Yes, indeed. We had such a good time talking, the afternoon went quickly."

"Thank you so much for your tea and your conversation. I really appreciated it."

"Well, we must do it frequently, all right? At least once a week."

"Absolutely. Thank you."

Melanie rode home, luxuriating in the Gardners' carriage, daydreaming about everything they had talked about. The ride was so smooth that she was sitting still, her eyes closed, when Ralph stepped up on the running board.

"Miss? We are at your home."

"Oh." Melanie started. "Thank you, Ralph." She almost tripped on the way down, but Ralph caught her in his strong arms and kept her upright. "Thank you again. I can't believe how clumsy I am." She wished she could have her jeans. This type of clothing definitely kept women dependent on men.

Ralph tipped his hat and watched her until she was at her front door, and then he drove off. Before Melanie had a chance to enter, the door flew open, and there was Athena, nearly jumping up and down at the door.

"Oh, you scared me! Are you all right?"

Athena grabbed Melanie's elbow, helped her off with her hat, and pulled her into the parlor, where she almost shoved her down onto the settee. Melanie felt a charge around Athena, the air almost vibrating with excitement.

"Oh, thank heavens you're home! I have been walking around, no, skipping around the house. My feet aren't even touching the ground. Jane's not home yet either. I had no one to tell! Now I can tell you."

"Tell me!" Melanie said, pulling on Athena's arm, but Athena couldn't sit. She paced back and forth in front of the sofa.

"They loved me." Breathless. "They *loved* me!" Athena finally sat down next to Melanie, and buried her head in Melanie's shoulder, her black curls bouncing as if they were animated by some internal energy.

"Of course they loved you, sweetie. What did they say?" She looked over at Athena, who had raised her head. Athena had tears streaming down her face. Melanie brushed them away with her hand, which was still in its silk glove.

"I am to return on Tuesday to take the entrance examinations. There will be written and oral examinations, and they are doing this only for me. The regular examinations were already held, but they are changing the rules so that I have a chance to start medical school in July. Because of my unusual background, they said the exams will be more exacting than normal, but I impressed them. They made that very clear!"

Melanie threw her arms around Athena and hugged her. "I'm so happy for you, Athena," she said, "But not surprised."

"Melanie, I have you to thank for this. This never would have happened if it hadn't been for your urging Tom to speak to me about it and then talk to the people at the medical school. It never would have happened." The sobs started again and were now becoming louder and wetter.

"No, no sweetheart. I don't believe that. It would have happened for you. I just quickened the process a little bit. I knew they would invite you to take the exams. You are an extraordinary person. You're going to be a doctor!"

Athena jumped up again, walked to the end of the parlor and back, holding her hands up to her head and swaying back and forth. "It's my dream, Melanie. It's always been my dream. But I honestly thought the dream was impossible."

"Well, some dreams come true. And I never doubted that this one would."

Chapter 21

Melanie couldn't believe how the days were dragging. Thomas was at the hospital every day, even Saturday and Sunday. Jane was spending all of her time at the Frog Pond, Athena ensconced in her room studying her books. On Tuesday, Athena got into the brougham early and rode to the South End for her entrance exams at Boston University School of Medicine. Jane, Thomas, and Melanie saw her off.

"Good luck!" Jane hugged her sister, and the two danced around in a circle like little children.

"You don't need good luck, Athena," Thomas said. "Just all of the information you've learned and taken to heart. I have no doubt you will pass with flying colors."

Athena saved her last good bye for Melanie. The two embraced, Melanie kissing Athena's flushed cheek and smoothing the tight black curls that emerged from her bonnet. "My heart and my mind are with you today," Melanie whispered in Athena's ear. "Don't think of anything but where you will be in four years, and how many people you will help. If you do that, you will succeed beyond all expectations."

"I love you, dear sister," Athena whispered, kissing Melanie back. "As if you were blood." And then she was off, Archie goading the horse down the street in the close-to-dawn dim light.

"I hope she'll be all right," Thomas said, sighing, when the brougham had proceeded out of sight.

"Don't waste your worries on Athena. She will be fine. Today marks the launching of the second doctor in the family."

"I know you're right," he said, "But I can't help worrying just a little. She's like my little chick going out into the big world. What if she gets there and forgets everything she ever knew?"

"You are such a papa," Jane said, laughing. "I keep reminding you, Athena is a little older than you are. And this is much too important to her to forget anything. You need to let go and have some confidence in her."

"I know, but I feel Mother and Father would approve my worrying about her, about all of you."

"Worry about yourself more," Melanie said. "Because tonight, we will be celebrating Athena's admission to medical school."

After Thomas left for the hospital, Jane and Melanie sat in the big kitchen, sipping coffee and eating the muffins Athena had made for them the night before. "All right, Miss Thornwell," Melanie said. "Now that we have gotten Athena started on her road, how about you? Soon it will be spring, and the ice will be gone, and then what for you?"

"I hadn't wanted to take the wind out of Athena's sails," Jane said, "So I haven't been talking much about what's going on."

"What?" Melanie set her cup down with a loud click. She heard the excitement in Jane's voice.

"A group of us, some of the girls and some of the boys, are looking forward to starting a skating club."

"A skating club?"

"Yes. It is to be an organization that lets individuals and

families participate in ice skating activities, and we will
hold competitions and training sessions, and we will raise
funds to keep it going, and perhaps even be able to build
skating rinks where people can come and learn and enjoy
the sport."

"That's fantastic," Melanie said. "When is all this going
to start?"

"We've already started, and what we'll do is meet in
people's homes and make plans about how we want to proceed. We've elected a president, and they offered me the
position of secretary."

"Did you take it?"

"Yes, although I'm not sure what I have to do. But my
friend Jared, who moved here from Philadelphia, was active
in the Philadelphia Skating Club, and all of this is basically
his idea."

"What does the Philadelphia Skating Club do?"

"Jared says they go to most of the outdoor skating areas
and patrol to make sure that people don't get hurt and injured, or to rescue people who have had an accident."

"Sounds a little dangerous?"

"Not really if you are trained to do the work, and Jared
has taken charge of the training." She paused, and Melanie
saw a blush overtake her very white skin, starting at the
neck. "Melanie, I really like him."

Melanie looked over at Jane and smiled. "Like him?"

"I think maybe I love him." Jane put her head in her
hands, as if she was defending herself against an emotional
slap.

"Oh, Jane, that is marvelous news. Maybe we'll have a
wedding around here one of these days?"

"You don't think I'm crazy?"

"Why would I think you're crazy for being in love? Love
is the best thing in the world."

"But I'm not sure he likes me in the same way."

"Is he handsome?"

"To me, very handsome. And he's strong. As strong as an ox. And a breathtaking skater."

Melanie laughed. "Well, I think he must like you in the same way, because you're so beautiful, and you are a breathtaking skater too."

"I don't know, every time I think he might, I convince myself that he doesn't. But I can't give up hoping."

"Never give up hoping, Janie, never." Melanie squeezed Jane's hand. "Would you like to have him over for dinner sometime?"

"If I can get my courage up to ask him."

"Perhaps Thomas could ask him?"

"Would he?"

"We'll ask him. He wants you to be happy, and it sounds as if you are well on your way. And Janie?"

"Yes?"

"Thank you for including me in this wonderful news. I feel so grateful that you did. Thank you."

Jane bowed her head, and when she raised it to look at Melanie, she was smiling, a broad smile. Melanie smiled back. A corner had been turned.

The two women went upstairs. After leaving Jane at her own bedroom door, Melanie sat down on the edge of her bed, put her head in her hands, and cried. Athena was going to be set on her way, and Jane was establishing herself and possibly getting married. No one could understand how she felt about her old life, how much she missed Justin. She got a chill and put her arms around herself, hugging herself tight. She would just have to continue hoping for the best. There was no other answer.

Melanie had no idea how much time had passed as she sat there, until she heard a clattering at the door downstairs. Whoever it was would have to make a great deal of noise for it to make its way to the master bedroom on the far side of the house.

She stood up, straightened her skirt, and walked to the top of the winding staircase. Athena and Jane were in the front foyer, holding hands, screaming and shrieking, dancing around in a circle. Melanie's mood changed in an instant, and she started to laugh at the sight of them cavorting around the room.

"What?" Melanie yelled down the stairs, as she skipped down, two stairs at a time. "What's going on?"

Athena was breathless, her eyes sparkling like dark brown diamonds, her mouth parted in a laugh. She could hardly speak. "Melanie!"

"Yes, what?"

"Melanie! Melanie!"

"Tell her, Athena." Jane let go of Athena's hands and tried to slow her sister down. "Tell her."

"I passed all the tests. I passed them all." Athena's words were jerky as she tried to catch her breath.

"Oh my God, that's wonderful!" Melanie grabbed both women, and they hugged each other. "I told you so." She led them all into the parlor and beckoned to Jane to sit down. Athena looked as if she couldn't stop, but Melanie tugged on her arm, and she sat down between the two of them. "Tell us what happened."

"Well," Athena seemed to be getting her breath back. "They couldn't believe how much I knew. Every time one of them gave me a quiz, they would call another to give me a harder question. They made me write first, and that was easy. But then all the questions. They said they were giving me trick questions, but nothing was difficult. Tommy's questions were harder. Then they all exchanged glances and raised their eyebrows. I don't think they noticed that I was spying on them, but I saw them do it. As if they couldn't believe it."

"So? What happens now?" Melanie had moved very close to Athena's face, as if she couldn't stand being far away.

Athena's voice became a hoarse whisper, the words coming out very slow. "I start medical school in July." And then a scream that permeated every corner of the room and blasted Melanie's head back. And then laughter. They were all laughing, and then silence.

"What in the world is going on here?" Thomas had come in quietly, as if he was looking at a performance of some sort. He was smiling, and Athena was the first one to spring up from the sofa and jump into his arms. She grabbed him around the neck and held on. He looked around her toward Melanie with a question mark on his face.

"Athena did it! She's admitted to medical school."

"Oh, my, little sister. I am so proud of you!" He kissed her on both cheeks and then kissed her on the top of her head. "This is the best present you ever gave me. We're going to be a two-doctor family. I'm amazed they told you right away."

Athena was nodding with authority, her eyes closed and her face frozen in a smile that looked as if it might be permanent.

"They must have been very impressed."

"How could they not have been impressed with her?" Jane said. "She is the smartest one in this family."

Thomas gave Jane a little slap on the shoulder. "Thank you, sister," he said, pouting.

"The truth hurts, brother," she said, smirking.

"Children, children," Melanie said.

"Oh, no," Athena dropped onto the wing chair closest to the foyer. She put her head in her hands.

"What?" Jane rushed to her and lifted her chin. "What's the matter?"

"What if they were wrong?" Athena looked up, and her brow was furrowed with horizontal lines. "What if I can't do it? What if it was just a fluke that I passed the tests? I fooled them, and now they will find out."

Jane giggled. "Athena, stop it this instant. You are going to be wonderful there. You will do it and do it magnificently. You are so smart, and besides, you want it so badly."

Melanie nodded. "Yes, no self-doubt allowed. You are on your way. Now I have to talk about Jane's news."

Jane made a little strangled sound and jumped up from her chair, her face flushing a deep pink. She looked at Melanie, her eyes wide with terror, and gave a little wave with her hand, as if she wanted Melanie to stop talking.

"Jane has a new man friend."

"What?" Thomas wheeled around, his eyebrows up. "Tell us, Jane. Who is this?"

"I didn't want to say anything. Melanie!" Jane looked as if she would either stamp her foot or run away.

"Jane met a man at the skating rink. His name is Jared, and he's from Philadelphia."

"Why didn't you mention this, Janie?"

Jane continued to stand there, her feet anchored to the ground, her voice mute, her face red. She didn't speak.

"I think we should invite him over for dinner. Would that be all right with you, Tom?" Melanie winked.

"Certainly. We'd love to meet this gentleman. Does he skate?"

Jane nodded. "It's just that I don't know how he feels about me."

"Well, we'll invite him over and tell him we want to know all about his skating," Thomas said.

"And all about Philadelphia," Melanie said, nodding her head. "It will be fine. We will be nice to him."

"I suppose that's all right," Jane said. "Maybe we should wait a while?"

"No time like the present," Thomas said. Jane got up and headed for the stairs.

"I hope I haven't embarrassed her too much," Melanie said. "I think this is wonderful, that Jane has even spoken about a young man."

"Everyone has good news," Athena said, standing up and heading for the kitchen. "I am suddenly ravenous. I'm going to start dinner."

"I don't think her feet have touched the floor since she got home from the school," Melanie said, blowing a kiss to Athena. "I'm so very happy for her. For both of them really.

I feel like my work here is done." She sighed.

"No, my dear, your work is just beginning. From now on, I will be your only project." Before Melanie could react, Thomas had swept her into his arms and was drawing her into a deep kiss. He had tried this before, and she hadn't allowed it, hadn't wanted to encourage it. But whether it was the festive atmosphere in the house, her worries about what was to come, or just the fact that he was so attractive and full of love, Melanie accepted the kiss. It was deep and searching, his tongue opening her lips, penetrating her mouth with hunger and longing. He brought his hands around and began to explore her body, unbuttoning the dress, caressing her breasts and then moving his hands down over her belly and below. She felt her body respond, every part of her tingling, and she pressed her body closer, feeling him get hard and wanting him. Then she thought of Justin, wished that it was Justin kissing her, wanting her. She pulled her head back and pushed Thomas away. He looked sad as she held him off, her hands on his shoulders. He didn't say a word.

"I didn't even ask you how your day was," she said.

Chapter 22

Justin Hilliard strode out of Penn Station toward the taxi stand. He took a deep breath. New York. It had a distinctive smell, something he didn't think much about until he left here and came back. It was a combination of roasted peanuts and chestnuts, hot dogs, garbage, the subway runoff, bus exhaust.

Boston didn't smell like this at all, and he realized it was notably warmer here, even though a mere two hundred miles separated the two cities. Although he'd grown up in Boston, in the Back Bay, like generations of his family before him, he'd wanted something different. He had bucked tradition and come to New York for college. He realized with some satisfaction that this was now home, and it felt like home. His business in Boston was taken care of, and he was happy to be back here.

There was a huge line for taxis, and as usual Seventh Avenue looked like a parking lot at this hour. He decided it might make more sense to walk the twenty blocks to the hospital. His weekender had wheels, and the streets were a little less icy than they'd been. He walked down Seventh, determined to stop in at the next Starbucks he passed. The coffee on the train was rotten, even on the Acela, and worrying about Melanie, he hadn't had a restful sleep since he'd left New York. He needed the coffee to wake up. *My veins have coffee running through them*, he thought. *I hope the next study I read says that coffee is good for you, not bad for you.*

He drank it black, always. Sugar was evil, and so were all of the artificial sweeteners people swilled down in their coffee, tea, and soft drinks. But caffeine was important. He never drank decaf. Caffeine had gotten him through these three years at the hedge fund where he was a rising star. The ridiculously long hours were fueled by coffee and then, afterward, Scotch, single malt.

In the Starbucks, he caught sight of himself in the plate glass window. *Christ, I need a haircut and a shave*, he thought. It had been a crazy week, what with his having to travel back to Boston to see to the final closing on the sale of his family's ancestral home, and what with Melanie's still being hospitalized, still in a medically induced coma. He hadn't wanted to leave her, but there was no choice, and at least her mother was with her. They'd assured him he wouldn't miss her waking up.

As much as selling the house had been the right thing to do, Justin needed one more look at it—needed to walk into all the rooms, look out the windows and see the "Comm Ave" sights, the magnolia trees getting ready to leaf. He, needed to put closure on all of it.

He'd laughed at the rectangular spot on the wall in the master bedroom where the portrait of his great-great grandparents had hung above the bed for more than a century, the rectangle so much darker than the faded wall around it. He had no idea what he'd do with that portrait, but he hadn't had the heart to get rid of it, so it was now in a storage unit with a whole lot of other family treasures he couldn't find room for in his apartment, including the wonderful Currier and Ives print that had hung on his bedroom wall over his bed for his entire childhood.

He'd sold the house mostly with all the furnishings, and he felt bad only about the beautiful carved rosewood headboard on his bed that had been imported decades before he was born from somewhere exotic.

But there was no one else left but him, and he knew that selling it all was the right thing. He loved his life here, and he had no plans to return as a permanent resident to his hometown.

So he'd gone, reluctantly, leaving Melanie in the hands of the doctors who had saved her after that horrible accident, but now he couldn't wait to get back. She was constantly on his mind, and he ached to see her awake, to tell her that he loved her, that he'd realized he loved her when she'd been nearly killed on the way to work. How often had he sat by her bedside, holding her limp hand, talking to her, whispering that he loved her and hoping she loved him too.

"Hello, Mr. Hilliard!" the security guard at the desk at the hospital entrance greeted him warmly. "I ain't seen you for a few days. On vacation?"

"Sort of, Julio," he said. "I had to go to Boston to take care of some family business. But I'm back now." It was funny that even the security guards recognized him. He'd been almost living in this hospital except when he had to be in the office. Luckily his manager had allowed him to bring his laptop here and work from Melanie's bedside unless he had to be at a meeting on site.

"I got a cousin in Boston," Julio said. "I like it there. Kind of different, you know?"

"Tell me about it." Justin laughed. "I grew up there, and my family lived there for generations. But you have to admit, New York is more exciting."

"Wouldn't know. I lived in Queens my whole life, and I only go to Boston about once a year, for family reunions. Never did much sightseeing. Anyway, welcome home. How's your girl doing up there?"

"Thanks, Julio. I'm hoping she'll be out of the coma soon. I can't wait." Justin gave a quick wave to the guard and then hopped on the elevator. He should probably have stopped at his apartment first, to see if there was any mail or if he needed to catch up on something, but he couldn't wait to see her.

He got off at the surgical ICU floor and almost tripped on his suitcase as he hurried down the corridor.

"Mr. Hilliard, you're back," a nurse walked toward him from the nursing station. She was smiling, and Justin noticed her red, tightly curled hair. It looked even redder than it had when he left.

"Yvonne, hi. Your hair looks different. How is she?"

"Oh, Miss Swift?" She winked at him, and he squirmed a little. "Still have your suitcase? Did you just get back from Boston? Mrs. Swift told me you had business there."

"Yes, I hated having to leave and couldn't wait to get back, you know? I wanted to be here when she wakes up. So I came straight from Penn Station."

"You're really sweet on her, aren't you, Mr. Hilliard? You spend an awful lot of time in her room. She's a lucky girl." The nurse closed her eyes and clicked her tongue. "You might be just in time. She's coming out of it," she said, "They even moved her out of ICU. She's got a private room down on Twelve. Her mother requested it. She's kind of a celebrity around here, Miss Swift is. Her recovery is pretty miraculous. Maybe it's because she knew you were there somehow and that gave her the motivation to wake up. You never know."

Justin was a little annoyed at the nurse. She should have told him right away that Melanie had been moved to the regular floor, but she was playing with him. They had been concerned about brain damage, about deficits that might be caused by the accident, but she was young and strong, and as the days went by, the neurosurgeons were more and more hopeful she would regain all her faculties. They all congratulated him on getting her to the hospital as soon as he could after the accident, although he realized the only thing he'd done was dial nine-one-one.

Even though he hadn't been able to communicate with her, he had the strong feeling she could hear him, so he talked to her constantly, told her he was sorry he hadn't admitted his feelings to her before she almost died.

"So, she's on Twelve B, room 1206."

He smiled at her, but she had already turned her back. So much the better. He headed back to the elevator, pulling his weekender behind him, and pressed twelve.

When he pushed open the door to her room, Melanie's mother was sitting in a chair, reading a book. "Mrs. Swift, how is she?"

"Oh, Justin. I'm so glad you're back. Melanie is coming out of the coma. You have been so dedicated to her these weeks, I knew you'd want to see her as soon as she was conscious. I missed you while you were away. I think I would have gone crazy if I hadn't had you to talk to when she was so critical."

Justin felt himself blush. "I know," he said, "We've been holding each other up through this, haven't we?" He wondered how much Mrs. Swift knew about him, whether Melanie had ever mentioned him to her mother. He tried not to worry that Melanie might not feel about him the way he felt about her.

"We certainly have, and I'm grateful," she said.

"I'm happy to be back, Mrs. Swift. Very happy." He approached the bed, looked into Melanie's face, which he thought was the most beautiful face he had ever seen. The scar along her hairline where they had removed the stitches was becoming less visible already. He didn't care if she had a deep red scar. To him, she would be beautiful no matter what. "Hello, Melanie," he whispered, "It's Justin." He picked up her hand, the one without the IV, and leaned down to kiss it. Her hand was warmer now, since they had raised her to normal body temperature, and the warmth of her skin shot feelings of excitement through his entire body. He leaned down over her and brushed her hair back gently. The nurses must have given her a sponge bath, because she smelled like fragrant soap.

He breathed in the smell and tried to hold it in his mind.

He wanted to leave his hand on hers, but with her mother looking on, he didn't feel he should.

Melanie's eyelids fluttered. She said something, but it was so soft that Justin couldn't hear her.

"Melanie?" he said. "I'm here. How are you feeling?" Stupid words, he thought as soon as they were out of his mouth, but he couldn't think of anything else to say.

"I can't tell you how relieved I am. I was so worried." Melanie's mother walked over and smiled at him, reached out her hand to grab his, and put her other hand on top. "I'm grateful to you for standing by her."

Melanie's eyes opened for a moment and then closed again. Justin's heart was beating so fast, he could almost hear it. "Mel?"

"Tom?" Her voice was so faint, Justin couldn't really tell what she had said. He looked at Mrs. Swift, raising his eyebrows in a question.

"I think she said 'Tom,'" Mrs. Swift said, and then she shrugged.

"Who's Tom?" Justin felt as though he'd been stabbed through the heart.

"I have no idea, none. Never heard her say that name before."

"Melanie, it's Justin. I'm here." He gave her hand a little squeeze, and she squeezed back. "Can you hear me?"

Melanie opened her eyes, blinking as though it was a terrible effort to open them. She squinted, a look of pain flashing over her face.

"Mrs. Swift, perhaps you could shut off the light in here? I think she has to get used to the bright light." Justin bent even closer to Melanie. Melanie's mother turned off the light, and Melanie tried to open her eyes again.

"Justin?" This time Melanie tried to say it louder, enunciating each syllable carefully. "Is that you?"

Justin almost burst out in laughter, restraining himself at the last minute. "It's me, Melanie. It's me. I love you." He said it softly, but it was out. He couldn't help himself. He had to tell her, had to let her know how he felt.

Her eyes fluttered closed again, but Justin saw the tears forming in the corners, and then, without any noise, Melanie was crying, tears streaming down her face. Justin grabbed a tissue from the bedside table and blotted them away, brushing her skin lightly with his fingers. He restrained an urge to reach down and take her in his arms, hold her tight. "You don't have to cry, sweetheart. I'm here for you. Are you in pain?"

But it would be a while before Melanie could explain herself. Her last memory, before waking up here in this hospital room, had been standing in Thomas's house and letting him kiss her, letting him explore her body with his hands, for the first time. She had given in, but then, when things became more intense, she had thought of Justin and pushed Thomas away. She tried to convince herself that she wasn't dreaming, that Justin was here with her, holding her hand and telling her he loved her.

"What year is it?" Melanie's voice was a little stronger.

Justin laughed a little bit. "It's still 2016, love. You haven't been out that long."

Melanie sighed. But what about the other family she had just been with? A minute ago? What about Thomas and Jane and Athena and the Gardners? What about Archie and the horse and carriage? She continued to cry. This was all too hard to understand. Justin continued to dab her eyes and touch her face. He leaned down and kissed her forehead. His kiss made her melt. Then she was exhausted, and she closed her eyes and drifted off to sleep, as much as she wanted to be awake and to tell Justin everything about what had happened to her. Her breathing became soft and regular.

"You don't think she's slipped back into the coma?" Melanie's mother looked alarmed.

"I think she's just gone to sleep," Justin said. She seems very peaceful. This must be so exhausting for her. I can't even imagine."

Several moments later the doctor came into the room.

"Is she all right, Doctor? She was talking a little, but then she just went to sleep."

"Perfectly normal," Dr. Morgan said. "She will need a lot of rest. I know it seems odd, when she's been unconscious for all these weeks, but her body has been working overtime to heal. You'll just have to bear with her."

"I'll wait an eternity for her if I have to," Justin said.

"Nice to see you back here," the doctor said. "Take care of that house business?"

"Yes, all taken care of. I don't have to worry about it anymore."

"I hope you got a bundle for it?"

"Probably not enough to live the way I'd like to in Manhattan, but possibly enough for a one bedroom in Washington Heights." The two men laughed.

"All right then, I'm going to have to wake her and do an examination, but she will be able to sleep after that. She's doing very well. She is our miracle patient."

"Funny to hear a doctor talking that way," Justin said.

The doctor shrugged. "Sometimes the science of medicine can't answer all the questions, despite the fact that we have so much wonderful technology," he said. "Having said that, the latest CT scan looks very good. Swelling's almost completely gone. I'm optimistic she won't have any permanent deficits."

"Thank goodness."

"Wonderful." Mrs. Swift had a broad smile. "What happens next?"

"We will work with her to make sure she can talk, that she has intact memory—you know, all the neurological testing. If everything is as we expect, we'll start physical therapy here. Depending on how she does, we'll discharge her either to a rehab facility or home with some home therapy. That depends on what PT recommends. For now—" He directed his gaze at Mrs. Swift, "My strong suggestion is that you to go home and get some rest. I understand you've been here all day, every day."

Melanie's mother looked concerned, her forehead raised in horizontal grooves. "Don't you think she'll need me to be here?"

"I think she's basically out of the woods, so maybe this would be a good time for you to take care of yourself. We'll take very good care of her here. Feel free to come back tomorrow."

"Maybe that's a good idea, Doctor. I've been neglecting things at home, and now that Justin is back, I won't feel terrible leaving her for a little while."

"Hopefully, there will be no complications. If not, there's nothing to keep her from being discharged soon. I'm going to wake her and talk to her now, check her reflexes, and we'll go from there."

She sighed. "All right, I'll go. Justin, are you all right to stay with her?"

"Absolutely," Justin said, "I'm sticking around. I've been away too long."

"Do you promise to let me know as soon as there's any news?"

"Of course," Justin said. "And feel free to call at any time if you want to. I'm going to sleep in that chair."

The mother stood up and gathered her things. She walked to the bed, leaned down and kissed Melanie on the forehead.

"Mr. Hilliard, would you please step outside the room while I examine her?"

Justin made a face, but he did what the doctor asked, following Melanie's mother outside.

"Please let me know when I can come back into her room," he said to the doctor as he went out into the hallway, where he began to pace back and forth. "I don't want to be apart from her anymore."

The examination took about twenty minutes, but to Justin it felt like hours. "All done," Dr. Morgan said, leaving

Melanie's room and grabbing Justin's hand. "It's looking very good. Don't tire her out too much, all right? She's trying to talk, but I don't want her to set her recovery back. There's time for everything."

Justin rushed back into the room. "Yes, Doctor," he called over his shoulder, but he couldn't contain his excitement. He placed his finger into Melanie's palm, and he felt a weak squeeze. The excitement that coursed through his body was electric. "Can you squeeze a little harder?" She did as he asked. "Can you open your eyes, Melanie? Can you look at me? It's Justin."

Melanie's eyes fluttered, as if she was trying. She made a little sound, like a moan, as if it was very hard to open her eyes. She still seemed somewhat dazed, but Justin hoped she would fight it and come back to him soon. After he coaxed her several times, Melanie half opened her eyes. The sudden harsh light made her wince, and Justin saw that she was having trouble focusing. He stood up and turned out the fluorescent ceiling light that the doctor had turned back on. She was trying to speak.

"What are you saying Melanie? Can you say it a little louder?"

"Where am I?" she said. Her voice was weak.

"You've been through quite a tough time," he said, stroking her arm. "You're still in the hospital, but you're getting better. Much better."

"Thomas?" Justin thought he heard her say Thomas again, and he questioned who that might be. "Thomas?" She said it again.

"Can you see me?" He leaned down closer to her face. "You may not be able to see things clearly yet. Your eyes will have to adjust to the light. You've been asleep for weeks."

Melanie continued to try to talk. At first, she had thought this was Thomas, leaning over her bed. There was something about his voice. It was so familiar, but she couldn't get his face into focus. But this man said he was Justin, and she had been filled with a rush of happiness. She wondered whether Justin could explain what was going on. She wondered where Thomas was.

Justin got up and filled a small cup with water. "Here, do you want a little water? Your mouth must be very dry." He tipped the cup slightly over her lips, but she didn't open her mouth and take it, and water dribbled over her mouth and chin. Justin leaned over and wiped her face with a soft cloth. He wanted to be the first one she saw, the only one. He couldn't keep his hands off her.

"Justin." Finally, she said his name. Then she started to cry again, and she opened her mouth as if she would sob, but only a choked sound came out. Tears streamed from her eyes, which she was opening wider now. Her mouth was slightly open, and she gripped his finger now with the hand that didn't have an IV attached. "Justin."

"Yes, I'm here. I won't leave you. Ever. Can you speak to me?"

Melanie shook her head and tried to lean back onto the pillows, but a nurse had plumped them up, so she was half lying and half sitting. Her arm was uncomfortable, her body ached from being in the bed, her head hurt, and she felt as if her mouth was glued together. She thought she might be dreaming. Justin approached with a cotton swab that he had dipped into the ice water on her bed table.

"If you open your mouth and suck on this, it might be easier to talk," he said. "Your mouth is just dry." Melanie did as he asked. "Better?" He smoothed the hair that was falling over her eyes. She let him do it. His touch was light and gentle. Thomas smoothed her hair like that all the time. The tears were still falling down both sides of her face.

"I thought you were Thomas," she said. "Where is he?" The words were clearer now, as if the ice water had helped. "I thought you were—"

"I'm not sure who Thomas is," Justin said. He sat on the edge of her bed, his brow furrowed. "Would you be more comfortable if they removed this?" He pointed to the board on her arm. Nothing was dripping into the IV, and now that she was back, breathing on her own, he surmised she wouldn't need it anymore. She nodded. "It looks very uncomfortable, I know. I'll call one of the nurses." He picked up the call button and pressed it. "Now, can you tell me who Thomas is?"

"He's—" Melanie said, her voice soft and mournful. "I thought you were—" she said again. Now that she could see better, she would have sworn she was looking at Thomas's face. The eyes, the nose, the mouth, they were all identical. There were some differences. The hair color maybe. Other than that, they looked alike, they sounded alike, but this was not Thomas. He said he was Justin, and she tried to understand what was going on.

"Does he live around here?"

"No. He lives in Boston. Please," she said, a shudder in her still-weak voice, "Am I really back? Is it you?" It took all her strength to get the words out.

"Do you know where you are?"

"Hospital?"

"Yes. Do you know where the hospital is?"

Melanie was conscious enough to know that this was not Boston General, and everything here was modern—the machines, the bed, the television, the electric doors. "Boston?"

"No, this is New York, where we live."

She didn't respond.

"You were in a terrible accident. You were hit by a truck, and you had a traumatic brain injury and some other injuries as well. They've been keeping you unconscious for quite some time so that your body could heal. But you'll be all right now, I'm sure of it. Melanie, I love you."

"What year is this?" She had a vague memory that someone had told her it was 2016, but she didn't trust herself. She knew there had been an accident, but she still remembered nothing after falling on the icy sidewalk. After that, her only memories were of waking up in Boston on a bench, and everything that happened afterwards. Adjusting to the light, she opened her eyes as wide as she could, and stared directly at him, taking in all the planes of his face. Perhaps this *was* real.

"Not sure? Don't worry. It will come back. It's 2016, baby. You haven't been out that long."

A gray-haired nurse came bustling in and pushed Justin away from the bed. Justin pointed to the IV. "Do you think you could remove that? It's not doing anything for her, and it's uncomfortable."

The nurse raised her eyebrows, watched Justin with the cotton swab still in his hand. "Do you want me to get rid of that for you, dear?" She smiled at Melanie and then reached over and plucked the swab out of Justin's hand, dropping it into the wastebasket beside the bed. "I don't see why not." The nurse went about her business. "There, dear," she said. "That should feel a little better. You're going to be just fine now. Is that it, Mr. Hilliard?"

"Yes, I think we're fine. Thank you."

The nurse shrugged. "All right. If you need anything else—"

"Thank you, we're fine."

Melanie had closed her eyes, but she felt the tears welling up again under her eyelids. She was almost positive this was not Boston General, and she thought of Thomas and their last meeting, remembered pushing him away because she couldn't get Justin out of her mind. And Justin was here, and he reminded her so much of Thomas. It was all too much to take in.

"Can you tell me what year it is?" he said again.

Melanie closed her eyes, shook her head no. "Is it 2016?"

"Right! Same year."

"Same year as what?" Her words were muffled by the pillow.

"I didn't catch that. What did you say?"

Melanie was afraid to hope. The entire time she'd been in Boston, she could think only of Justin. But now that she was with him, she thought of Thomas and how he must feel with her gone.

"I'm so glad you're back with us. You can't believe how I missed you! It's all going to be fine now."

Melanie hoped it would be fine. All of her senses seemed heightened. The beeping of the machines, the squeaking of the door, the scraping of his shoes on the polished floor gave her exquisite pain. Justin reached over to pat her shoulder, and she gripped his arm with her hand, which felt much better without the board attached. Talking was easier, now that her mouth wasn't so dry. "I thought about you the whole time," she said.

"Seriously? You were thinking about me? Those are the best words I've ever heard," he said, breaking into a smile. "I thought you were dead to the world...well, in a manner of speaking."

Melanie was tired of talking. She nodded her head, but she felt her eyes closing again. "I never stopped. Justin, my head still hurts."

"Do you want to nap a little more? Should I ask the doctor if you can have some more pain medication?"

But she had drifted back into a restful sleep. He sat on the edge of her bed, holding her hand, leaning down to kiss her cheek, feeling as if he had been given the greatest gift in the world. Justin gazed at her face, which was relaxed now as she slept, without any indication that she had ever been in pain. She was the most beautiful woman he had ever seen. He hated himself for not realizing he had loved her before, but he wanted to know who Thomas was. He couldn't understand how she could have been thinking about him, but that made him so happy, he decided not to worry about it.

Chapter 23

Justin didn't sleep well. Not only was the chair uncomfortable, but he got up and checked on Melanie every time he was awakened by nurses' footsteps or other hospital sounds.

As happy as he was that she would be all right, he was impatient for her to get well enough to talk to him. She had responded to him, but he was confused about the "Thomas" she continued to ask for. He had dozed off when the doctor and a group of residents walked into the room during rounds.

"Good morning."

Justin jumped up. The light was just starting to seep in through the blinds. He looked at his watch. Through bleary eyes he thought it said six-thirty. "Good morning, Doctor."

The doctor nodded and then approached Melanie's bed. "Miss Swift? Good morning. How are you feeling? Mr. Hilliard, would you mind leaving the room for a few minutes? We need to examine the patient."

Justin didn't want to leave, but he thought it might be a good time to splash some water on his face and see if he could find some strong coffee. He tiptoed out of the room, even though the doctor was waking Melanie.

He found the coffee he was looking for, although it wasn't very good, and tried to eat a muffin, but it sat in his stomach like a rock, so he threw out half of it and then returned to Melanie's room.

The doctors were just leaving. Justin met Dr. Morgan at her door. "How is she, Doctor?"

"She is doing well physically, but there are some issues."

"What issues?"

"She's coming along well, seems to be focusing better, but she's very emotional, can't stop crying, and continues to ask about Thomas."

"Do we know who that is?"

"Not sure. Perhaps you could talk to her about it some more? She seems to trust you."

"I'll try, Doctor."

"After such a severe brain injury, the emotion doesn't surprise me, but the sooner we can help her work through it, the better for her."

"I'm happy to do whatever I can."

"And if it continues, I'd suggest a psych consult."

"Whatever you think is best."

"I think you should keep her mother informed as well."

"Certainly, Doctor. I'll call her this morning."

"I'll order the psych consult right away." The doctor and his entourage went down the hall to the next room.

Justin opened Melanie's door and looked in. He didn't want to upset her any more than she already was, but he was curious to find out who this Thomas character was. He wasn't sure whether he was disappointed or relieved that she had fallen back asleep. He sat down in the chair and called her mother.

"Hello?"

"Oh, Mrs. Swift, this is Justin."

"Is everything all right?" Her voice was tense.

"Yes, yes. Everything's fine."

"That's a relief. I thought I'd come in this afternoon, after I take care of some things here."

"Melanie keeps talking about someone named Thomas?"

"Yes, I know."

"Do you know where we can reach him? The doctors think it might be important to help with her recovery."

"Well, that's the thing. I have no idea who he is. I've never heard her talk about anyone named Thomas, either a boyfriend or a friend. I'm afraid I can't help you with this one."

"She seems to be very upset about it, and Dr. Morgan suggested a psych consult, given the severity of her injuries?" He paused, waiting for Melanie's mother to react. She remained silent. "Meantime, if you think of anything, would you please let me know right away?"

"I certainly will. I'm just as confused as you are. And if a psych consult can help her, it's fine with me."

Justin said good-bye and opened his laptop. He tried to do some work, but he couldn't concentrate, spent some time playing "Angry Birds" on his phone, answered a couple of emails that had accumulated. But his mind was consumed with Melanie, and he was determined to get to the bottom of her agitation. He wasn't sure how much time passed.

"Excuse me, I have to take her vital signs." Justin hadn't noticed the nurse walk into the room. He moved his chair away from the bed.

"Oh, sorry. I'm thinking about something, kind of off in my own world."

"Sorry, honey, I have to wake you up for a little while."
Melanie stirred and opened her eyes. "Justin?"

"I'm here, Mel. Do you need something."

"This is New York?"

"Last time I checked." He was heartened that her voice sounded stronger this morning. Perhaps they would be able to talk.

"All right, I'm done here." The nurse packed up her equipment and put it back on the cart she had wheeled into the room. "She's doing great, Mr. Hilliard. Maybe you should go home and get some shuteye? You've been here a long time, you must be tired. It couldn't be comfortable sleeping on that chair."

Justin had no desire to leave now, especially since Melanie seemed more alert than she had before. The nurse left, and Justin sat on the edge of Melanie's bed. "Are you comfortable in that position, honey?" Melanie was almost flat on the bed.

"Could you move the bed up so I can sit up and look at you?"

Justin felt a surge of optimism course through his body. He pressed the button, and the bed rose slowly. "Is that better?" He reached over and brushed the hair off her face. She took his hand and held it.

"Yes. Thank you. Is it really you?"

"In the flesh!" He kissed her hand and squeezed it.

"I need something."

"Anything. Your wish is my demand."

Melanie giggled a little. "I need to talk to you. It's important."

"You can tell me anything. Melanie, do you understand how wonderful it is to see you like this? Awake? Talking? Yourself! You're back."

Melanie's expression darkened, vertical lines rising above the bridge of her nose. "I'm not sure you'll think I'm myself when I tell you what I have to."

"Should I worry?"

"Just...the only thing..." She hesitated.

"What?"

"Just try to believe me. Do you promise?"

"I love you. Of course I'll believe you."

"It makes me very happy when you say you love me, Justin. I didn't know I felt this way about you before." She started crying again.

"Shhh, honey, you don't have to talk about it now if it's too painful. Yes, I love you, and I didn't realize it either, until I almost lost you."

"But..."

"But?"

"But the whole time Thomas loved me, I was aching for

you, wishing I had told you how I felt before—" She looked down, wouldn't catch his eye.

"I don't know what you're talking about, Melanie. And who is Thomas? You have repeated his name, but your mother doesn't know, and neither do I. I don't know whether I need to be jealous." He drew his hands to his mouth, trying to hide the frustration.

"Hello? Miss Swift? I am Ellen Romano."

The tall, middle-aged woman walked into the room. Justin looked at her. She was dressed in a gray pantsuit with a colorful scarf around her neck, her dark hair pulled back into a ponytail with a blue scrunchie securing it in back. She was attractive, but Justin thought she seemed a bit over-solicitous. He couldn't figure out what she was feeling. She smiled at Melanie, ignored him. She reached out to Melanie and touched her shoulder.

"I'm a psychologist here in the hospital," she said. "Your Dr. Morgan asked that I stop in and talk with you a bit." Ellen turned to Justin, who hadn't moved, and looked him up and down. "And you?"

"Justin. Justin Hilliard."

Ellen looked at Melanie. "This is your…" She paused.

"My friend," Melanie said.

"Ah, Mr. Hilliard, would you mind stepping out for about a half hour? I'd like to talk with Melanie about her ordeal. She's been through a great deal."

Melanie looked worried, her eyes open wide and her mouth open slightly. "Ms. Romano, would you mind if Justin stayed while we talk? I feel very safe with him."

"If you insist," Ellen said, "But it's irregular. Usually I like to have a private conversation with my patient." She glanced over her head at Justin, who was hoping he didn't have to go.

"I would prefer it," Melanie said. "There's nothing I have to say that I don't want him to hear, and I feel more comfortable with him here. He makes me feel safe."

"If you'd like, I'll take that chair in the corner," Justin said, relinquishing his bedside perch to the doctor. "Please, Dr. Romano, feel free to sit close to Melanie. Forget I'm here."

She took a spiral-bound notebook and a pen from her bag and sat down. "Miss Swift—may I call you Melanie?" Melanie nodded. "You may call me Ellen." Melanie nodded again. "According to Dr. Morgan, you have been having some episodes of emotional despair. Is that true? And if so, do you want to talk about it?"

Melanie didn't answer for a moment, but as if on cue, tears started forming in her eyes. Ellen brought out a tissue and handed it to Melanie, who took it but didn't use it. "I'm a little confused," she said, choking on the words. Justin restrained himself from jumping up and coming to her rescue, taking her in his arms. He bit his lip. He realized this woman was there to help, and Melanie needed the help.

"That's understandable," Ellen said. "What is confusing you?"

"I know I'm in New York, and this is 2016."

"Yes," Ellen said. "That's good!" She smiled.

"But I have been in—" She looked over at Justin, a pleading look he thought. He wanted to protect her from the hurt. He stayed on the chair, grabbing the arms as if that would keep him sitting there. "Boston."

"Boston?"

"Yes."

"When were you in Boston?"

"I just came from there. I'm not sure how I got back here. Actually, I'm not sure how I got there in the first place."

Ellen was writing fast in her book, glancing up every few seconds at Melanie, her brow furrowed. "Now I'm confused, Melanie. When do you think you were in Boston?"

"No, I *was* in Boston," she said. "Just before I got here."

"You mean before your accident?"

"No, after the accident. I was in the hospital there, and I was taken in by a family to recuperate."

Ellen drew in her breath, making an audible sound. Then she regained her composure. "I understand you've been through a major traumatic brain injury, Melanie, but I believe Dr. Morgan said you've been right here the entire time."

"No!" Melanie's frustration was making her tears more prominent. "I know where I was, and I was in Boston."

"Is there someone there we might call?" Ellen couldn't mask the sarcasm in her voice, despite her best efforts, and Melanie cried some more.

"No."

"All right, then. I think you've had enough for now. I will be back, however. Mr. Hilliard, would you please see if you can calm her down?" She stood up and patted Melanie on the hand. "I didn't mean to upset you, Melanie. You need some more time to get stronger, and I will be back." She turned her back on Melanie and walked toward the door, raising her eyebrows at Justin as she passed him. Then she left and closed the door behind her.

෧෨෧

In the hallway, Ellen ducked into a small office and called Dr. Morgan. "Do you have a few moments?" She paused. "All right, I'll be right up." The elevator was slow, so she hurried up two flights of stairs and rushed into his office.

"That was fast, Ellen. What's up?"

"Well, originally, from the patient's history, I thought maybe it was PTSD, or some sort of depressed state caused by the brain injury. You know, recommended treatment talk therapy, antidepressants, lots of patience, physical healing along with the emotional healing." She paused, waiting for Dr. Morgan's response. He nodded.

"But in the fifteen minutes it took me to get her talking, I'm just not sure what it is. Whatever, it is serious and needs all of us to sit down and figure out next steps."

"Next steps?"

"Medication? Possible admission to a psych unit?"

"Whew." Morgan blew a low whistle through his teeth. "I am sorry to hear that. What did you get from her?"

"Well, the short story is that Miss Swift claims she was in Boston, living with a family who took her in to recuperate."

"Really? When?"

"Well, that's the issue. She claims she was there after she had the accident. She's obviously delusional. I tried to steer her away from that notion, but she just became almost hysterical, and insisted she had been in Boston."

"I've never seen a patient do that before."

"Exactly. I suppose it makes sense to wait a little while longer and see if these delusions dissipate."

"Yes, but if they don't, and if they continue to make her this emotional, I might have to recommend inpatient care in a psychiatric unit."

He shrugged, raised his eyebrows and rubbed his eyes.

"We know for a fact that she lives in New York, correct?"

"That's my understanding."

"And we know that she's been here in the hospital since her accident, correct?"

"Yes."

"And she hasn't gone anywhere?"

"No, she was in a medically induced coma. She couldn't go anywhere. She was unconscious. She hasn't left that bed since February eighth."

"Well, according to her, she has been living in Boston. I didn't see any signs of auditory or visual hallucinations, at least not at the moment. She knows she's here now, knows what the date is, all of that. Has she been on any medication that might cause this type of delusional thinking?"

"No, we try not to use any type of sedatives for people with this kind of brain injury."

"To your knowledge, is there any history of mental illness in her or her family?"

"Not to my knowledge, but you should take a history from the mother."

"So, what would you like me to do? We can start medicating her, at least until she calms down. Perhaps an anti-anxietal? If the depression continues, an anti-depressant? I'm worried that her mental state is going to affect the physical healing process."

"I'd like to talk to her before we start any medication course, all right? And I'd like to discuss it with her friend, Mr. Hilliard, and her mother. They have been providing twenty-four-seven bedside vigil." He wasn't keen on dulling her newly revived consciousness with psychotropic drugs.

"Whatever you'd like to do, doctor, but my advice is don't wait too long. I'm very concerned about her mental state."

"Thank you, Dr. Romano. I will talk with Melanie and get back to you."

"Please, as soon as possible." She stood up and backed out to the door. "This poor girl's been through enough."

Chapter 24

Melanie was relieved. She didn't want to talk to the psychologist anymore. She was sitting up in bed, grateful not to be encumbered by the IV board on her arm. She rubbed her arm. It hurt, and she wished she could get rid of the pain. It interfered with her trying to relax, and she was also worrying about how to tell Justin about her time in Boston.

Harsh fluorescent lights shimmered from the ceiling, and the television stared down at her from its mount at the top of the wall. Something was playing on the screen, but the sound had been turned off. She tried not to look at it. Television. She'd been prepared never to look at one again. For the first time, she noticed that someone had placed a small radio on the table beside her bed, and soft classical music was playing; maybe Mozart? It was a piano concerto, and it was pretty. She let herself listen for a moment. Thomas loved Mozart. They had gone to hear the Boston Symphony play, and she had loved listening to that music with him.

"Sweetie, are you all right?" Justin was at her bedside again, and she grasped his hand, entwining her fingers through his. Every time he touched her, she felt her body responding with an electricity she loved. She wanted to jump into his arms.

"There's something I have to tell you, and you have to promise you won't think I'm crazy. Because I am not crazy." She sighed, felt her hands shaking a little. This reminded her of the scene in Boston General when she arrived there the first time.

"What's this thing about Boston?"

"I know, that's what it's about. Do you promise?" She felt like a little kid, making her "best friend" promise not to tell a secret. "It's important. I don't want them to send me to a mental hospital."

"I promise I won't let anyone send you to any mental hospital. Just tell me everything." He leaned over and kissed her softly on the lips. "I've got your back, babe."

Melanie leaned in for another kiss, and Justin kissed her again, this time somewhat more hungrily. Neither of them wanted to stop, but she pushed him lightly and he moved back. "I have to tell you this," she said. "I remember being hit hard. My face was in the street. I didn't know what hit me."

"Yes. It was awful. It was a pickup truck that came around the corner too fast. I was scared to death. If you had—no, I don't want to think about that."

"I know. I don't specifically remember anything that happened after I felt the impact, but I do remember being on the ambulance, and I could hear everything that was being said. But I couldn't respond, couldn't move at all."

"You could hear?"

"Yes, and I knew you were there with me, because I recognized your voice. I was wishing I could tell you that I wanted to be more than your friend. And I was frustrated I'd never told you before. I didn't know whether I'd ever be able to tell you. I think I was crying."

"Oh, Melanie, I felt the same way. I've never been so

frustrated in my life, but then and there I knew I'd never leave you."

"Then they must have anesthetized me when they took me in for tests, because everything went black. I didn't hear anything anymore. And then..."

"Then?"

"Then, somehow, I was sitting on a bench in my hospital clothes, nothing else, and it was freezing, and I thought I'd freeze to death. And I was in Boston."

Justin sucked in his breath, his hand over his mouth, his eyes wide.

"Really. I knew it, because I saw Trinity Church from the bench." She looked up at him through half-slit eyes, to try to see if he really did think she was a lunatic. His face had gone back to normal, as if he wanted to show no emotion.

"How could that be, Mel?" he said. "It just doesn't make any sense."

"I know, but that's not all. Not only was I in Boston, but it was more than a century ago. I found out later that it was 1886."

Justin stifled a laugh. Part of him thought she must be joking, but he knew she wasn't, and she started to cry again. "No, please don't cry," he said, "I'm with you. Tell me more."

"I was rescued by a doctor who happened to be on his way home from work. He got an ambulance—a horse-drawn ambulance—and took me to the hospital. After I was released, he let me move in with him, in his big house." She realized she was talking very fast, as if her fast talking would make her more believable. Justin's mouth was open, and his eyes were wide now.

She waited to hear whether he would respond, but he did not. She continued.

"He had two sisters who needed guidance, and I helped

them. But the thing was, he fell in love with me, and he wanted me to marry him."

"Oh." Now Justin had a look of pain on his face, and she pulled his hand to her mouth and kissed it.

"But I said no, that you were here, in 2016, and you were the one I was in love with." Justin relaxed a little. "But Justin, I swear he looked just like you, he really did. He reminded me of you. He even sounded like you. He kept pleading with me, saying I might never see you again, that you weren't even born yet."

"Sweetie, you realize this does sound completely wacky?"

"Just as wacky as they thought I was when I said I had traveled there from 2016. Justin, I met people there, famous people."

"What? Who?"

"The sad part is that just before I got back here, I thought I might give in and see if I might fall in love with Thomas. But I could only think of you. Now I'm with you, and I'm worried about what happened to Thomas." She felt her body lurch a little. "It's true, and I'm not crazy, but I am confused."

"It's going to take some time for me to get my head around this," Justin said.

"So, you don't believe me, huh?" Melanie tried to make light of it, but she felt herself losing composure again. "It really happened, Justin."

Before he could answer, there was a knock at the door. "Hello, Miss Swift? I'm Fran, your physical therapist. I'd like to work with you for a few minutes. Is that all right? You need to get up and start exercising your muscles, and I need to evaluate any physical deficits the accident and the immobility might have caused."

"I'm tired," Melanie said, looking to Justin for support.

"Another reason why you need to get up and start moving. The quicker you do, the sooner you'll feel like yourself."

Fran was dressed in gym shorts and sneakers, and she was holding a large green balance ball.

"Maybe it's a good idea, honey. Maybe some exercise will help clear your mind." He reached around and hugged her.

"My mind is clear," Melanie said, her words clipped with annoyance.

"Yup, your friend here is right," Fran said. "Come on, I'll help you." She reached her free hand out to Melanie, who sighed and let herself be pulled up. "Maybe you'd like to go and get a cup of coffee or something, sir? It'll be about a half hour."

"Does he have to go?" Melanie was sitting on the edge of the bed, her head hanging and her hand across her fore-head.

"I think it's better. He'll be back soon."

Justin gave a pleading look to Melanie. "Just a half hour, okay? I'll be in the cafeteria. I will come back in exactly thirty minutes. I promise." He backed out the door, threw her a kiss, but she didn't notice.

On line to pay for his coffee, Justin saw Dr. Morgan. "Good morning, Doctor."

"Good morning, Mr. Hilliard. How's our patient?"

"She's with the physical therapist. She wasn't keen on it, though. I think she's very tired."

"That's understandable. Any more information from her?"

Justin sighed. "Well, she told me that she was living with a family in Boston, in 1886."

The doctor tipped his head to the side, put his index fin-ger to the side of his nose. "I'm not sure how to respond to that." The two men stood, each with a cup of coffee, staring at each other. "I'm glad I requested a psych consult."

"She insists she's not delusional, that this actually hap-pened. She doesn't seem mentally ill to me."

"But, Mr. Hilliard, you of all people know she never left this hospital."

Justin shrugged. "I don't know how to explain it."

"What else did she say?"

"That somehow she got there, but she didn't know how, and she was rescued by someone named Thomas, who let her move in with him." Justin left out the details about Thomas's falling in love with Melanie and trying to court her. "I tried not to act shocked, Doctor, but it was weird. It's obvious she believes what she says, because there was no hint of any type of lying. Dr. Romano said she didn't think there were any hallucinations. You can just tell when some-one feels they are telling the truth. Heaven knows, she was lucid and spoke intelligently about everything, and I just didn't get any kind of psychotic vibe from her, like she was hearing voices or anything. She was being straight, and that is the strangest part."

"Well, thank you for the report," Dr. Morgan said. "I ap-preciate it. We'll just have to see what the psychologist thinks. I guess I'd say, just humor her for now. No sense in upsetting her more than she already is. We don't want to impede her recuperation."

"I'm glad you feel that way."

"Perhaps she'll tell you more. Did she give you any de-tails about anything else?"

"No, she was pretty vague about it."

"Wait-and-see attitude, Mr. Hilliard." The doctor clapped Justin on the back and, with a wave, he was gone.

As he promised, Justin returned to Melanie's room, try-ing to formulate a plan about what he was going to say to her. But his thoughts were even more jumbled when he got there.

"Hi Melanie," he said.

She was sitting up in bed, her eyes swollen from all the crying. He wanted to kiss her. He stood at the foot of the bed, thinking he should restrain himself.

"Hello, Justin."

"Did you have a good session with Fran?"

"I like her," she said. "She was only here about twenty minutes. She told me that I won't need much therapy."

"You're in very good shape," he said. "That's great."

"I know. Fran couldn't believe it. I didn't tell her what I told you, though. I'm tired of having people look at me like I'm off my rocker."

"Do you feel like talking any more about Boston to me? About Thomas?" Justin sat down on the edge of the bed. He wanted to get to the bottom of it, to help Melanie plead her case for sanity.

"He's a doctor."

"Right, you said he was a doctor at the hospital?"

"Yes, a doctor." Then she looked startled, as if she had forgotten something. "I meant to ask Fran, but I'm wondering if you could do me a favor?"

"Absolutely. Anything."

"When I got out of bed to work with Fran, I dropped something out of the pocket of these hospital pants onto the floor. I didn't realize it until afterward. Would you mind reaching under the bed and getting it for me?"

"No, of course not." He knelt down and felt around under the bed. "Is this it?" He held his arm up to her.

"Yes, that's it," she said.

Justin brought the object, a gold pocket watch, up and handed it to her. "That's a beautiful pocket watch," he said. "It looks very old."

"Yes, Thomas gave it to me. He had proposed to me, and I turned him down—I couldn't stop thinking about you. Thomas was a wonderful man, but he wasn't you." Justin leaned over and kissed her on the cheek. "So he told me he wanted to keep this watch for him, until I decided to marry him, and then he'd exchange it for a ring. It's a family heirloom."

"May I see it?"

She handed it to him, and he pressed the little latch and looked inside at the inscription: *Edward Thornwell, MD, May, 1853.*

Justin reeled, looked as if he might faint. He put his hand on the wall behind the bed for support. "*Where* did you get this?" he said, grasping the metal railing at the side of her bed as he tried to avoid losing his balance. The room was spinning, so he reached for the chair at the side of the bed.

"Are you all right? I told you, Tom gave it to me."

"Where did you get that?" he said again, grasping the watch, the color draining from his face and from his fingers.

"Justin, you're scaring me."

"Tom who?" Justin's voice was strident, almost angry.

"Thomas Thornwell." She started to cry again.

Justin stood up and glared at Melanie. She held her arm up across her face, as if she were afraid he might strike her.

"That can't be." His voice now softer, breaking, "It can't be."

"I told you—" Melanie stopped talking. She reached for the watch, but Justin gripped it as if he'd never let go. "Why are you so angry? Did I do something wrong?" she asked.

"Thomas—Thornwell," he said, articulating the first and last name carefully, leaving long spaces between each one, "Dr. Thomas Thornwell was my great grandfather."

The room became completely silent. Melanie looked straight into Justin's eyes, and he looked back at her with a look she couldn't interpret, but the fear had disappeared. Now she knew why this man reminded her so much of Tom.

"Oh my God," she said. And again, "Oh my God." She put her hand up to her mouth.

Justin reached the hand with the watch to Melanie, and she tried to take it from him, but he didn't let go, and their hands touched, the watch held between them. Melanie felt a current of electricity shoot through her body.

"The disappearance of that watch has been a mystery in our family for decades. For as long as I can remember," he said. "Originally it was my great-great grandfather's, and when he died, my great-great grandmother gave it to her son Thomas, and it was supposed to have been left to a child in every succeeding generation, the first one who graduated from medical school. But after my great grandfather died, no one could ever find it. We are a family of doctors, for over a hundred years, really until I decided not to continue in the family tradition. That watch was meant to be present- ed to the first one in each generation who became a doctor. I can remember my grandmother tearing apart the rooms of the house looking for it. But it was presumed lost—until this very moment."

"I'm so sorry," Melanie said.

"No, don't be. I'm just thrilled that it's back. But—"

"But now you are questioning why I have it?"

"Yes."

"I told you. I know you're having trouble believing me, but it's true. How else could I have it?"

"All right, now I'm listening. Tell me everything again, please, starting from the beginning." He continued to hold her hand, stroking it with the hand holding the watch.

"My hand is sweating," she said, feeling sheepish. "Can we put the watch down?"

"I don't want to let you go."

"I'll hold hands with you," she said, as he placed the watch on the table beside the bed.

She reached for his large hand again. He wrapped it around her smaller one, their fingers intertwined. She felt such love for this man. It felt as if she had been waiting a long time for him. She was sad he was so taken aback.

"How could you possibly have known my great grandfa- ther? You're only in your twenties, aren't you?"

"I have no idea how it happened. I had that terrible acci- dent, and then all of a sudden I was in Boston and it was 1886 and Thomas was there, and he fell in love with me. Do you believe in love at first sight?"

"I didn't used to," he said, gripping her hand.

"But then I realized I was in love with you and only you. I was frustrated that it took the accident for me to realize that. And I couldn't tell you. I even wrote you a love letter, as silly as that seemed."

"What happened to it?"

"It's a long story. Thomas's sister Jane hated me at first.

She did everything she could to make my life miserable. I'd crumpled it up and left it in my room, and she took it and waved it in Thomas' face. Then I just threw it in the fireplace.

Justin sighed. "I wish I could have had that letter," he said.

Melanie continued, trying to include as many details as she could remember. They sat there for several hours, Justin rapt with wonder at her intimate knowledge of his family and their history.

"And Jane? Finally she came around, but it took a while. What happened to her? Your great-great aunt? She was embarking on an exciting career in figure skating when I—last was with her. But she was so jealous of losing Tom's attention, she did everything in her power to make my life a living hell. Then, when I realized she was such a talented ice skater and got Tom to allow her to follow that dream, our relationship had begun to turn around."

"Jane Thornwell made a name for herself in the figure skating community in Boston," he said. "She was instrumental in helping found the Skating Club of Boston."

"Oh, when was it founded?"

"I think it was in the early twentieth century sometime, maybe 1910 or so? I'm not exactly sure."

"Did she marry? Have children?"

"She did marry. A fellow figure skater I think. It was around 1890. They didn't have children, but I remember being told that she was very happy and that they both lived in the family house. Until—"

"Until?"

"It was tragic. She died in the influenza epidemic of 1918. They were all relieved they had escaped it that spring, and then a virulent strain came back in the fall, just as she was getting ready for the new ice skating season. She contracted it, and it turned into pneumonia and killed her. She was the only one in the family who died from it. She was forty-six years old, fit, healthy, active, with everything to live for. But she died. Apparently, it hit my great grandfather very hard."

"Oh God, no." Melanie had started to cry again. "She was so talented. Skating was a true calling for her. She lit up when she was on skates—luminous, beautiful, and amazing. Her parents' death hit her hard, and skating was the only thing that drew her out of her depression." She sighed, closing her eyes. "Athena clued me in to that. I convinced Thomas to let her pursue it, and he finally did, against his better judgment, I think. He was completely convinced she should be a nurse. But he loved me so much, he would do anything I asked." Melanie started weeping again. This time Justin leaned over and embraced her. She put her head on his shoulder, and he felt her warm tears on his neck. He wanted to be awash in her tears. He sat up and looked into her eyes.

"So you knew her and Athena?" He couldn't fight his urges anymore. He leaned over and pulled her into a gentle embrace.

She wrapped her arms around his waist and reveled in his touch, his smell. It amazed her that he smelled like Thomas. She wanted to melt into his body. "I never had a sister of my own, and I was frustrated when Jane disliked me so much, but we were working through that." They stayed there, holding each other, for several minutes, until Melanie pulled away. "What about Athena? Did she finish medical school?"

"Athena Thornwell was an amazing, brilliant woman. You know her history?" He leaned back, closed his eyes, a smile forming on his lips.

"Yes, I know how she joined the family."

"A legend among the Thornwells. She did graduate from medical school, when hardly any women, let alone African American women, ever did. She had always wanted to go back down south and care for the children and grandchildren of former slaves whose lives were almost worse than they had been when they were slaves. They lived in shanty towns, were forced to do menial work for low pay. According to family lore, she wanted to give back to that community because she had been given such an amazing gift."

"Did she accomplish everything she wanted to do?"

"She did. I'm embarrassed to say I'm not sure where she went, but I think it was somewhere in Georgia or Alabama. She married, had kids, and continued working in the least serviced rural areas, providing medical care for people who otherwise would not have been able to get it. I believe she lived a long life, died in her nineties."

"I'd love to try to find some of her grandchildren if they're still alive. Or maybe great grandchildren?"

Justin raised his eyebrows. "You and she were friends, then?"

"When I got there, Athena was being treated like a domestic. She cooked, sewed, took care of the house, and in her spare time read all of Thomas's college and medical school text books. Everyone just took her household talents for granted, and she was so grateful to the Thornwells that she never protested. But she never stopped dreaming of being a doctor. She just never told anyone—until I got there. I was so impressed with her, I think she already knew more about medicine than any other new medical student. I'm so happy she realized her dream."

"So, then it seems you had something to do with that too?"

"I hope so."

Justin pushed Melanie gently away, his hands on her shoulders. He squinted at her. "How do I know this is all real?"

"What about the watch?"

"You could have found that somewhere. Picked it up at a pawn shop or something?"

"Really? You think so? Then how do I know about all of your ancestors?"

"Maybe you're like one of those fake fortune tellers. You just listen to me, and then you say things based on things I've said to get me to believe you're not a fraud."

"I'm not a fraud," she said, smiling now. "I don't know how I can convince you, but somehow, I have to. I was there, I was with all of them, I helped those two girls fulfill their dreams, and your great grandfather fell in love with me. But I couldn't get you out of my heart, ever, even though I tried."

Justin winced.

"And now I'm back, and I love you. And you love me." She closed her eyes, put her hands over them. "I don't think I've ever cried so much in my life."

"You make it all sound so real, Melanie."

"It *is* real, Justin. If I closed my eyes and tried to dream myself back there, I couldn't make it happen. Somehow, some way, I was transported there to help Jane and Athena. I feel awful that I absconded with Tom's beloved watch! And I hope I didn't break his heart too terribly. What happened to him? While I was there, he was promoted to attending physician at Boston General Hospital. If they had neurosurgeons then, I believe that's what he would have been called. Was he all right?"

Justin breathed in, and then he said, "There was a family story that my great grandfather had a tragic loss. I always thought it might be family lore, you know? Like when you were a kid at a birthday party, and the game was for the first person to whisper some story in the second person's ear, and then by the time it got to the last person it was a completely different story?"

She nodded.

"So, the story goes that he fell in love with a woman who appeared out of nowhere, possibly a patient, a woman who was a little mysterious—no one in the family seemed to know where she came from—and he fell fast and hard for her. It was kind of a scandal at the time, because he took her home to live with him."

Melanie smiled. "So far the story is spot on. Tom was a little worried about that, but we didn't *do* anything. We had separate rooms. It's because that mysterious woman was carrying the torch for one Justin Hilliard, who wasn't even born yet. Yikes, this does sound crazy."

"But she simply disappeared and was never seen or heard from again. My great grandfather apparently went into a deep depression. His sister Jane nursed him out of it, waiting on him hand and foot until he recovered a little, and then he went back to work and spent sometimes eighteen hours a day at the hospital, doing nothing but work, having no serious relationship but burning the candle at both ends, drinking hard, having affairs with women he picked up at bars. He grieved over the loss of his mystery woman for many years."

Melanie started to cry again, this time softly. *That woman was me*, she thought. *I did that to him.* Justin took her hands again. If he had been unsure of his love for her before, he was sure of it now. He couldn't help himself.

"What happened after I—she—disappeared?"

"He did get married, eventually."

Melanie perked up. "I guess so, or you wouldn't be here. Was it a happy marriage?"

"Not sure. It was much later. 1910, I think. He would have been in his fifties."

"Who was his wife?"

"She was a nurse from the hospital. Letitia. Much younger, twenty or twenty-five years younger. Story is that she went after him like a dog after a bone until he just surrendered and married her."

Melanie smiled through her tears. "Yes, he was very handsome."

"They had a baby girl in 1911, my grandmother."

"Oh, that's wonderful. He must have been very happy."

Justin put his head down, as if he didn't want to give her the rest of the story. "He didn't have time to be very happy, I'm afraid. His wife died in childbirth."

"Oh no! Poor Thomas. He was such a good man. He dedicated his life to taking care of other people, and he had such a difficult life, from beginning to end. I feel so guilty that I contributed to that difficulty. How does that happen to such a man?"

Justin shrugged. "I don't know. It doesn't seem to make any sense. None of this does." He looked at her, his teeth biting down on his upper lip, his eyes narrowed, as if he was trying to understand how this could all be. "But he did live a long life."

"Did he?" She thought at least he'd had one great love, even though it was unrequited.

"He died in 1941. He lived long enough to see his daughter, my grandmother Melanie, married to my grandfather, Mark Hilliard, and he met his grandchild Edward, my father, who was born in 1938. According to my father, Thomas loved him when he was born, although my father has only vague memories of his grandfather."

"Did you say your grandmother's name was Melanie?"

"Oh. That's a coincidence. Her name was Melanie Jane."

"Justin, think about it—do you really think that is a coincidence? Doesn't this make you realize that I'm telling you the truth about all of this?"

"Mr. Hilliard, I need to come in and take vitals now," the nurse at the door of Melanie's room had one hand on her hip, the other pointing at him, her index finger extended. Justin pulled his arm quickly off Melanie's knee. Melanie stared at him. To her, he looked more perplexed than ever, his brows knit, his green eyes dark and deep. She had an urge to hold him, kiss him, smooth out his troubled face.

"Okay, I'll disappear for a few minutes, but I will be back, and we can continue this conversation."

"Okay, I'll see you soon. I think might try to sleep a little. All this talk is making me exhausted."

"Do you need anything else? Maybe a milk shake from the cafeteria or something?"

"Oh, I almost forgot—there is something." She pointed to the table beside the bed. "Does you have a phone charger? My phone is dead."

"An iPhone? Sure, I have a charger in my apartment. I'd be happy to take it and charge it for you. Probably a good idea for me to go home and see what's up there. Is that all right? You get some rest, and I'll be back with the phone."

"I'd appreciate that," she said.

He picked up the phone and put it in his pocket. "No problem."

"Thanks. I miss it."

Justin put his hand on her shoulder, and then kissed the top of her head and walked toward the door. The nurse came in and took her vitals, and afterwards Melanie pushed the button to lower the bed, and she turned on her side. "Would you mind turning the light out?" she said. She fell asleep almost before she closed her eyes.

Chapter 25

When Justin got home, he plugged Melanie's phone into the charging station on his desk. He looked at the phone. It was in a case with brown teddy bears on a pink background. He laughed. *Silly that she would have a teddy bear phone cover*, he thought, but then it struck him as endearing, a little poignant. This sophisticated young woman who had been through a chilling, near catastrophe was still a girly girl. *It makes me love her more*, he thought, missing her already.

The mystery of the pocket watch, the intimate knowledge about his relatives—what was the chance Melanie would know anything about any of this? He had sat by her bed talking to her all those weeks she was in the coma, but he had never mentioned any of these things about his great grandfather or his family history.

Justin took a scalding hot shower. He stood there, his skin turning red, wondering how he'd tell Dr. Morgan about the things Melanie had said. She was lucid, rational—he was almost convinced she was as sane as he was. But how could any of this had happened? It gave him a headache, but he continued to mull over the entire thing. After the shower, he wrapped himself in a towel and walked into the living room, where he stared at her phone in the charger, with its cheerful little teddy bears. It was all so illogical. He sat down on the sofa, dripping warm water onto the leather, watching the city view out his window. Everything looked normal out there, but his life was anything but normal, had been turned upside down. Sometime later, he dozed off, as if sleeping might give him some respite from his disorganized thoughts. When he woke up, shivering, he forgot momentarily why he was here and what he had been doing. He turned around and saw the iPhone. *Of course,* he thought, *It's all about Melanie.*

Justin reached over to his desk and pulled the little phone out of the charging cradle. It was about halfway charged. He held it in both hands, caressing it as if it were Melanie herself. He felt a little like a lunatic. Perhaps he was the crazy one? Then Justin was compelled to do something he knew was wrong, that he would never have done in the past. He pushed the "on" button and watched as the phone powered up. He felt instantly guilty. He turned it off, put it back down on his desk, and then picked up the phone again, pressed the button.

Shit, it's asking for a password. How ignorant of me to forget I'd need one to get into her phone. That wasn't enough though, he was now a man on a mission, and he couldn't stop. He had to find out everything he could about this woman who had affected him so deeply and so quickly. He tried some combinations: "MELS," "SWIF," "JUST," but nothing worked. Then, on a whim, he pressed: "1111." And the phone made a little "ding" and booted up. He felt like a little kid who had gotten away with stealing a candy bar, guilty but invigorated at the same time, breathing hard, feeling very proud of his prowess. Now he could eat the "candy" in the privacy of his own home.

She had dozens of apps on her phone. GPS apps, social media apps, music, "YouTube," weather, "Starbucks." He laughed when he found "Angry Birds," because that was one of his guilty pleasures too, but nothing really struck him as out of the ordinary. She had everything that any young urban professional would feel necessary. Then he noticed it, the "Photos" icon at the top of the phone, its multicolored, overlapping petals inviting him to take a look. With a shaking hand, he pressed it. This was like looking into someone's private boudoir with a telescope out your window, imposing on her privacy like a peeping Tom. He rationalized that people send around their photos, text them, email them, so what was the difference. Then he reminded himself that people share only the photos they want to. They don't assume that strangers will have the opportunity to look at all of them. But he and Melanie weren't strangers. They had been friends, and they would be lovers. If she could forgive him for breaking into her phone.

Justin flipped through the camera roll. Pictures of her mother, of little children, a dog, some photos that looked like work parties. Many pictures of cats. He would have to ask her if she liked cats. A photograph of the "Mona Lisa" in what looked like its regular setting at the Louvre. He was surprised that people could use their cameras in there. Melanie must have visited Paris at some point. Justin loved Paris. He had a fantasy about taking her there, getting down on one knee and proposing to her on the Pont Saint-Louis or at the Tuilleries, or perhaps at Sacré-Coeur. She was his sacred heart. He shook himself back to reality. Finally, scrolling down to the very bottom, he saw them—three photographs that made him gasp. Although he was sitting, he felt as if he had lost his balance, started to fall sideways and grabbed the arm of the sofa for support.

Breathing hard, Justin allowed himself to look at the pictures. They were pictures taken inside his Boston house. He recognized them right away. There was one of the very bedroom he had called his own for his entire childhood. In that one, there was the ornately carved rosewood headboard that had been imported from Brazil. She must have appreciated that headboard. The second was a selfie of Melanie and a man who had to be his great grandfather, Thomas Thornwell, standing under the Currier and Ives print hanging on his wall. In the photograph, the two of them were smiling, although Thomas had a look of surprise on his smiling face, his eyes very wide. Their heads were close together, touching. Justin thought he could be staring at himself dressed in an old fashioned suit that looked like a costume. The third photograph was of two young women, one black and one white—the black girl had opulent curls and was wearing what looked like a domestic's uniform. She had a broad smile and was holding up a wooden spoon. The other girl, a pale blonde, was frowning, as if she had a headache or was angry about something. Obviously, Jane and Athena Thornwell, caught on an iPhone camera in the late 1800s, from the looks of the ages and dress of the two girls. The kitchen had been renovated several times, but Justin recognized the room, the plaster molding, the black-and-white checkered porcelain tile floor. So this was a modern kitchen from before the twentieth century. He stared at the photograph, unable to take his eyes off it. He went back and forth among the three photos, over and over, breathing hard. There was no question. Somehow, some way, Melanie had been there, in his house, with his great grandfather's family, in 1886, just the way she said she was. She had helped to launch both of those sisters on their dreamed-of paths. But she had never left her hospital bed.

Justin clicked the phone off and sat there, amazed, wondering what he should do next. He decided he should return to the hospital and apologize to Melanie first for hijacking her photos and next for ever doubting her story. Life was strange, but he had no idea his life would turn out to be this strange.

At the hospital, Dr. Morgan had stepped into Melanie's room, where she was sleeping peacefully. Justin burst in and beckoned for him to come out into the hallway, putting his finger over his lips. The doctor wheeled around, frowning at the younger man.

"Excuse me, Mr. Hilliard, but I need to examine my patient."

"Dr. Morgan, I apologize for the intrusion, but we need to talk. I know what happened now. It's important. Melanie has not gone off her rocker. Everything she said was true."

Dr. Morgan rubbed his chin with his index finger and thumb. "Have you gone off yours?"

"I see why you might think so," Justin said, half to himself.

"Just tell me what's going on." He followed Justin, closing Melanie's door behind him.

"Is there a place where we could go to have a private conversation?"

Morgan ushered Justin into a small, windowless office. They sat down on the two chairs in there. Justin faced the doctor and related the entire story, from beginning to end. The doctor took a deep breath, whistling as he let his breath out. He didn't say a word. Justin told him about the pocket watch. Morgan's eyes widened, the vertical lines across the bridge of his nose deepening by the second. When Justin was done, he looked up at the doctor, trying to catch his eye.

Dr. Morgan looked away. "Someone's in la-la land here," he said. "I'm worried it might be you."

"There's one more thing," Justin said, picking up the phone. "You need to look at these photos."

"That's her phone? What are *you* doing with it?"

"She asked me to take it home and charge it for her."

"Yes?"

"After I did that, I couldn't resist looking at the photos..." Justin powered up the phone and scrolled down to the pictures.

The doctor frowned. "She gave you her password?"

Justin laughed, embarrassed. "I figured it out."

"You hacked into her phone? Are you sure she's all right with our looking at this?"

"I didn't ask her, but I am fairly sure she will be happy to be exonerated. She's not insane." He powered up the phone and offered it to the doctor.

Dr. Morgan took the phone and looked at the pictures as

Justin pointed them out. "What are you saying, Justin?"

"That's my great grandfather, Dr. Thomas Thornwell."

"How do you know?"

"Look at him. Don't you think we have a strong family resemblance?"

Morgan looked at the picture and then looked closely at Justin and shook his head slowly. "You could look like someone who wasn't your great grandfather. Or maybe you were dressed up as someone from a different time? This is all too unbelievable."

"I'm positive that's my great grandfather. I've seen old photos and portraits of him, and I can tell by the background. These were taken a long time ago in my bedroom in my house...well, the house I just sold."

"Is she—"

"Yup, that's Melanie. Don't you recognize her?"

"This is impossible."

Justin opened the photograph of Jane and Athena. "Those two women are my great grandfather's sister Jane and his adopted sister Athena. She was one of the first African-American women to graduate from medical school. This picture was taken in 1886."

"She graduated from medical school? In this picture she looks like the maid or the cook or something."

"Yes. Before Melanie got there, she was acting like the maid and the cook. But after she became a doctor, she practiced medicine in the South for decades, helping to provide medical care for freed slaves and their families. My great grandfather funded her free clinic in Georgia. She was quite a remarkable woman, actually a legend in our family."

"But how could this be?"

"I have no idea. Somehow, Melanie was there, and because of her intervention, two women were able to have extremely productive lives. I don't know how it happened, but you have to agree, this is evidence enough that it did happen. She came back when you brought her out of the coma. I have no idea what any other answer could be. You're the doctor."

"I have to be honest with you, part of me wishes I never knew anything about this. I don't know what to do with it. You know what the kids say, 'too much information'? My teenage daughter would say, 'This hurts my hair.'"

"Well, you can just feel free to forget it. I'll take care of everything. Are you all right? You look a little pale."

"I feel a little pale."

"So tell the psych consult that Melanie is okay, she's not crazy. Then discharge her. She can continue her physical therapy outside the hospital, can't she? If she's medically ready to be discharged?"

Dr. Morgan stood up, scratching his head. He backed out toward the door, one hand behind his back, searching for the door handle. "I don't want anyone to get wind of this." He snapped his fingers. "Please promise me you will keep mum. We don't need any press hanging around outside the hospital. Everyone will say we've all lost our marbles."

"I'll talk to Melanie. I don't think she'll have any objections to keeping it all on the down-low."

"That is a necessity." Morgan opened the door and walked out, half slamming the door after him.

Chapter 26

Justin waited a few moments, pulled himself together. Then he went back to Melanie's room. The doctor was nowhere in sight, so Justin approached the bed and leaned down and kissed her. She woke with a start.

"Oh, Justin, you scared me!"

"I'm sorry, love. I couldn't think of a better way to wake you up."

"I was having a nice dream."

"I'm sorry! I charged your phone, thought you'd like to have it."

"Oh, thank you, sweetie!" She pushed herself up as he handed her the phone.

"I saw some pictures of my house." He looked down at his hands, hesitant to look into her eyes until he knew what her reaction would be.

"*Your* house?"

"My house in Boston."

"Oh!" Melanie put her hand over her mouth. "I forgot I took those pictures! Your house? I don't understand."

"There's a picture of you and a man in my bedroom."

"What? Now you're confusing me." She rubbed her forehead. "Justin, what are you saying?"

"At first I thought it was a picture of me. But it's a picture of my great grandfather, Thomas Thornwell. It was taken in the bedroom that was mine. I recognized the bed." Now he looked directly at her.

"Oh my God, Justin. Is this possible? That was *your* house?" she repeated.

"It gets stranger and stranger, doesn't it?"

"Justin, I was ready to get angry with you for breaking into my phone, but—"

"Melanie, I felt bad about doing that, but do you understand? Those pictures are the evidence that you were really there. I need to be serious about this. I saw the pictures of Jane and Athena. And the Currier and Ives print on my bedroom wall."

"Okay, please, just say it again—Tom Thornwell was your great grandfather? But why isn't your name Thornwell?"

"Right," he said. "Remember I told you Tom Thornwell only had a daughter, no son? And his daughter Melanie Jane married a man named Mark Hilliard, my grandfather."

"Holy shit!" she said, and the two of them burst into laughter. "That's right. Tom named his daughter after me." Melanie sighed.

Justin leaned over and hugged her, and she hugged him back. Then he did what he had been wanting to do, kissed her first on her mouth and then all over her face, her hair, her neck, her lips again. She kissed him back, and then he kissed her the way Thomas had kissed her the last time she had seen him, but this time Melanie didn't push Justin away. She wanted all of him. It felt so right. Their tongues met, and electricity shot through her. She never wanted to let go. Finally, they stopped, and she let her head rest on his shoulder. They remained in a tight embrace.

"Listen, I showed Dr. Morgan the pictures."

"You did? Did he have a cow?" She burst into laughter again.

"Sort of. First he got mad at me for looking at the pictures on your phone. Said I was violating your right to privacy. But of course he looked at them, and then he almost threw up."

Melanie giggled.

"Then he said that if we don't tell anyone about this, he'll discharge you, and you can continue your physical therapy on an outpatient basis. But he doesn't want any publicity about this. Is that okay with you? I kind of answered for you and said you wouldn't object."

"Yes, of course. It's fine. Perfect. As long as you love me and believe me and agree I was telling the truth."

"I have no idea why any of it happened, although I suspect it had something to do with your taking on my great grandfather and paving the way for his sisters to succeed in their lives. How you did it, I have no idea, and why it was my family you, um, visited, well it's beyond my comprehension. It's too freaky to be a coincidence, but I suspect we will never be able to explain it."

"Jesus, so I was transported there to put Jane and Athena on the right path?"

Justin shrugged.

"But what about Tom? The mission was only two-thirds a success," she said, serious again. "Was I supposed to stay there and be his life partner?"

"I don't know. I don't know anything about anything, it seems."

Melanie shuddered, and Justin held her closer. "You know, if they had kept me in this coma any longer, it's possible I would have succumbed to Tom. It was starting to happen, and I was starting to lose hope that I'd ever see you again."

Justin kissed her again. He held her hands in his, and she felt a charge of excitement, a closed circuit that seemed to have no beginning and no end. "But they didn't and you didn't and it didn't," he said. "Thank heavens."

"But poor Thomas. Every time I feel happy to be here

with you, I feel sad about how I left him. He was obviously terribly hurt. I'll never understand any of it."

"Call me a selfish man," he said, "But I have no guilt about my great grandfather. He had you for a while. And you fixed things there. He had a good life. I don't think there's anything else for us to say about it."

"I have learned to expect the unexpected," she said, very serious.

Justin laughed. "A good thing to do, I'd say." He kissed both of her hands. "I have another confession," he said.

"What? What else did you do to me besides breaking into my phone?"

"No, it's nothing I did to you, but I've known for a while that my feelings for you were more than friendship. I just never knew how you felt. I thought it would be unprofessional to suggest we see each other socially, especially where I was supposed to be your more experienced mentor at work."

"I knew too, Justin, but it took that awful accident for me to admit it to myself. But then, when I ended up with Tom and his family, I thought I might never know how you felt."

"I love you so much," he said.

"What is it about the men in your family?" she said, a half-smile on her face. "I seem to be irresistible to you guys." She shook her head slowly from side to side and laughed. "Guess I'm just irresistible."

"And your modesty amazes me," he said, laughing.

"Well, there's that," she said, winking, patting his face with her hand.

"As soon as I worried I might lose you, I stopped fighting the fact that I'm in love with you. And I promised myself that as soon as you came out of the coma, I'd let you know. I only dreamed you would feel the same way."

Melanie had closed her eyes and was leaning back on the pillows. "And I do feel the same way. Tom was so in love with me, from the very start, that he was hard to resist. But my love for you was so strong—the kind of love I never thought possible. He was so good to me. I just couldn't return his love."

"Well, you did go back and change history. Selfishly, I can't worry about how disappointed he was. If you hadn't come back to me, I would have longed for you forever."

"So, my love, you won't have to long for me." She smiled, kissing her fingers and then moving them gently over his lips. "But when do I get out of here? I want to see 2016 outside of a hospital room. I have to convince myself this is all real."

He grabbed her hand and kissed it. "You're going to be out of here soon. PT told Dr. Morgan you're in really good shape."

"Yeah, we had to do a lot of walking back in 1886. No one had cars. Great exercise."

He chuckled but then got serious and leaned in. "I need to kiss you again." Justin leaned down and kissed her gently on the lips. He didn't linger there long, gave her one more kiss and then stood up. "If I'd had my way, I would have jumped into bed with you and done it right."

Melanie laughed. "I can't wait for that! I wish we could do it right here, the hell with the doctors and nurses."

"You could move in with me when you leave here, you know? You'll need a little TLC."

"Whoa, I'm not moving in with any more Thornwell/Hilliards after I get discharged from a hospital."

Justin made a sad face, his mouth turning down at the corners. Melanie giggled. "I have my own apartment, and frankly, it will be nice to see it again. My mom will visit and give me all the TLC I need. Of course, you are welcome to come over every night."

Justin continued to pout. He still held her hand.

"And I'm starting to worry that no one paid the rent and my stuff will be out on the street. How about my job? Do you know what happened to that?"

"They're holding your job for you."

"That's a relief. In 1886 every time I told Tom I wanted

to have a job, he looked at me funny." She laughed. "He said, 'Women work?'"

"Well, luckily I am fine with women working. We can still go to work together."

"Yes, but I need to get a good pair of snow boots, no more trekking through the snow in high heels."

"I'll buy you cleats!"

Melanie laughed again. She hadn't laughed this much in ages, and it felt so much better than crying.

"If you're worrying about all of that, you're recuperating. That's a good sign. Someday, mark my words, you and your teddy bears will be moving in with me."

"We'll see, won't we?" She sighed. "For now, when I get out of here, how about a date to the Met Museum?"

"Sure, if that's what you'd like. I know you were an art history major. You need to teach me more about art."

"There's a specific painting I want to see. John Singer Sargent's 'Portrait of Madame X.' I know it's there. Isabella Gardner wanted it so badly for her collection, and I knew she'd never get it. Sargent told me so. I just couldn't bear the thought of telling her. It would have broken her heart." Melanie was staring off into space, and Justin wiggled his fingers in front of her eyes. She shuddered and looked at him.

"What are you talking about? Where did you go just now?"

"Someday I'll tell you the whole story. She did get one of Sargent's studies for the painting, though. It's in the Gardner Museum in Boston."

"So one of the things I found in the house when I was packing it up were some very old photographs. She was in one of them, with my great grandfather. Their names were on the back with the date 1918. He had his arm around her. It looked as if they were good friends."

"They were. Great friends. She took care of him and his sisters after their mother died. Aunt Isabella. She was a pistol." Her eyes were moist and shining again. "I hope she took care of him after I—disappeared." She focused on Justin, her eyes wide as if she'd just had a great thought. "I'd love to have that picture if you wouldn't mind."

"Of course I'll give you that picture and any other pictures you'd like." He bent down and kissed her again. "You can probably tell me lots of other things about my family I didn't even know. You can tell me when we're in bed, after I've made unbelievable love to you."

"Promises, promises."

"It's going to happen soon, I promise you. Sex is great exercise, you know? You need to get all of your muscles back in shape." He sat on the edge of the bed and pulled her into an embrace, kissing her deeply, running his hands over her body. "I've wanted to do this for so long," he said. "I love you so much."

"A nurse could come in at any moment," she whispered, responding to his touch, the shock waves coursing through her body from top to bottom.

"I don't care. We'll tell her that we're both crazy, and crazy people have to kiss and fondle one another."

Melanie laughed, and Justin pulled away. "Are you laughing at my love making?" he said, pouting.

"I don't know," she said. "But I can't wait to find out.

Isabella Stewart Gardner

Isabella Stewart Gardner, known also as "Mrs. Jack," referring to her husband, Jack Gardner, was born on April 14, 1840 and died on July 17, 1924. She was one of the nineteenth century's most prominent patrons of the arts. She was a friend of many artists and writers of the day, including John Singer Sargent, James McNeill Whistler, and Henry James. Prominent in Boston society, she supported the Boston Symphony Orchestra and was a fan of the Boston Red Sox and Harvard College football. She is responsible for amassing one of the most remarkable private art collections in the world today.

Over the course of thirty years, Mrs. Jack traveled all over the world and acquired an impressive body of art. In 1903, she completed the construction of a mansion in the Fenway section of Boston to house her collection so that people could visit and appreciate the paintings, sculpture, decorative pieces, and tapestries. A vibrant member of society, she was always the object of journalistic curiosity in her time, and she engendered a great deal of interest by a press that longed for sensationalist material, whether or not she was involved in scandal.

She always wanted to acquire John Singer Sargent's "Portrait of Madame X," a painting that had created a scandal of its own in Paris, for her collection, but Sargent stubbornly refused to sell the painting to her, and she was able only to acquire a study he had done for the painting. The painting itself now hangs in the Metropolitan Museum of Art in New York.

In 1990, two thieves disguised as Boston Policemen entered the Isabella Stewart Gardner Museum and stole thirteen priceless works of art, including works by Rembrandt, Vermeer, Degas, and Manet, among others. Although the investigation continues, the works have never been recov-

ered or the thieves caught, despite a $5 million reward of-
fered by the museum. For more information on the Isabella
Steward Gardner Museum, see www.gardnermuseum.org.

John Singer Sargent

John Singer Sargent, who was born January 12, 1856 and died April 14, 1925, was the most successful portrait painter of his time. Sargent was born in Florence, Italy to American parents. He studied painting in Italy and Paris, and in 1884 he caused a sensational scandal at the Paris Salon with a painting of Madame Gautreau, which he called "Portrait of Madame X" because of the scandal. The press was so merciless and the woman's husband so angry, that in 1886 Sargent left Paris and relocated to London. Although he was renowned for his portraiture, "Portrait of Madame X" was his favorite, and he wanted to keep it for himself, but he eventually sold it to the Metropolitan Museum of Art in New York.

As well as being a gifted artist, Sargent was also a talented pianist and musician. He was quite private about his personal life, but he was rumored to have had close relationships with both men and women during his lifetime.

Although Sargent lived his life in Europe as an American ex-patriot, he traveled to the United States many times to paint commissioned portraits. Isabella Stewart Gardner was a great friend and colleague, and she frequently sought Sargent's advice and counsel on her notable acquisitions of art.

About the Author

Rebecca Marks practiced law and worked as a technical writer in Boston for years. With her husband Frank, a policeman-turned-glassblower, she raised six kids, performed in many choral groups, and trained and showed their German Shepherds and Belgian Tervuren dogs. After Frank passed away, she moved back to her hometown of New York and began writing fiction in earnest. She studies at the Sarah Lawrence College Writing Institute.

CPSIA information can be obtained
at www.ICGtesting.com
Printed in the USA
BVOW10s1105130517
484071BV00014B/142/P